Death of Anton

Death of Anton

Alan Melville

With an Introduction
by Martin Edwards

Poisoned Pen Press

Originally published in 1936 by Skeffington
Reprinted by kind permission of Eric Glass Ltd on behalf of the
Estate of Alan Melville
Copyright © 2015 Estate of Alan Melville
Introduction copyright © 2015 Martin Edwards
Published by Poisoned Pen Press in association with the British
Library

First Edition 2017
First US Trade Paperback Edition

10 9 8 7 6 5 4 3 2 1

Library of Congress Catalog Card Number: 2017938969

ISBN: 9781464208720   Trade Paperback
        9781464208737   Ebook

Poisoned Pen Press
4014 N. Goldwater Boulevard, #201
Scottsdale, Arizona 85251
www.poisonedpenpress.com
info@poisonedpenpress.com

Introduction

Alan Melville's *Death of Anton* is a lively whodunnit in which murder stalks a travelling circus. First published in 1935, this is another lost gem from the Golden Age of Murder between the two world wars which has been rescued from oblivion by the British Library. "The greatest show on earth" provides an engaging backdrop for an example of "the grandest game in the world", to use a favourite phrase of John Dickson Carr, one of the finest practitioners of traditional detective fiction. Melville's brief contribution to the genre is much less celebrated by mystery fans than Carr's, but this story shows that his work does not deserve to be forgotten.

The eponymous Anton and his seven Bengal tigers form "the Most Fearless and Sensational Act in the History of Animal Training", and when Anton is found dead in a cage in the company of his tigers, the obvious assumption is that he has been mauled to death. Things are never so simple in a detective novel, however, and after Joseph Carey, the circus owner, invites Detective Inspector Minto from Scotland Yard to look into what has happened, it emerges that Anton was murdered by one of his enemies in the circus. But which one? Suspects include the man who takes over Anton's act, a trapeze artist, a clown, and Carey himself.

Minto's methods are frequently unorthodox, as when he pretends to be a housing inspector ("Did you get the form?… it's just a formality you know, Housing Act of 1935") in order to gain access to suspicious premises, but he is decent and likeable. So is his brother Robert, a Catholic priest, who provides him with a crucial lead as he sets about untangling a web of criminality, but is unable to disclose who has, under the seal of the confessional, admitted to killing Anton. Fresh dramas unfold, involving both the trapeze and the tigers, before justice is done.

The story is told with a youthful exuberance, which is unsurprising, given that the author was still in his twenties. It tends to be forgotten that much of the best Golden Age fiction was written by young men and women. John Dickson Carr, for instance, was also in his twenties when his early crime novels were published, while Agatha Christie, Dorothy L. Sayers, and Anthony Berkeley, the cream of the crop, also started young. This helps to explain why they were able to write about the serious business of murder with an irrepressible *joie de vivre*.

Alan Melville (1910–1983) was a man of many parts. Born William Melville Caverhill, he began his working life at Berwick-upon-Tweed in the family timber business, and ended it as a well-known wit, raconteur, and television celebrity. Along the way, he tried his hand at many forms of writing, and produced half a dozen detective novels in a brief flurry during the mid-1930s, before abandoning the genre for richer pickings elsewhere. He did, however, adapt his first whodunnit, *Week-end at Thackley*, into a play, which duly became *Hot Ice*, a film screened in 1952.

Melville showed that he had a way with words early in life, and he won a return trip to Canada as a prize in a literary competition at the age of 22. He started writing lyrics for songs, and joined the BBC as a scriptwriter in its variety department. Having gained experience as a radio producer, he proceeded to combine writing revues with war service; he enlisted in the RAF, rising to the rank of wing commander, and taking part in the Normandy landings. He wrote several popular light-hearted plays, and the book and lyrics to Ivor Novello's final musical, *Gay's the Word*.

The television era saw his career take a fresh turn. Before long, it was hard to avoid Alan Melville, as his range of interests was matched by unfailing industry. He became chairman of *The Brains Trust*—on one programme he sparred with Nancy Spain, another TV celebrity who dabbled in humorous detective fiction. Later he hosted a satiric revue series called *A–Z*, and was a panellist on *What's My Line?* and a "castaway" on the long-running radio show *Desert Island Discs*. In the 1960s, he presented *Before the Fringe*, a series focusing on the genial humour popular in the days before *Beyond the Fringe* took comedy in a new and edgier direction. As an actor, his credits included parts in a televised adaptation of Noel Coward's once-controversial play *The Vortex*, and in *By the Sword Divided*, a costume drama set around the time of the English Civil War. Melville spent his last thirty years or so resident in Brighton, and became a regular at the Neptune Inn in Hove, a haunt of many of his contemporaries in the theatre. Versatile as ever, he was occasionally to be found serving behind the bar. A.S. Byatt's description of him as a "chameleon" seems apt.

He used the title of one of his television shows, *Merely Melville*, for an autobiography, but in later life he had little to say about his work as a detective novelist. Probably, like so many of his contemporaries, he regarded his crime writing as akin to a guilty secret, considering his other work to be much more important. But the appeal of detective fiction is enduring, and Melville made a lively if short-lived contribution to the genre. Its rediscovery by the British Library will be welcomed by readers in search of light-hearted escapism.

Martin Edwards
www.martinedwardsbooks.com

Chapter One

The circus came to town.

It arrived, not with any of the majesty and excitement which herald the arrival of a small circus in a small town, but with all the modern efficiency for which Joseph Carey's World-Famous Circus and Menagerie was famous. There was no triumphal procession through the streets of the town to delight the youngsters, give a brief preview of the circus's delights, and act as a powerful piece of publicity; instead, the two special trains which pulled Carey's Circus around Britain during the summer months rolled more or less smoothly into the station between eleven and twelve o'clock on that hot July night.

From the first of these trains there stepped out a small army of human beings, well-dressed and apparently prosperous. If every available hoarding in the town had not been plastered with those well-known blue-and-gold posters announcing the coming of Carey's, it is certain that not one of the passengers waiting on the platform that night would have recognized any of these human beings as circus people. At a pinch, they might have taken them for the cast of some extravagant and successful musical comedy which had condescended to visit the town. But never as people of the circus.

The porter who attended to Herr Ludwig Kranz's suitcases and travelling-rug, for instance, would never have imagined for one moment that this tall, distinguished, and good-looking young man with the slightly foreign accent who was inquiring about the locality of the best hotel in the town was none other than Anton, whose name appeared at the top of the blue-and-gold posters. Anton and His Seven Bengal Tigers, The Most Fearless and Sensational Act in the History of Animal Training. Direct from His Continental Successes, First Time in Britain, Secured at Enormous Expense. There were many more-than-life-size posters of Anton besprinkled over the town, showing the gentleman clad only in a small triangle of tiger-skin (doubtless made out of one of his former conquests) and surrounded by seven ferocious tigers, all sitting on their rear portions on boxes of varying heights.

Until he paid a visit to the circus on its opening night, the porter would never have associated that sparsely-clad figure with the elegant gentleman who gave him a tip several times larger than he was accustomed to receive. Herr Ludwig Kranz, buried deep in an expensive camel-hair overcoat and smoking a cigarette which conjured up visions of harems and Eastern potentates in the simple mind of the porter, was a very different-looking personality from Anton, the gentleman who appeared with next to nothing on inside a cage which also housed seven none too friendly tigers. These two beings were, however, one and the same person, as the porter found when he sat down on the hard one-and-threepenny benches, which was the cheapest way of seeing Carey's World-Famous Circus and Menagerie. "Gorluvaduck!" as the porter remarked to his best girl. "That's the lad what slipped me a couple o' bob tip last night. 'Struth!…I hope them ruddy tigers don't do nothing to him."

"Why not, Bert?" inquired the best girl.

"Well, he'll be going away by train again, end of the week. And I know who'll be looking after his bags all right. Yours truly, if there's another couple o' bob going."

The small gentleman who followed Anton out of the compartment was even more difficult to place in his true light. He was dressed quietly in a well-cut, dark-grey suit. His collar was of the stiff variety which is now even losing its grip on its last stronghold, the necks of successful stock-brokers. A bowler hat crowned his head and a neatly rolled umbrella dangled over his arm. He, too, passed on the job of coping with his luggage to a porter, for he was carrying—in addition to the umbrella and a Burberry—a copy of *Seven Pillars of Wisdom*, which is enough for any man to deal with and at the same time manage to get out his ticket in time to be punched at the barrier.

The few people on the platform, if they troubled to think about him at all, would almost certainly have put this gentleman down as a sober and successful business man, a man who dictated letters all day to a pretty stenographer without ever splitting an infinitive or leaving a preposition at the end of a sentence…and who never thought of his stenographer as anything but a stenographer.

The lady standing beside the chocolate machine on the platform went, in fact, a stage further in guessing the business of this immaculate little man. She was a teacher of mathematics in the local elementary school, and as soon as he stepped down from the train she scented danger on the following morning. Miss Jenkins was perfectly certain that the immaculate little man was one of those archfiends, His Majesty's Inspectors of Education; she rushed at once to warn the other members of the staff of the impending peril. He looked exactly like an inspector, and it was fully two months since one had swooped down on the school. Yes, an inspector, without the slightest doubt: the bowler and the umbrella gave him away at once, and *Seven Pillars of Wisdom* settled it.

Miss Jenkins spent a horrible morning the next day, with her class taut and tense, waiting for the classroom door to open and the immaculate little man to walk in and start asking awkward questions. He did not come. Miss Jenkins, in fact, did not see him again until she visited the circus on the Thursday evening, and even then she was unable to penetrate the immaculate little man's disguise. It was not easy to do so: a white face, a red nose, a ginger wig, baggy trousers of an enormous check pattern, a tiny comic hat, and a waistcoat with the Union Jack stitched on the back—all these made a great difference to the soberly dressed individual who stepped down from the train that night. He was, however, Dodo—King of Clowns.

The platform filled up with the discharge of people from the train. They stood about in groups—acrobats, bare-back riders, the owner and trainer of Horace (the World's Most Intelligent Performing Sea-Lion), clowns, trapeze artists, jugglers, and the rest. They had none of the glamour and excitement which would be so much in evidence at this hour tomorrow night, when they would be wearing considerably less and doing considerably more than at present. Only one of the battalion, in fact, seemed to be doing anything at all, and he was certainly making a great deal of noise. Mr. Joseph Carey, proprietor of the most famous touring circus in Britain, lost no time in letting the townspeople know that Carey's Circus had arrived.

"Don't suppose there'll be taxis in a place like this, eh?" demanded Mr. Carey, throwing away the stub of a cigar on to the rails.

"Yes, sir. Outside the station, sir."

"Enough for all this bunch, eh?"

"Well, sir—I don't know about that, sir."

"No. Didn't expect you would. Mr. Johnston! Where's Mr. Johnston? Get Mr. Johnston, will you? 'Ere—Mr. Johnston…are you in charge of the advance arrangements for this circus, or aren't you?"

"Yes, sir. I mean, I am, sir."

"And 'aven't I told you a 'undred times that being in charge of advance arrangements means looking after the comfort of the artists, as well as letting the public know what's coming to 'em?"

"Well, sir…I mean, yes, sir."

"And doesn't looking after the comfort of the artists include such-like things as carting 'em from the station to their hotels, eh?"

"Well, yes, sir. I suppose so, sir. But I thought—"

"I don't pay you to think, Mr. Johnston. If I'd wanted someone to think I wouldn't 'ave engaged you as advance manager. Get a couple o' dozen cabs. And make it snappy, will you?"

"Yes, sir."

The overworked and underpaid Mr. Johnston flies off to round up all available forms of vehicles, however ancient or unreliable, and the army saunters down the platform and across the bridge and out, via the booking-hall, into the town, and are bundled into the various vehicles, and discover (as Mr. Johnston discovered when he paid his first visit to the town six weeks before) that their hotels are mostly less than five minutes' walk from the station, and that they could have been safely inside them long before this had it not been for the Boss's concern for the comfort of his artists.

Caravans? Tents? Such things are simply not mentioned in connection with a circus like Joseph Carey's, which has appeared by Royal Command and has been patronized by most of the crowned heads of Europe, not to mention a certain well-known politician who very nearly threw up his portfolio in order to become a trapeze artist. There are, certainly, a number of lesser persons who put up for the night in caravans dotted over the field where the circus is to be held, but these are mainly the corps of workers whose job it is to put up and take down the big tent in an amazingly short time. These men, and the men responsible for looking after the animals and cleaning out their cages, live in the shadow of the big tent and are the only remnants of the good old days when a circus was a circus and not a mammoth touring variety show. But the actual performers are all housed under proper roofs and on more or less proper beds in various establishments in the town, according to their prominence in the bill.

Anton, the gentleman who befriended the Seven Bengal Tigers; Dodo, the highest-paid clown in the business; Lorimer and Loretta, the world's most sensational trapeze artists; the stars of the show, such as these, have the best rooms reserved for them in advance in the Station Hotel. A little further down the scale, Lars Peterson and his Intelligent Sea-Lion will be found in the second-best hotel in the town, the King's Head. (Or, to be more accurate, Lars Peterson will be found there, most probably drinking a succession of quick whiskies in the bar; Horace, his sea-lion, is living happily in his tank at the back of the big tent.)

And so on, right down the programme, until one comes to the lesser clowns, the foils to Dodo, and those rather pathetic females who are now losing their figures and whose job in the circus is to hand a great variety of articles to the jugglers, or to stand in the middle of the ring and make "allezoop!" noises whenever their more famous colleagues have brought off some particularly daring feat. This last category will be found in some rather dilapidated boarding-house in the town, grumbling at the hardness of the beds and the softness of the drinks, and talking nineteen to the dozen about the days when they were on the legitimate stage (which means the music-halls), and actually took part in the acrobatic feats instead of merely standing to one side and bowing, in a tired fashion, to applause that is not for them.

There is one exception to this rule. However hard you may look, you will not find Mr. Joseph Carey himself in any of the hotels or boarding-houses. You will find him instead on the scene of battle, in an enormous green-and-white caravan pitched in a corner of the field where the circus is to be held. It is one of Mr. Carey's little idiosyncrasies. He insists on his artists being put up in the best hotels (or in the worst, according to their value in the circus); but he himself always stays in his caravan beside the big tent. Asked for his reasons for this, Mr. Carey will reply that he likes to hang on to the glorious traditions of the circus, that he is a Regular Trouper, that a caravan was good enough for his father and is good enough for him. An answer, incidentally, that is usually taken with considerably more than the average grain of salt, and even greeted on occasions with murmurs of "Baloney!" … for Mr. Carey only came into the circus business three or four years ago, after losing a great deal of money on three revues called, successively but not successfully, *Femmes de Paris, Nuits de Paris*, and *Joies de Paris*.

Joe Carey, at any rate, sleeps in his caravan, which is a noble affair and fitted with all the very latest contraptions, including a well-stocked liquor cabinet; and certain unkind persons have been known to suggest that the real reason why Mr. Carey prefers living in a caravan to living in an hotel is that it gives him more scope for his amorous adventures. Which, taking a quick look at Mr. Carey's beery face, bald pate, and overhanging stomach, seems a little surprising.

The light is switched on in Joe Carey's super-caravan, at any rate, just as the lights are switched on in a number of rooms in various hotels in the town as the Town Hall clock strikes a quarter to twelve. Herr Ludwig Kranz is in his room in the Station Hotel, sitting on the edge of his bed and drinking hot malted milk…thereby proving that there is, after all, some truth in his unsolicited testimonials which appear so often in the advertisements of the stuff: "The training of wild animals, and of tigers in particular, is a task which requires absolute physical fitness and the steadiest of nerves. I have found that, since taking a nightly tumblerful of…" He has unpacked, and pinned a number of photographs of himself, surrounded by tigers, round the walls, as well as a picture of a young Hungarian girl whom he hopes to marry when he is running a circus of his own.

Further along the corridor of the same hotel, the immaculate little man who is appearing tomorrow night in a grotesque make-up as Dodo the clown, is lying on top of his bed and turning over the pages of his *Seven Pillars of Widsom*. Not reading, merely turning the pages. Mr. Mayhew (for that is his name in real life) has been looking for a suitable place to begin reading the book ever since he bought it, but up to now has failed to find one. He has enjoyed looking at the pictures, however, and it gives him a definite superiority complex to be seen carrying the volume about.

In the King's Head, Lars Peterson, owner of a sea-lion a great deal more intelligent than himself, has taken a bottle of whisky up to his bedroom and is undressing and drinking in turns. In Mrs. Wilkinson's High-Class Boarding-House (Terms Moderate, Accounts Weekly) a little group is eating cold meat and pickles and talking loudly of the days when they were at the top of the bill. Or as near the top as makes no matter.

Midnight.…

The second of the two special trains which carry Joseph Carey's World-Famous Circus and Menagerie up and down the country steams into the station, and this time there is no doubt that its occupants have something to do with a circus. The trucks are oddly assorted and of various sizes, and out of them comes a great deal of stamping and shuffling and scraping and growling and roaring. They are all shunted into a siding and left there until five o'clock in the morning, to the annoyance of everyone living near the station and trying to get to sleep. Quite a few of these unfortunate citizens, in fact, make up their minds shortly after midnight to write a fairly snorty letter to the local papers about this unholy row; one female goes so far as to sit up suddenly in bed and demand that her husband does something about it at once. Though, as the husband meekly points out, it is difficult to see what can be done about five elephants, seven tigers, twelve lions, fifty or more horses, and a great collection of other animals, if they have set their minds on yowling and stamping and roaring all night in the siding.

The biggest noise of all comes from the long wagon near the end of the train, where Anton's Seven Bengal Tigers have made up their minds to spend the night by pacing up and down, backwards and forwards, from one corner of the truck to the other, reaching out their smooth, well-kept necks and shattering the night with one roar after another. Peculiar behaviour for the tigers; the attendants who have been left on guard over the wagons cannot make it out, for usually Anton's seven tigers are so bored with night travel that it takes a great deal of persuasion and bad language to wake them up and get them to leave the train. Peter, the oldest and biggest of the seven, has certainly a sore paw which was giving him trouble at the last stop of the circus, but Peter's sore paw could not be responsible for making all seven beasts create such an unearthly din, and keep it up all night.

Perhaps—who knows—the seven Bengal tigers are wiser than most of us, and have an inkling of the tragedy that is coming to their cage so very soon.

Chapter Two

One of the most recurrent posters advertising the various attractions of Carey's Circus was the one which depicted a young man and woman, showing a complete disregard for the laws of gravity both in what they were doing and in what they were wearing, hurtling through the air with (apparently) no hope of touching terra firma without breaking every bone in their bodies.

The young man, shown in the top right-hand corner of the poster doing a triple backwards somersault some two hundred feet in the air, was Lorimer, otherwise Mr. Lorimer Gregson. The lady in the bottom left-hand corner, sailing through the air with arms outstretched in the seemingly vain hope of connecting with her partner in mid-air, was Loretta, otherwise Mrs. Lorimer Gregson. A charming and talented couple, aged twenty-seven and twenty-six respectively. They had been doing this sort of thing since childhood, and had brought down the roofs of several music-halls as the Child Trapeze Wonders when neither of them had reached the age of ten. They had been married under the roof of the big tent of Mendl's Circus four years ago; they had joined Carey's the season before last and were now equal leading attraction with

Anton and his tigers. And they were paid, grudgingly, eighty pounds a week for risking their young lives twice daily and laughing at the idea of using a net in their act.

Caught unawares in the seclusion of their bedroom in the Station Hotel, Lorimer and Loretta were not quite as exciting a couple as their posters made out. Loretta, to be perfectly frank, was covering her face with a clammy coating of some beauty preparation, and Lorimer was thoughtfully engaged in bursting a pimple on the point of his chin. These two occupations took up the whole of Mr. and Mrs. Gregson's attention: not a word was spoken until the pimple was successfully burst and the face cream smeared thoroughly on, and then just as thoroughly removed with a towel. Then Lorimer, having sent up a mute prayer to heaven expressing the hope that the blessed thing wasn't going to bleed all night, broke the silence.

"I'm not exactly a fool, you know," he said.

"No? Well, as long as you say so, dear..."

"I've been watching you for the last month or so."

"Yes. I've noticed that all right. Proper little sleuth, aren't you? Perhaps if you stopped carrying on like Sexton Blake and paid a little more attention to the act, you'd do your stuff a bit better. You're getting later with that back somersault drop every night."

"That's meant," said Lorimer. "The later it's done, the better it looks to the audience."

"Really? That's fine. I suppose one of these nights you'll leave me dangling in mid-air for a quarter of an hour—just to give the audience its half-crown's worth, eh?"

"I'm not talking about that. I'm talking about you and Joe."

Mrs. Gregson sat up in bed and opened her eyes very wide.

"Well! Now this is going to be really interesting! If there's one thing I love, it's a nice fairy story before I go off to sleep. Tell me all, darling. What about me and Joe?"

"Well, I'm not exactly a fool—"

"No, dear. You said that before, didn't you? We've only your word for it, but we'll take it as agreed. You're not exactly a fool. So what?"

"Well, I've seen the way you and Carey are playing about."

"Yes?"

"The whole outfit's talking about the pair of you. The way you went on with him in the train…I'm just warning you, Loretta, that's all. I know the kind of man he is, and I know you've got to be nice with him. But don't let it go any further than being nice, for God's sake."

"Lorrie—take your clothes off and get into bed."

"I've seen Carey break up more than one act before now. Women are his profession—the circus is just a side-line."

"Oh, shut up…turn off the light and get into bed. I'm dead."

"You…you aren't gone on him, are you?"

Loretta sat up again and became vehement.

"Sure. I'm mad about the man. He's my dream idol. So handsome, so strong…whenever I feel those manly arms around me, crushing my poor weak little body, drawing me closer and closer towards him—hi!…Lorrie…"

But the other half of the World's Most Sensational Trapeze Artists had gone out and rudely banged the door in the middle of his wife's rather lovely sentence.

"Oh, well…" said his wife, and went off to sleep.

On the other side of the door, Lorimer stood still for a moment and then decided wisely on a little fresh air. He had taken off his collar and tie, but the night was stifling and it was almost one o'clock; there would be no one about. He walked along the corridor and, turning the corner, bumped into Dodo the clown as he came out of his room.

"Hullo—not in bed yet?"

The immaculate little man looked worried.

"Er—no. I've been sitting up, reading. Can't get to sleep. I was just going down to try and get a tonic water. I—I've rung the bell, but no one seems to be up."

"That's not surprising. Cheerio."

Lorimer let himself out of the hotel and stepped out into the empty streets. He looked back up to the third fourth-floor window of the room which he and Loretta occupied. The light went out just as he turned his head. He walked on, hands in pockets.

Maybe he was all wrong about Loretta and Carey... maybe it was just Loretta fooling about, like she always did. But Carey was a nasty piece of work, all the same... you couldn't trust a man like that with a woman, let alone with a good-looker like Loretta. She knew how to look after herself, though; she wasn't the same as the other women in the circus, who were ready to leap at anything in trousers.

Lorimer rather prided himself on the fact that Loretta and he were a class above the other circus artists—all except Dodo, and possibly Anton. They weren't high-class, but they were decent middle-class; they might have come out of poor families, and had to work like slaves ever since they were kids, but they'd done their best to improve themselves. He used to get ragged unmercifully for going to night-school classes when they were with Mendl's. Old Mendl had been pretty decent about it, fixing in their act early in the first performance and late in the second so that he could get away...but the rest of the crowd thought he was cuckoo. Mendl understood, though; so did Loretta.

And it had been worth it: they were top of the bill now, and though Lorimer found it a little difficult to explain how night-schools and studying had helped to get them there, they had all right. They'd taught him one thing...refinement. That was what people were after nowadays; they didn't like things being thrown at them to the accompaniment of a blare of trumpets, like they used to. They liked cleverness in an act, quietness and subtlety. If you did a daring bit of trapeze work while the tympani crashed and the drums rolled they clapped all right; but if you did the same act, quietly and as though it were of no importance at all, they clapped a damn' sight harder. There was a little piece of business in their present act which illustrated this very well: while Loretta was swinging towards him, stretching out her arms to be caught in mid-air, Lorimer sat on the higher of the two trapezes which they used, putting straight the beret he wore in his act and apparently paying no attention to his partner's actions. At the very last moment he dropped and gripped her wrists, as though it had suddenly occurred to him to do something about it.…That always went down well.

Yes, it had been worth it. He was able to talk to people—not just about the circus, which was all that the other circus folk could talk about—but about anything, taking his part in a normal conversation. He wasn't in the same class as Dodo, who spent all his free time reading thick books and bringing out quotations from Plato and all those guys. Maybe not even in the same class as Anton, who had come from a good family and had been to a public school and a respectable business before he went nuts and joined up in a fifth-rate travelling show. Hardly in the same class as Anton, who could take more than his share in any conversation, though Lorimer suspected a good deal of it to be bluff…But, all the same, he was a class above the rest of them. Thank God for that.

Loretta and Carey, though. He wasn't sure of Loretta. He never had been sure. Sometimes he thought she was of the same type as himself, anxious to get on, keen on the right things. At other times, she went on like any other circus woman. She had a common streak in her which kept on bobbing up every now and then. Maybe he was all wrong about her and Carey, of course. But if he were right?…

He remembered Raquel, who had been Vincent Varconi's partner in the high-wire act in Carey's last season. She had started with Joe Carey in just the same way as Loretta was doing now. Nothing serious; seeing a lot of each other, getting people talking about them and nudging each other and hinting things, though. Then there'd been the flare-up. Varconi had caught her in Carey's caravan, preparing to sleep with him. That had been a hell of a night, all right. Varconi was Italian; he'd wanted to get the thing settled right away…with a knife. Carey had knocked him out with a left to the chin which took the wind out of everyone's sails, particularly Varconi's. He'd booted the pair of them out of the circus first thing next morning—said he had no use for a husband who used a knife, and less use for a wife who was foolish enough to own a husband like that. They'd gone—separately, of course. Raquel was selling chocolates and cigarettes in a dirty little dance-hall somewhere in London now; Varconi was dragging along, doing high-wire stuff on his own in three-night stances with touring shows. Two lives smashed in one night. That mustn't ever happen to Loretta and himself…but it might.

He stopped and asked the one policeman still out of bed where Martin's Field was.

"Martin's Field? What do you want to go there for at this time of night, eh?"

Lorimer didn't know, really.

"I've got to go and see about something, that's all. I'm with the circus."

The policeman flashed his torch in Lorimer's face.

"You're the trapeze bloke, aren't you? Lorimer?"

"That's right. Lorimer and Loretta."

"Thought I recognized you. I've seen your pictures in the papers. Saw you when you were here last year, as well."

"Good. Did you enjoy the show?"

"First-rate. I'd sooner have my job than yours, though. Flying through the air with the greatest of ease—not for the likes of me. Not with a figure like mine."

"What about this field, then?"

"Less than five minutes from here. First on your left, and then straight ahead. You can't miss it."

"Thanks. Good night."

"In case you don't know—good morning."

Lorimer walked on, feeling considerably brighter. That was the sort of thing that made it worthwhile. Complete strangers—people on the street, policemen on their beat—stopping you and saying, "You're the great Lorimer, aren't you? Of the World's Most Sensational Trapeze Artists, Lorimer and Loretta?" Perhaps not saying so in so many words, but that was what they meant. The bobby had seen his pictures in the papers. He remembered him from last year's show. Fame...that was the thing that mattered. And, having got it, Lorimer was quite determined not to lose it, through Loretta and Carey, or through any other means.

He went straight to the corner of the field where Joe Carey's green-and-white caravan had been parked. He had left the hotel without any intention of doing more than clearing his head by a sharp walk. Now his mind was made up: he was going to have a chat with Joe Carey. A nice quiet chat—no rough business—just to find out exactly how things stood. He walked across the soft grass and came to within thirty yards of the caravan. The lights were still on inside it; the green oil-silk curtains were only half drawn across the windows. The headlights of a car passing along the road at the side of the field threw up the bright paintwork of the caravan, and the neat black lettering on the side: Joseph

Carey, Sole Proprietor, Carey's World-Famous Circus and
Menagerie. One day, Lorimer thought, a caravan would stand
in a field with lettering on it announcing that Lorimer was
sole proprietor of a circus, and a better one even than Carey's.

He was just going forward to the caravan when he realized
that he was not alone. Two men were crossing from the far
side of the field, making towards the caravan. There were
some piles of scaffolding poles and bundles of canvas lying
about, sent on by the advance men. Lorimer sat down on
one of the canvas bales and watched.

The men came straight to the caravan, looked round, ran
quietly up the four steps. The taller of the two stood on the
top step and whistled…a short, peculiar whistle. The door
of the caravan opened no more than a couple of inches. A
narrow slit of light shone out far across the grass. The taller of
the two men came very close to the door, which was opened
no further. He stayed there for perhaps half a minute, then
elbowed his way past his companion, down the steps, and
hurried off across the field. The performance was repeated
with the other man. He, too, turned and disappeared. Not
a word had been spoken. The night was still and Lorimer
could easily have heard any conversation from where he was
watching. The narrow slit of light vanished. The door of the
caravan closed softly.

"Queer," said Lorimer. "Who the hell were those two?"

He lit a cigarette and walked slowly up to the caravan.
He was within a dozen yards of it when the curtains were
drawn quickly across the windows. Old Man Carey preparing to go to bed, no doubt. Alone? No, not alone…sounds of
conversation plainly audible as Lorimer came near the caravan. Heated conversation, too, and not a lady. All humble
apologies to Mr. Carey for doubting, for one brief moment,
his morality. A man's voice, and the voice of a man in a
temper. It was impossible to make out what was being said,

for the windows of the caravan were closed, but there was not much doubt that something approaching a free fight was going on at that moment inside Mr. Joseph Carey's elegant green-and-white caravan. Not knowing quite why the affair should interest him, Lorimer walked silently round to the back of the caravan. Just as he did so, the door opened. He stubbed out his cigarette and pressed himself close against the curved coachwork. He stood still and listened.

"Now get out," said Joe Carey. "And keep your dirty little nose out of other people's business, see? If you value your job at all, that is...."

The door slammed. Whoever was being shown out so politely came down the steps, turned, and came to within a foot of where Lorimer was standing. It was Anton. Anton, top of the circus bill, and trainer of the seven Bengal tigers who were at that moment causing such a commotion in their railway siding a mile away. Lorimer thought it best to speak before being seen.

"Anton..." he said.

The other man turned round and stared at him.

"Good God!" he said. "Are you another of them?"

And walked away.

This, thought Lorimer, was too much for one night. To set out for a quiet stroll to get over the effects of a tiff with one's wife, to be drawn to Joe Carey's caravan, and to witness goings-on such as these, to get a remark like that from Anton, with whom he had always been on as friendly terms as is possible between the two leading attractions of the circus...far too much for one night.

"Are you another of them?" Another of what? What the devil was going on in Joe's caravan? Was it, after all, something more serious than women? There was no answer to these questions....For a moment he thought of hurrying after Anton and getting to the bottom of it; then he gave up the idea, and decided to wait until the morning. The idea of his quiet chat with Carey was also forgotten. He felt suddenly tired, and set off across the field on his way back to the hotel.

He was just leaving the field when he heard the whistle again. The same short, peculiar whistle used by each of the two men whom he had watched. He'd get to the bottom of this, at any rate. He turned and ran quietly across the grass until he reached the caravan. He walked round the side of it, and waited until the door shut and the latest visitor was heard coming down the steps. This time the visitor prepared to leave the field by the other gate; Lorimer could stare at his back without being seen himself. In doing so, he got the biggest shock of the night. For the last man to visit Joe Carey's green-and-white caravan was the immaculate little man whom he had last seen going in search of tonic water at the Station Hotel. The clown—Dodo.

Lorimer was still young, young enough to lick his lips at the thought of adventure, which rarely came his way in the everyday life of the circus. The thrill of falling fifty feet through the air, knowing that a second miscalculated or an inch misplaced meant certain death—that was no adventure to him, and never had been. That was his job; this sort of thing was much more intriguing. He made up his mind as soon as the clown had disappeared. It might lead to something, or it might not. He'd take a chance, and hope it led to a lot.

He ran up the steps of the caravan, and whistled, the same short, peculiar whistle which he had heard the clown and the other two men use—or as near to it as he could manage, having come from an unmusical family which even objected to the *Blue Danube* waltz being played while they were doing their trapeze act.

The door opened. Two inches, no more. An arm was pushed out and a small cardboard package placed in his hand. He took hold of it in silence and waited.

"Well?" said Carey's voice. "Come on, then…."

There being nothing to say, Lorimer kept silent. The door was flung open and Carey stood silhouetted against the light inside the caravan. He was a huge man, coarse and broad-shouldered. It was evident that he had been drinking. He stared at Lorimer for a moment; Lorimer could not see his face, which showed up as merely a round bullet against the light of the lamp.

"What the hell…?" said Carey.

His right arm shot out. The knuckles of his hand caught Lorimer on the point of the chin, making it unnecessary for him to have wasted so much time and trouble on the bursting of a single obstinate pimple. He swayed and crashed headlong down the steps. He lay still, his head on the damp grass and his body stretched up the steps.

The door of Mr. Joseph Carey's caravan shut with a bang and the key was turned quickly in the lock.

Chapter Three

Mr. Minto came down to breakfast at the Station Hotel on the following morning, and wondered just why he was such a mug.

Why had he been mug enough to promise to look into this business of his sister's wedding and actually take part in the ceremony? Why had he left London a week earlier than was necessary and come to stay in this excellent, but unsociable, Station Hotel? Why had he tolerated a bedroom that was next to a bath-room which gurgled and spluttered and generally behaved like Dante's Inferno all night? And why, in the name of heaven, had he been mug enough to rise at this unearthly hour of the morning, when it was perfectly obvious that there would be nothing to do, after eating his breakfast, but to sit in the lounge and read *The Times* until lunch? Why?

"Echo," said Mr. Minto, coming into the dining-hall and taking a sad look over its wide, open spaces—"echo answers 'Why?'"

It was Robert who was really responsible for his visit. Mr. Minto had not seen his brother Robert for over three years. His own business kept him in London, and Robert's business only allowed him to come up to town on occasional hectic one-day excursions.

"Business" is perhaps not the right word to use in connection with Robert Minto's life work, for Robert was a clergyman. To be strictly accurate, he was a priest, and second-in-command of the Catholic Church in this town. Mr. Minto had never quite understood the reasons which led Robert to taking the cloth; for, throughout his childhood, the only leanings he had towards religion showed a desire merely to take the collection. However, Robert had become a priest. It embarrassed Mr. Minto slightly, and he saw no more of his brother than was absolutely necessary. He was a Catholic himself, like all his family; but the presence of a priest in a family like his, and especially in a business like his own, was rather apt to cramp one's style. However, that was entirely Robert's own affair, and as long as he kept his religion a matter between himself and his flock and did not try to make his own family see the error of their ways, Mr. Minto had no objections. To be on the safe side, however, he made a point of only meeting brother Robert at the Christmas family reunions…and occasionally managed to skip even these.

Robert Minto (the family could never get used to the idea of him being called "Father Minto") lived quietly and seemingly happy in this provincial town, appeared to be worshipped by every poor person in it, and occupied a microscopic flat presided over by the youngest member of the Minto clan, Claire. And, going right to the root of the trouble, it was really Claire who was to blame for Mr. Minto suffering the rumbles and gurgles of the hotel bath-room.

Claire Minto was several years younger than her brothers, and had a most awkward habit of suddenly deciding to do surprising things. And an even more awkward habit of doing them—at once, right away, before anyone could get their breath and suggest that such actions were not altogether wise. As soon as a revolution or a war broke out in any part of the world, Claire Minto packed her bag, left her clergyman brother to look after himself as best he could, and made a bee-line for the affected part for a holiday.

Claire had gone to Austria at the time when Dolfuss was assassinated, and Mr. Minto had been put to a great deal of trouble getting her out of that country and back to England. Claire, it seemed, had insisted on taking photographs of the Chancellery in Vienna where the murder had taken place, and had said exactly what she thought of the various officials who tried to stop her. She had been promptly locked up as a suspected foreign spy. As soon as Britons became really unpopular in Italy, Claire Minto had hopped on a convenient train, arrived in Rome, and started asking for trouble right away by suggesting in a loud voice that Signor Mussolini was an ass. Only the combined efforts of her two brothers had stopped her from going to Abyssinia itself for a month's rest. And now it seemed she had made up her mind to set out on an even riskier journey. Marriage.

Mr. Minto, hard at work in London, had received a frantic letter from brother Robert. Brother Robert had a perplexing habit of beginning a letter as though he were resuming a conversation which had been interrupted for a moment. He started in the middle, and ended in the same place. He held no brief for punctuation of any kind, put a great deal of his thoughts in brackets, and underlined every second word. Mr. Minto took some little time before he was able to gather what was biting his brother. At last, however, he grasped the situation.

Claire had got engaged to a young man whom she had met at a League of Nations Rally. The young man was called Briggs, and Robert Minto seemed to think that the engagement made the reform of the League of Nations even more necessary than ever. Mr. Briggs, when not attending League of Nations Rallies, was a vacuum-cleaner canvasser, and Robert did not think him at all a suitable match for Claire. He had nothing against vacuum-cleaner canvassers as a clan; many of them, he felt, were to be numbered among the salt of the earth…but he could not help feeling that Claire was being just a little hasty over the matter. Would Mr. Minto come down at once, meet Mr. Briggs, have a serious talk with Claire, and see what he could do about the business? (Mr. Minto, reading between Robert's lines, gathered that Robert was a good deal concerned at the thought of Claire marrying and leaving him alone in the flat with a housekeeper.) Come at once, said Robert, underlining this heavily, and ending up rather surprisingly by saying that the wedding had been fixed for the following Saturday, and that he had better bring his morning-dress and top-hat in case he wasn't able to change Claire's mind.

Mr. Minto had arrived the previous night, had seen Claire and realized that her mind was made up and that nothing short of a real good earthquake would stop her from marrying the vacuum-cleaner gentleman on the following Saturday. He had also met the young vacuum-cleaner gentleman, and found him a nice, reliable young man, if inclined to have clammy hands and to say "Pleased to meet you" when introduced. He had paid a quick visit to his brother Robert, assured him that nothing could be done about the impending disaster, and that he had better carry on with the arrangements for the wedding—for Mr. Briggs was also a Catholic and the ceremony would take place in Robert's church.

Mr. Minto had then gone back to his hotel and become involved in what seemed to be a high-class conducted tour which had just arrived in town. It was, in fact, the star performers of Carey's Circus. He had had a drink with a man who looked like a stockbroker and who turned out to be some kind of an acrobat, and then went up to bed. The circus people, tired and dirty after their long railway journey, all elected to have noisy baths in the next-door bath-room, and even after they had gone to their rooms the bath-room took the rest of the night to settle down. It gurgled, rumbled, spluttered, groaned, wheezed, and made peculiar plopping noises. Mr. Minto sat up in bed and read the advertisements in a copy of *Punch*, dated August 1935, which happened to be lying on the table beside him. At a quarter to eight he rose in none too mellow a mood, and now, less than an hour later, he sat down at a window table in the dining-hall and scanned the menu.

"Grape-fruit, sir?" said an aged waiter. "Or porridge?"

"What's the name of the chef?" asked Mr. Minto.

"Bernstein, sir."

"In that case, grape-fruit," said Mr. Minto. "If it had been McKenzie or McDonald, we might have risked the porridge. Being Bernstein, we'll have the grape-fruit, please."

The waiter, unable to follow this line of thought, shuffled off to the serving-hatch and reported that one portion grape-fruit was required for a gentleman who was crackers.

Mr. Minto launched his attack on the grape-fruit, and ordered a light meal of finnan haddock, double egg, and sausage with a couple of rashers of bacon—"fat and crisp, the kind that breaks on your fork"—toast, marmalade, and black coffee. He then removed an offending flower-vase, folded his *Times* and set it in front of him, and started to read how right the Government had been in dealing with the recent tricky international situation. The Government, he gathered, had given a lead to the other nations of the world by sitting on the fence and doing nothing. Many other Governments would no doubt have dashed in wildly and done something in the recent spot of bother; the British Government, by doing nothing, had restored confidence and brought relief to what had threatened to be a very serious situation.

Mr. Minto was half-way through the third paragraph of this and rather more than half-way through his second sausage when he realized that he was no longer the only nit-wit to be eating breakfast at this hour. He looked over the top of his newspaper and saw a small, carefully dressed gentleman with a bald head sitting down at the next table.

"I suppose it's tinned?" the gentleman was saying.

The waiter looked pained.

"Oh no, sir. Fresh grape-fruit is always served in this hotel, sir."

"Can you say the same for the porridge?"

"I'm sure you'll find the porridge excellent, sir."

"If it isn't a rude question, what nationality is your chef?"

The waiter took some time to grasp this. Two customers of this kind in a single morning is more than any waiter can stand.

"Er…I think he's a Pole, sir. But I'm not quite certain. I could make inquiries, sir."

"No. Don't bother. I'll have the grape-fruit. I was just hoping that he might be a Scot, and then I could have the porridge. The English don't know how to make it, and I shouldn't think a Pole would be very good at it. Grape-fruit, please."

"Yes, sir."

The waiter shuffled off again, and told the kitchen staff that there must be some kind of educational conference on in the town, since both the blokes taking breakfast were quite obviously mental.

Mr. Minto, hearing this conversation, brightened up. Here was a kindred spirit—a man who shared his views on the major issues of life, such as porridge. He lowered his newspaper screen and beamed across to the other table.

"Good morning," said Mr. Minto. "I'm so glad to hear you say that about the porridge. As a matter of fact, I'd just said exactly the same thing myself."

"Only the Scots can make porridge," said the little man seriously. "With all other nationalities, it's a toss-up between two evils. The lumpy, congealed variety—and the runny, dish-water stuff."

"Agreed," said Mr. Minto, who held strong views on the proper consistency of porridge.

"Mind you, one occasionally comes across a Scot who can't make porridge. It's this modern craze for synthetic breakfasts, done up in cardboard boxes with high-sounding names, that's doing it. The industry is dying. I came across three lumps the size of halfpennies in a plate of porridge I had at Inverness this spring. In Inverness, mind you. The heart of the porridge country."

"Dreadful," said Mr. Minto. "You wouldn't like to come and sit here, would you? It's so pleasant to meet anyone who shares one's views on things like porridge."

The little man collected his *Seven Pillars of Wisdom* and his serviette and moved across to Mr. Minto's table.

"My name is Minto," said Mr. Minto. "I'm staying down here for a few days. I can't think why—but I am."

"My name is Mayhew—Ernest Mayhew," said the little man. "I'm here for a week also—because I can't help it."

"Ah," said Mr. Minto sympathetically. "Not exactly a bright spot, is it?"

"There are some very interesting Norman ruins, I believe. And the local Catholic Church dates back several hundreds of years. It was originally a tavern. Cromwell, so they say, stabled his horses there when he passed through the town on his way North."

"Dear me," said Mr. Minto. "I hope they've cleaned it out since then. I've got a wedding there on Saturday."

"Really? Congratulations. I can't say I'm absorbed in this grape-fruit, can you?"

"It's not my wedding," said Mr. Minto. "It's my sister's. I'm giving her away."

"I always say 'I suppose it's tinned, is it?' in a sneering sort of way, you know, because it almost always is nowadays. And whenever I get the real stuff, I'm so very disappointed. It's not nearly as good as the tinned variety."

"She's getting married to a vacuum-cleaner canvasser," said Mr. Minto.

"And, in any case," said the little man, "I always squirt."

Mr. Minto began to feel that the conversation was getting at cross-purposes. He tried a new tack.

"I see you're reading *Seven Pillars*," he said.

"I'm not," said the little man. "I'm carrying it about with me. I do it to create an impression. People say, 'Look, he's reading *Seven Pillars*.' And they at once think that I must be not only an intelligent sort of man, but—what's more important—that I must be able to afford thirty shillings for a book."

"Both of which are probably true, I imagine."

"Thank you. Do you know what I am—what my occupation is, I mean?"

"I've no idea."

"Have a guess. I'll give you until the fish arrives. That will probably be some considerable time. The service in this hotel is *largo*."

"You aren't a solicitor?"

"God forbid."

"A novelist?"

"I've been talking to you for five minutes, and I haven't yet mentioned one of my masterpieces. Therefore I cannot be a novelist. Try again."

"A low comedian?" said Mr. Minto, being facetious.

"Perfectly correct," said the little man. "Not on the stage, I may say. I'm with the circus. Perhaps you have noticed there is a circus in the town this week? There are posters of it everywhere, even on the Norman ruins. I've spoken to the publicity manager about it, but he won't listen to me. I wouldn't mind it so much if the posters were true, but they're not. They'll all exaggerations and more than half of them are downright lies. Isn't there a law about posters, Mr. Murdo?"

"Minto."

"Minto. I'm sorry. There ought to be. If I were to advertise this grape-fruit as the Sweetest Grape-Fruit in the World, I'd soon get into trouble about it, wouldn't I? The sugar, please, if you don't mind…thank you. But if people advertise a circus turn as the Most Daring Act of its Kind in the World, no one bothers to question it. Whereas it's nothing of the kind. There are probably a hundred similar acts, or more daring acts, being performed in lesser-known circuses and not being advertised nearly as well. However, that's by the way. There's my card. I'm a clown. You may have heard of me. The name is Dodo."

Mr. Minto took the card solemnly and studied it. "Dodo, Carey's World-Famous Circus and Menagerie. London Address: 3 Hanover Gardens, S.W.I."

"It must be a very interesting life," said Mr. Minto.

"It's a very difficult one," said the little man. "In the music-halls, for instance, you can be certain of the same audience night after night. Or, at any rate, of the same sequences of audiences. You know that on Monday night the only people who matter are the newspaper critics, and so you play to their level."

"Up to it?" said Mr. Minto.

"Down to it. From Tuesday to Friday, you get the ordinary lower- and middle-class audience, and you play as intelligently as possible. On Saturday you get an audience who have come merely for a night out, most of whom have had already too much to drink, and who don't care what happens as long as the intervals are timed to suit the licensing hours. So you play down again, even lower than to the critics."

"I see," said Mr. Minto, and poured out another cup of coffee.

"But in the circus you never know what kind of house you're going to have. It's especially difficult with children. You may have a house packed with children, and you think that this is going to be easy. All you have to do is to fall down as many times as possible, landing in a pail of whitewash whenever you can—and you'll be a riot. And what happens? You find that these wretched children have been to the cinema twice already that week, have been lapping up Noel Coward epigrams, and are bored to tears with whitewash. They want a good smutty line, and the smuttier the better. Sad, Mr. Purdoe, but true."

"Minto," said Mr. Minto once again. "But surely—"

"Again, you have an evening performance, when there are very few children in the house. You decide to put on a rather more subtle performance. It falls completely flat. And if you do try landing on your backside, just to see how they take it, they hold up the show for five minutes, laughing themselves silly."

"But—"

"On the other hand—was your haddock all right?... there's something a little peculiar about this one—on the other hand, you may find yourself in a town where children are still children and still laugh at the throwing of custard-pies. I've never played in this town before, for instance. When the circus was here last year I was away, helping to bury my brother-in-law. It was the only thing I ever did for my brother-in-law that I didn't regret immediately afterwards. Now, I'm going on in the opening performance this afternoon without having any idea what kind of children are bred in this town. They may be custard-pie children. Or they may be what I call Lonsdale children—the playwright, not the peer. Or they may be the sticky, half-way-in-between kind. They're the worst. I'll have found out before the end of the performance, of course, and I will be able to alter my tactics in time for the next show. Which will probably have just the very opposite kind of audience. It's very tantalizing."

The little man pushed his fish away with a melancholy air.

"What kind of a circus is Carey's?" asked Mr. Minto.

"Between you and me and the gatepost," said the clown—"though where the gatepost comes into it I can't quite make out—between you and me, Carey's Circus is a hotbed of crime."

"Crime?" said Mr. Minto. It was not a word of which he was particularly fond.

"There's more crime going on in Carey's Circus than in the whole underworld of London, and I happen to know the underworld of London pretty well. I lived in it for three years, and a tamer and more respectable lot of people you couldn't find. Except when a gang of foreign crooks crop up and start giving the place a bad name. No, Mr.—"

"Minto."

"No, Mr. Minto, if it's crime you're after, Carey's is the place for it. Theft, immorality, blackmail—you'll find all the pretties there. There was an act with us last season—Raquel and Varconi. A couple of high-wire artists. They weren't very good on the high wire, and Raquel wasn't particularly good off it. She was Mrs. Varconi. She was living with Carey, the proprietor of the circus, for a while. Varconi heard about it, and the act smashed up. But not before Carey had a very ugly scar down his left arm…from Varconi's knife. There might have been murder that night. There has been murder once, but that was hushed up."

"Dear me," said Mr. Minto. "And I always thought that circus people were just one big, happy family."

"You've been reading the novelists who join up with a circus for a fortnight and then go home and write a book about it," said the clown. "There's crime going on at Carey's right now—plenty of it. I could tell you of one certain piece of blackmail, of a repeat performance of the Raquel and Varconi business that'll be coming to a head very soon… and of something a good deal worse."

"Go on. Tell me," said Mr. Minto. "I lead such a quiet life myself…this is all very exciting for me."

"Well—I'm not boring you? I've talked all about my own life. I haven't let you say a word, have I?"

"The only important words I have to say this week are after my sister's wedding," said Mr. Minto. "I've got to propose the toast of the happy pair, blast them. Carry on with Carey's crime. Maybe I'll write a book about it myself."

"Why? Are you an author?"

"No. I'm a detective," said Mr. Minto, who liked to be honest about these things. "I'm from Scotland Yard. Detective-Inspector Minto, to give me my full title."

The little man stopped in the middle of raising a forkful of sausage to his mouth, and stared at Mr. Minto. He seemed a little shaken.

"Are you really?" he said. "Well, of course, that doesn't make any difference. It'll be all the more interesting from your point of view, won't it?"

"Yes. Go on."

"Well, what I was going to tell you was…dear me!"

"Anything the matter?"

"I've just remembered—I have to be down at the circus at nine-thirty. I'd no idea it was so late. We've got a new band,

and we're running through some of the acts this morning to get them sure of their cues. I'm so sorry. Perhaps some other time....Good morning."

And, having folded his serviette and collected his *Seven Pillars of Wisdom*, the clown left the dining-hall at what seemed to Mr. Minto an unnecessary speed.

"What a terrible drawback to have to go through life with," said Mr. Minto to himself. "Being a detective. It makes them all shut up just when they're going to open out."

Chapter Four

Anton stood waiting his turn, wrapped in a dressing-gown of apricot silk. The wings of a circus are even more draughty than the wings of a stage, and in Carey's they were merely two canvas alleyways leading from the ring out to the caravans and tents where the performers, human and animals, idled away their time before and after their acts. It was in the left-hand alleyway that Anton was waiting, standing behind the heavy curtain of red plush which the artists pushed aside to enter the big tent. Between that and the other entrance, the circus band was thumping out a Strauss waltz while Miss St. Clair and her Educated Ponies went through a series of rather jerky manoeuvres supposed to be an old-fashioned waltz. The band, by keeping strictly in time with the ponies' hoofs, was usually able to persuade the audience that the animals were waltzing in perfect time; today, with a new band, Miss St. Clair's ponies seemed a little less educated than usual, and appeared to have lost a good deal of their sense of rhythm.

On the other side of the band platform, a long tunnel of steel sections had been stretched out through the alley, connecting the ring with the cage in which Anton's seven tigers were housed. At a certain chord from the band (or, more likely, at an uncertain chord, for the new trombone player had not yet accustomed himself to fitting in his blowing with the rapid succession of acts in the ring below him) the door of the cage would be opened, and the seven tigers—after a good deal of prodding and poking—would slouch lazily down through the tunnel and into the ring.

Anton walked across to find out what mood the animals were in. The tigers were very like Dodo's audience: you never knew quite how they were going to behave. Four of the seven were reliable; they had been with Anton since they were five weeks old and he could take them on a shopping expedition along the main street of any town, knowing that they would behave themselves a great deal better than any of the pedestrians. He had once done this, when the circus was in Edinburgh, parading the four cubs along the full length of Princes Street on the end of four chains which looked much too slender for their job; and the Princes Street cafés have never done such business in their lives, for the good people of Edinburgh decided unanimously on a nice quiet cup of coffee as soon as they saw the four beasts strolling along the pavement.

The cubs were all right; they had been caught young enough to have the intelligence drilled out of them, and a fearful obedience installed in its place. The other three tigers were different; they still knew perfectly well that the whole idea of being subdued and made to go through stupid tricks by a single puny man was absurd. Three full-grown man-eaters in a cage with a nearly-naked and unarmed man…one of these days they would do a great deal more than merely growling and snarling and reaching out their paws to try and cuff this helpless mortal….

Peter, the oldest and largest of the seven, was the one who would do it. The duel between Anton and Peter was always the star turn of the act, and the audience, sitting back and telling each other how clever this fellow Anton was, never realized how slender was the borderline between Anton's mastery of Peter and Peter's conquest of that mastery. Peter was always left to the end of each trick: when the other six had been cowed and placed meekly in their positions on top of the bright yellow boxes, there was always the long battle with Peter until, with a last vicious snarl, he climbed up on his own box and completed the picture.

Less than a month ago, when Anton was putting his tigers, one by one, through a hoop of flaming rope—and fire is the thing a tiger hates more than any other—there had been a tense struggle before Peter could be persuaded to follow the others. The act had played four minutes longer than its scheduled time that night, and Anton had not enjoyed those four minutes at all. He knew, however, that if he gave in and contented himself and the audience with putting six of his seven beasts through that flaming hoop, Peter would realize that he was getting on top…and God alone knew what would happen at the next performance. So he carried on until the thing was done; and the attendant standing outside the cage put back his revolver and mopped his forehead, and Anton, after bowing and salaaming to a packed house, ran out of the ring, sweating.

He put his arm through the bars of the cage and scratched the ear of one of the cubs, who was lying asleep on the floor of the cage and could not be bothered to do its silly tricks twice today in this heat. Most of the others were sleeping, too, or stretched out blinking their eyes in the sun and occasionally flogging their tails to keep off the flies. Peter was pacing backwards and forwards along the full length of the cage. He was in one of his moods all right. Anton called to him by name; he paid no attention, but continued to trek silently up and down the cage.

"Peter!" said Anton. "Peter...come along, Peter....All right, if you're going to be high-hat..."

He went on scratching the cub, which woke up, stretched itself, and rumbled with pleasure, for Anton had hit on exactly the right spot for scratching.

"Is that good, Rene? That good, old girl?...Are you very itchy there, eh?"

Peter sprang. One quick, enormous bound from the other side of the cage to within six inches of Anton's face. Its claws could not have been an inch from Anton's hand as he drew it out between the bars. He could feel its breath in his face. It stood over the drowsy cub, staring straight into Anton's eyes.

"Now then, Peter!" said the trainer. "What's the matter with you today? Touch of liver, eh?"

He walked back to the other alleyway and lit a cigarette. It was satisfying to note that his hand was perfectly steady as he held it up to shield the flame of the match. He peered through the heavy plush curtains: Miss St. Clair was on her second-last movement, the Rumba. Anton smiled; it was funny to think that this was the dance that was thought most of by the audience, when it was by far the simplest to do. Pull back the bit in the ponies' mouths as tightly as you could, give them a little encouragement with a jab from your heels in their flanks, tugging them back as hard as possible at the same time...and the result was an unsteady, jerky motion which, with a little help from the band, was at once recognized as a perfect Rumba step. Not that Miss St. Clair was getting very much help from the band today, for the trumpeter seemed to have got *My Muchacha* mixed up with *Moment Musicale*. Two minutes, and Miss St. Clair would be off and Anton on.

A young man in grey flannels and a canary sweater came up to him.

"I've been wanting to see you, Anton," he said. "What did you mean last night?"

"You know damn' well, Lorimer," said Anton.

"I'm sorry—I don't. As far as I can remember, you said, 'Good God—are you another of them?' Another of what, if it isn't a rude question?"

"What were you doing at Joe's caravan at that time of night—if that isn't a rude question?"

"That's a personal matter."

"Exactly. You take my tip, Lorimer, cut out the personal matter before it finishes you and your act."

"I still don't get you. Is there something shady going on at Joe's caravan?"

Anton turned to face him.

"What did you do after I left you?"

"I went and knocked up Joe."

"Exactly. I thought so. And you got what you were after, I suppose?"

"I did not. I got a first-class, grade 'A' sock on the chin. I wasn't after it. I wasn't even expecting it, otherwise I wouldn't have taken it as easily as I did. The funny thing is that I'm beginning to doubt if I really got it. I went to play hell with Joe about it this morning, and one of us is a liar. His little story is that I was found out for the count on the other side of the field, half a mile away from his ruddy caravan. Tight, so it seems."

"That's a polite way of putting it, isn't it?"

"What the devil are you getting at?"

"You know, Lorimer."

"I don't. Honest to God, Anton, I don't. I'll tell you quite frankly—I went to have a heart-to-heart talk with Joe... about...well, about Loretta. You know the way she's been playing about with Carey lately. I didn't want a repeat of that Raquel and Varconi business. I got down to the field round about one o'clock. I saw a couple of blokes—I don't know who they were—going up to his caravan. They gave a queer sort of whistle, and the door opened and they went off without a word."

"Whistle, eh?"

"That's right. Then I started off again to get in and see Joe, and I realized that he had company. You, in fact. Then you came out and saw me, and said your little piece about me being 'another of them'. You cleared off, and I was going to do the same thing when Joe had another visitor. The place was quite busy, I tell you. Same whistle—same funny business at the door—same lack of idle talk. I saw who this one was, though. It was Dodo."

"What?"

"Dodo—the clown."

"Good God! I can't believe that he's…"

"That he's what?"

"Never mind. Carry on. What happened then?"

"I thought it might be rather fun to look into the business. I hopped up the caravan steps and—like a damned fool—gave the whistle. Joe opened the door and socked me. At least, that's what I thought happened. Joe doesn't seem to agree with me, and he's been very pleasant to me all day. Maybe I'm going potty and imagined the whole thing. I can't have dreamt it, because Loretta says I wasn't in bed the whole night. She's full of nasty insinuations about where I spent the evening."

Anton threw away his cigarette.

"Lorimer," he said, "is that the truth? You've no idea what has been going on at Joe's—honestly?"

"Honestly. What has? Come on…tell a fellow."

"I can't tell you just now. That's my cue. And I can't see you after the show. I'm busy. I've got to get into the town and do something. Listen—I'll see you after tonight's show. Dodo's giving a party. Are you going?"

"Yes."

"Good. I'm not. Sneak out of it round about midnight. I'll meet you at the back of the tigers' cage. I'll tell you something that'll make you sit up. I'll tell you this now, though. Keep that girl of yours away from Joe Carey. He's not a very suitable companion for a nice girl like Loretta."

"I know it," said Lorimer.

The band blared out, hanging grimly to a triumphal chord. The plush curtains parted, and Miss St. Clair's Educated Ponies trooped through and were led away for a wash-down and a meal. Miss St. Clair appeared, said: "Hullo, darling!" to Anton, disappeared again, took a number of bows to the accompaniment of some rather half-hearted applause, appeared again, said: "Lovely house—just listen to the dears!" disappeared again, took a few more bows to applause that was now only a ripple, came back through the curtains, debated for a moment about taking a third call, decided against it and went off to her dressing-tent for a cup of tea.

The band struck up Anton's music. On the other side of their platform, the door of the tigers' cage was opened, and the cubs roused and sent down the tunnel into the ring. The two older animals followed after a brief argument. Peter was left alone in a corner of the cage. The two attendants responsible for getting the animals into the ring armed themselves with sticks, and prodded Peter viciously in the behind. Anton, flinging off his dressing-gown, ran round to see what was holding up his act.

"Don't do that, you damned fools! Leave the beast alone—he'll go in all right if you leave him."

"Yes—but when?"

"Well, stop punching him like that. It's all right for you. I've got to go into the ring with him, after you've made him mad."

The tiger gave a lusty roar and slouched off down the tunnel.

"He's losing his nerve," said one of the attendants, who would no more have thought of appearing unarmed in the ring with the smallest of the cubs than have contemplated climbing Mount Everest on roller-skates. "Losing his nerve, that's what he's doing."

Anton parted the curtains and ran to the side of the ring. The house was filled mainly with children, who rose and cheered wildly. This was the kind of thing they were after; for, having been let out early from their schools in order to attend the opening performance of the circus, they had very little use for Miss St. Clair and her Educated Ponies. The less education the better. The tigers and the elephants and the comic little clown were what they were after. They had studied the posters of Anton's act each day since Mr. Johnston and his advance staff arrived in the town and plastered them on all the hoardings...they had studied them, and weaved highly imaginative tales around the gentleman and the things he did to his seven tigers. He held the biggest one up in his arms, high above his head, and made the others jump over it. That was what he did: there was a picture of him doing it on the hoarding beside the station. They had not yet reached the age of realizing that circus posters, like the advertisements of patent medicines, are a little too freely studded with superlatives to be taken literally. They cheered and yelled, and suddenly subsided and waited in silence.

Anton opened the door of the huge cage which had been erected right round the ring—to the great annoyance of Miss St. Clair. Miss St. Clair made out that it spoiled her act and put the idea into her ponies' heads that they were dangerous animals. He banged the door shut, locking it behind his back. The tigers turned round to face him on hearing the door clang to, and the four cubs went meekly into the positions for their first trick without even waiting for a word from Anton.

He was unarmed, without even a whip: that was one of the great features of his act. The first few tricks were schedule stuff and went through smoothly, though Peter was plainly in no mood to be played with on this sultry afternoon. The high-jump apparatus was placed in position in the middle of the ring, and the rope hoop set on top of it. The tigers were back in their positions round the edge of the ring; the cubs had gone off to sleep. Anton, with his eyes fixed on Peter, walked backwards to the bars of the cage and took from one of the attendants outside the torch which was to set the rope hoop alight. Peter gave a lusty snarl on catching sight of the flame, and ran quickly round to the far side of the ring. Anton lit the hoop, which was soaked in petroleum and burned up quickly. He roused the cubs and sent them one at a time through the hoop without any great difficulty. The children got off their seats again and roared their approval. The two older beasts took a good deal more trouble before they could be persuaded to leap through the hoop. He got them at last and they retired, grumbling, on to their boxes. Anton walked up to Peter.

Peter was damned if he was going to go through any hoop of fire to please any animal trainer, however brilliant and well-paid. It was hot enough this afternoon without hoops of fire; he'd been rubbed up the wrong way by those attendants shoving him out of the cage; in any case, it was beneath his dignity to show himself cowed by a mere man in front of a house of yelling children. Peter sat very still on his box, his jaws wide open, but no sound coming from his powerful throat. Anton came up to within a yard of him, calling him by name. Peter looked down on him with a pair of bright green eyes. Anton took another step forward. A huge forepaw flashed out within inches of his face; he leapt back into the middle of the ring. The children sat tense, leaning forward on the edges of their seats. Anton walked slowly up to the tiger again.

"Peter!…come down, Peter!…Peter—here, Peter…"

The tiger roared and slouched off his box down on to the sawdust. Anton felt better—he had the upper hand now. He started to manoeuvre the beast round to the other side of the ring. Peter went, meekly at first, and then suddenly turned to face his trainer and made one lightning dash into the centre of the ring. Anton jumped aside and ran backwards to the bars of the cage.

"Whip!" he said.

He knew that, with Peter in his present frame of mind, it was merely inviting trouble to try and finish the act without a whip. The attendant passed it through the bars to him with a muttered, "Stick it, lad!" Anton grasped the whip without taking his eyes off Peter.

The two older beasts decided to come off their boxes and join in whatever fun happened to be going. It was the one thing Anton had hoped would not happen. He could deal with Peter alone all right; Peter, in his present mood, plus two other none-too-genial tigers at his back, was a different kettle of fish altogether. He cracked his whip; the two tigers went slowly back to their positions. Peter stood his ground in the middle of the ring, his neck stretched out and his jaws wide apart. The whip cracked again. The tiger went slowly round to the side of the ring from which he started his run up to the hoop of fire.

"Now, Peter…jump!"

The tiger jumped—at Anton.

A woman in the dearer seats—one of the few people at the matinée who had paid the necessary amount of money to be given a piece of carpet instead of a plain board to sit on—screamed shrilly. The attendant standing below

the band platform had his finger taut on the trigger of his
revolver. Anton was all right, though. He had the tiger back
in position again, and the long cord of the whip cracked
smartly against the beast's hind-quarters. It was the first time
that he had used the whip on any of his tigers for months.

"Now, Peter…up!"

The beast began its run. Just before it jumped, Anton
stepped back into the middle of the ring, satisfied that he
had got what he wanted. Peter, catching sight of the movement, side-tracked as if to spring at him, caught sight of
the whip in Anton's hand, and jumped. Instead of clearing
the hoop perfectly, he grazed the rim of the rope with his
body. The burning rope scorched his skin, and the animal
gave a roar of genuine bad temper. In the same moment
as his landing after the jump, he turned on Anton for the
third time. Anton backed towards the door of the cage
leading out into the tunnel, and cracked his whip twice
in quick succession.

"Open the door!"

The two attendants pulled back the latches and the door
to the tunnel shot open. Peter, turning round at the noise,
saw the open door and ran out of the ring and up through
the tunnel. The other beasts followed him, all except the
baby cub, who was by this time sound asleep and had to be
pushed out of the ring. The door shut, and another clang,
a few seconds later, told Anton that the second door, at the
other end of the tunnel, had also been shut and that his
seven Bengal tigers were back in their cage.

He took his applause, ran out of the ring, and came back
for several vigorous calls. He pushed aside the plush curtains
and took his dressing-gown from an attendant.

"Bit frisky today, sir, aren't they?" said the attendant.

"Yes. It's this heat," said Anton, and realized that his whole
body was trembling. He ran off to change his clothes. He

had an appointment to make—an appointment with the local superintendent of police.

The attendant who had handed him his dressing-gown crossed over to where a grotesquely dressed clown was standing, waiting to go on while the cage was being taken down. The clown had his face completely whitened, save for two enormous eyebrows of black, fully an inch in thickness. He wore a tiny bowler-hat, and a harlequinade costume of red and yellow silk. He carried a heavy book under his arm.

"Those cats'll get Anton one of these days," said the attendant.

The clown patted his wig into position and gave the man his book to hold while he was playing the fool in the ring.

"Yes," said Dodo, "they'll get him all right. Perhaps it would save a lot of trouble if they did."

Chapter Five

In a weak moment Mr. Minto had invited his brother and sister and sister's fiancé to dinner at the Station Hotel, and afterwards to the evening performance of the circus. Claire had said that she was quite sure that Mr. Minto, after spending an evening in the company of her Ronald, would realize the other side of the young man's character, and would see how wrong his brother had been in summing him up.

Mr. Minto, as early as the soup course, was forced to the conclusion that Claire's young man had not been fitted out with a character at all, let alone a character with more than one side. He was shy and ill-at-ease and with no conversational powers at all; and Mr. Minto did not hold with the way he gripped his knife and fork in mid-air while masticating each mouthful. He tried his best to persuade young Mr. Briggs to open out: he asked him about business, and pumped him for details of the vacuum-cleaner industry, only to receive the information that it "wasn't a bad life". Mr. Minto asked him if he liked circuses; young Mr. Briggs replied that they weren't bad. Mr. Minto asked him if he was enjoying his dinner; young Mr. Briggs said that it, too, wasn't bad. A queer young man, Mr. Minto decided, and fell to brooding moodily on this thing called Love.

Honestly, you could never tell what Love would be up to next. Here it had got hold of Claire Minto, a sensible and normal female if ever there was one, and reduced her to a state of jelly-like devotion for this pale and rather mannerless youth. Claire, of all people: a girl who enjoyed life to the full, who was intelligent and appreciated intelligence in others...what on earth had made her fall for a vacuum-cleaning youth like Ronald Briggs? Mr. Minto had no idea, and sighed mournfully as the relics of his fish were taken away and the entrée put before him.

"Was that a sigh, darling?" asked Claire. "Or just your asthma?"

"It was a sigh," said Mr. Minto. "'I sip no sup, and I crave no crumb, and I sigh for the love of a ladye.'"

"That's poetry, isn't it?" said Mr. Briggs.

"Do you mean you want an affair?" asked Claire. "Or are you just quoting from Gilbert and Sullivan?"

"I was quoting."

"Well, you might at least be accurate. You're sipping your sup pretty well—pour me out another glass, Robert—and you seem to be craving your crumbs all right. Who's the ladye in question?"

"You," said Mr. Minto.

"Well, you can't have me. Ronnie got me with his strong, he-manly personality. Didn't you, darling?"

Young Mr. Briggs gave a little giggle and continued to pick at his entrée.

"He swept me off my feet—just as though I were a speck of dust and he was demonstrating one of his vacuums."

"I wasn't wanting you," said Mr. Minto. "I was sighing for you, but I wasn't wanting you. As a matter of fact, I was just wondering how you would settle down to married life. You're making a terrible mistake, you know, young man. She's an awful woman."

The husband-to-be made a series of clucking noises with his teeth, intended, presumably, to convey the impression that Claire wasn't an awful woman at all, that Mr. Minto really shouldn't say such things about his own sister, but that of course he must have his little joke.

"No, but I mean it," said Mr. Minto, pouring out more champagne. "Do you remember, Robert, the time she stood up in the middle of one of your sermons and shouted out 'Bosh!'?"

The priest, who had been concentrating on his dinner up to now, dropped his knife and fork with a clatter and went pink at the thought of the incident.

"I don't see anything wrong in that," said Claire. "It was both. Utter bosh. By the way, have we got to go to this circus?"

"There's nothing else to do in this town. There isn't a theatre and all the films I see advertised were in London round about the time of the first Wembley Exhibition. So we're going to the circus."

"Ronnie and I thought of spending a quiet night, planning things."

"If you think I'm going to waste a whole evening watching you two canoodling on a sofa with sappy expressions on your stupid faces, planning the colour of your spare-bedroom curtains—if you think that, you're very much mistaken," said Mr. Minto. "No, we're going to the circus, and after that we're going to Dodo's party."

"Who, might I ask, is Dodo?" said the priest.

"Dodo is the leading clown in the circus. A very intelligent little man. He's staying in this hotel, and we had a most interesting talk at breakfast this morning. About porridge. He's giving a party, and we're all invited. Beer and bangers."

"Bangers?" said Robert, suspecting that they had something to do with the Fifth of November.

"Beer and bangers and lots of Camembert."

"Gorgeous!" said Claire. "I shall eat until I burst, and rumble the whole night."

"If you burst first, you won't rumble," said Mr. Minto, whose police training had made him a stickler for accuracy in such matters. "And if you are going to burst, do so at the circus and not here. They'd charge it as extra on my bill—it's that kind of an hotel. What do you say to the circus and supper idea, Mr. Briggs?"

"Not bad," said Mr. Briggs.

The party broke up and prepared to leave for the circus. In the hotel *foyer*, Claire drew Mr. Minto aside and whispered to him.

"What do you think of him?" she asked. "Ronnie, I mean."

"Not bad," said Mr. Minto.

The circus was a huge success. Mr. Minto had by this time befriended almost all the artists staying in the hotel, and he was able to tell the other members of his party the inner history of each act. The priest spent the evening staring open-mouthed at the goings-on in the ring, and raising his eyebrows higher and higher as Mr. Minto took the gilt off each turn's gingerbread by revealing that the artists concerned suffered from rheumatism, spent their spare time knitting socks, or were secret drinkers when not actually doing their stuff in the show.

The clown, Dodo, recognized them on his first appearance, and introduced one or two personal allusions which were greatly appreciated by Mr. Minto, but which left the rest of the audience rather cold. Mr. Minto's brother, being a priest, thought them a trifle outspoken, but did not say so. Lorimer, perched high in the very roof of the tent and waiting for Loretta to get into position for the beginning of their act, waved down to Mr. Minto, and Mr. Minto waved back with his bowler-hat. His stock at once soared in the eyes of the surrounding audience, and one discerning youth of about six years left his parents in the half-crown seats and clambered up to sit beside Mr. Minto, who was obviously the man to settle one or two knotty points which his father and mother had been unable to answer.

"My name's Bobby," said the youth.

"So is that funny-looking gentleman's," said Mr. Minto, pointing to his brother. "But we're not allowed to call him Bobby, because he wears his collar that way round. We have to call him Robert. Father Robert at that."

The youth, after thinking this out for a moment or two, got down to business. Was it true that Anton caught all his tigers when they were baby tigers and taught them to do their tricks then? Mr. Minto was not sure, but thought it highly probable. Was it true that Anton's tigers had all their claws and teeth taken out, and really weren't a bit f'rocious? Oh no, said Mr. Minto, shocked at such an improper idea; Anton's tigers were the most f'rocious tigers in the whole world, and it was very, very brave of Anton to go in beside them and make them do all those clever tricks. Would he (Mr. Minto) go in a cage beside seven tigers? No, not unless it was absolutely necessary. Would he do it for a million pounds? No, certainly not for a million pounds. Would he do it for a billion pounds? No, Mr. Minto didn't think he would do it even for a billion pounds. Would he for a billion billion pounds? Mr. Minto, realizing that this sort of thing might go on for some time, said that he wouldn't do it for any amount of money.

"You're a funk," said the youth.

Mr. Minto admitted that perhaps he was; where tigers were concerned, at any rate.

The youth took out a sticky slab of chocolate after this last answer, and said, "My daddy's not a funk. My daddy would go in beside them all right. He'd do it for only a hundred pounds."

Mr. Minto resisted the temptation to ask why the young man didn't go and sit beside his daddy, if he were that kind of man; and the boy passed on from Anton and his tigers to the baby elephants, who were being put through their paces in the ring at that moment. If a baby elephant sat down on you, would you be squelched to death? Mr. Minto thought it highly probable. If the great big daddy elephant sat down on you, what about that? Mr. Minto, after consulting with his sister and her young man, gave it as his considered opinion that squelching to death would be a certainty in such an event. That would be awful messy, wouldn't it? Mr. Minto agreed.

The boy then explained at some length how he had been very nearly squelched to death himself that very afternoon, owing to Podgy Simpson landing on top of him while practising for the school sports. Mr. Minto had then to answer a number of highly technical questions concerning the relative size, weight, and squelching properties of baby elephants, full-grown elephants, and Podgy Simpson. At which point the boy's father, goaded on by his wife, came up and redeemed his offspring and carted him back to his rightful place in the half-crown seats.

"That gentleman knows a lot more about the circus than you do, Daddy," said the youth on being carried down to his seat. "Did you know that if a baby elephant sat on you…" Mr. Minto saw that the father was in for an awkward night.

The elephants finished their act, bowed clumsily, and shambled out of the ring. Their place was taken by twenty-four beautifully kept chestnuts, held in tow by a single slender blonde. Mr. Minto, feeling himself almost part of the circus, informed young Mr. Briggs that the blonde was forty-two years old, had been married twice, and that it was her eldest son who was fired out of the cannon a little later in the programme. Young Mr. Briggs made his clucking noise again, and his wife-to-be told him that he would have to give up these farmyard imitations when he was married.

Outside the big tent, Mr. Joseph Carey sauntered up and down on the already well-worn grass, in the splendour of full evening-dress, and pulling at a fat cigar. Mr. Carey was in a good mood: business had been above the average for an opening day, and promised to be better; he had just fixed up a contract for a resident season in Glasgow during the Christmas and New Year Carnival, and another with a new team of Cossack riders who, being aristocrats, had considered it beneath their dignity to haggle over terms. He puffed contentedly at his cigar and decided to overlook the events of last night. They had been awkward enough, but it seemed that they had blown over. Except for the attitude of one young man who would have to be carefully watched....

Mr. Carey, catching sight of Lorimer coming out of his dressing-tent in time for his turn, called him across and offered him a cigar—knowing quite well that a trapeze artist needs all his wind for his acrobatics, and is not likely to accept a large and powerful Corona just before going on to do his act.

"By the way," said Mr. Carey kindly, "what was it you wanted to see me about last night, Lorimer?"

"It doesn't matter," said Lorimer. "You didn't seem too pleased to see me then so I won't trouble you with it now."

"Now, look 'ere, young fellow, I never interfere with the private lives of my artists—"

"Don't you?"

"No, I don't, young man. If they want to go out and get tight, I let 'em. It's no business of mine, as long as it doesn't interfere with their acts, that's to say. But you must 'ave been pretty bad to get it into your 'ead that I socked you last night, Lorimer. You were found lying at the back of Miller's caravan, out for the count. As far as I know, you never came near my place the whole night."

"All right. If that's your story, Carey, stick to it."

"It's not my story, lad. It's the truth. I'm just telling you for your own good. I've known too many acts in my day ruined through that kind of thing. In a turn like yours, young man, you want to climb up on the water-wagon and never come down."

"Thanks very much. You say you never interfere with the private lives of your artists, Joe."

"That's my motto. I never 'ave done, and I never will do."

"Okay. In that case, just leave Loretta alone from now on, will you?"

Mr. Carey took the stub of his cigar from his mouth, threw it on the grass, and prodded it into the earth with his heel.

"And just what d'you mean by that, eh?" he asked.

"You know damn' well what I mean. You've been playing about with Loretta these last two months. The whole circus is talking about it. You got a nasty scar on your arm last time that happened, didn't you? Well…I might balance things up for you—give you one down the other arm."

Mr. Carey lit another cigar.

"When a bloke's in love as much as you are, Lorimer," he said, "'e sees things what aren't there, and misses things what are bang in front of 'is eyes. And that's what you're doing, son. There's nothing between me and Loretta, and you can take that as gospel. She's a nice girl and a good-looker all right, but if I want a woman to brighten up my little life I can get one without risking a bust-up in one of my star acts."

"You didn't seem to think that way about Raquel and Varconi."

"Oh, shut up about Raquel and Varconi! 'E was an oily little Dago, 'e was. Got ideas into 'is 'ead, and couldn't resist flinging a knife about the place. Listen, Lorimer…I don't say you're not wise to keep your eye on that pretty little wife of yours, but you're on to the wrong man, see?"

"What do you mean?"

"Ask Loretta 'ow she enjoyed Anton's company, night before last. Just ask 'er."

"Anton?"

"Yes—Anton. You're blind, son. Just because I'm friendly-like towards your girl and 'ave a bit o' fun with 'er, you start getting all these daft ideas into your 'ead. And all the time the real thing's going on and you can't see it. You'd better get going—there's them chestnuts finished. And you take my tip, son. You 'ave a little talk to Loretta about our friend Anton."

Mr. Carey walked away.

Lorimer went slowly to the entrance to the tent. Anton… Anton and he had always been friends. Anton wouldn't do anything like that; it was just one of Carey's yarns, to get himself out of a hole. He'd have a word with Loretta about it, all the same. He slipped off his dressing-gown and smoothed down his white tights. Loretta came running up and asked him what the house was like.

"Packed. That fellow Minto's here—he's coming on to Dodo's supper after the show."

"Did you know he was a detective?"

"Yes. Loretta…"

"What is it?"

"Has Anton been making love to you lately?"

The girl stood still, staring at him.

"Has he?"

The band inside the tent brought its march tune to a crashing finale, and launched out on the music which introduced Lorimer and Loretta to the ring.

"That's us," said Loretta. "Come on—let's go."

Mr. Minto clapped politely as the pair ran into the ring, and told his brother that he had had a double brandy with Lorimer just before dinner. The priest, after consulting his programme to find out what Lorimer did in life, said that he could hardly believe it possible that a man engaged in such a strenuous and dangerous pursuit as this could be a consumer of alcohol. Claire, taking advantage of this, leaned across and said that it just showed how wrong Robert had been in wanting cider cup instead of champagne at the wedding reception.

Lorimer and Loretta shot up a lengthy rope ladder to the very top of the tent at a considerably faster speed than the ordinary mortal takes to come down an ordinary ladder, and stood for a moment on the little platform high above the ring. Lorimer waved down to where he had noticed Mr. Minto sitting, and Mr. Minto waved back.

"I wish you wouldn't show off, darling," said Claire. "You're behaving just like that man we met in Venice. The one who'd been before, and knew all about the Doge's palace and everything."

It was at this point that the small boy detached himself from his parents and took up most of Mr. Minto's attention.

On the platform up in the roof of the tent, Lorimer pulled the centre trapeze towards him.

"Has he, Loretta?" he asked again.

"Don't be such a damned fool. Get on with it."

"You haven't answered yet."

"Go on—the band's waiting."

Lorimer pulled the trapeze back over his head, pushed himself off the platform with a kick of his feet, and swung out above the centre of the ring. Gathering speed each time he swung across the roof, until his back touched the canvas at the top of the return swing, he suddenly let go of the trapeze and sailed head downwards through the air. The crowd, telling each other quickly that there was no net, gasped and (in the case of a few elderly ladies) shut its eyes and hoped for the best. Lorimer connected, surprisingly but surely, with another lower trapeze which no one seemed to have noticed before. The jerk of his landing on it sent it soaring out over the heads of the people in the cheap seats, and then back right into the middle of the ring. Another leap through the air, another connection with the first trapeze—sent out to meet him with perfect timing by Loretta, another swing, and he was back again on the little platform.

Through the applause, Lorimer said, "If he has, I want to know right now, Loretta."

"All right. He has. He's been making love to me. He's crazy about me. Now, are you satisfied? If so, we'll carry on with the act."

The drums in the band rolled again. Both Lorimer and Loretta sailed out, hanging to the bar of the trapeze with their hands. This time Loretta went on her way to the other trapeze, shot out over the cheap seats, and was swung back again into the middle of the ring. Lorimer, hanging to the bar by his ankles, shot out his arms and seized her round the wrists. In the same movement he drew her up to catch on to the ropes of the trapeze, and swung himself and his partner back on to the platform.

"Oh, dear," said Claire. "Very bad for the heart, isn't it? We must try this, Ronnie, after we're married. We can start on the chandelier in Robert's sitting-room. They're marvellous, aren't they?"

"They're not bad," said Mr. Briggs.

In the roof of the tent, Lorimer put forward a question which invariably causes more embarrassment to the person who asks it than to the person of whom it is asked; a question that is still a sure laugh in any film or play.

"How long," said Lorimer, "has this been going on?"

"Oh, never mind."

"I mind all right, if you don't."

"Two months then. Longer, maybe. Come on—double somersault."

"And I suppose you've given him every encouragement, have you?"

"Oh, shut up!"

And Loretta sailed out on her own, turning a couple of graceful somersaults high in the air, dropping twenty or thirty feet, catching hold of the second trapeze by what seemed to be either a miracle or a mistake, shooting out and back again, passing Lorimer in mid-air, landing on the first trapeze, shooting out again without stopping for a second, whisking Lorimer's beret from his head as they passed the second time, clinging with her feet to the other trapeze, being hurled back again, and landing in comparative safety by catching hold of a long sash which Lorimer threw out to her and which uncurled, allowing her to drop head downwards towards the ring below and making the audience squeal, cry out, hold their breaths, cover their eyes, and finally heave a sigh of relief and burst into tremendous applause. Loretta climbed up the sash like a monkey and put back the beret on Lorimer's head. The pair bowed, smiling down on the thousands of tiny, upturned faces below them.

"If you were a really jealous husband," said Loretta, "you'd have been a second late in dropping that sash, wouldn't you?"

"Loretta...have you let him make love to you?"

"Yes. I have."

"Has he...?"

The drums rolled out again for the final turn in their act. Loretta was off once more, shooting out to the other trapeze and catching it this time by one foot. Lorimer, hanging by his ankles, swung himself out to catch her on the rebound.

Father Minto found it a little difficult to believe that this slender, rather attractive piece of womanhood could really have done three complete backward somersaults through the air in such a short space of time; but his brother had told him that this was what she was going to do, so it must be true enough.

Lorimer, now on the lower trapeze, appeared to be taking no interest in the proceedings as his partner righted herself after the final somersault and sailed towards him. He was patting his beret into shape as though that were the only thing that mattered in the world, and as though the spectacle of a woman sailing through the air towards him was none of his business. At the very last fraction of a second he suddenly dropped on the trapeze; his ankles caught round the bar, his body stretched down taut and his left hand only outstretched to meet her. She gripped it with her right hand—not quite correctly. Lorimer's hand was slippery with the oil from his hair…she felt her own hand sliding out of his grip. She jerked herself up and hung tightly to his wrist. Lorimer pulled her up to the bar of the trapeze above him and the pair swung back on to the platform to take their applause.

"You were late that time," said Loretta. "I nearly didn't get hold of you."

"I know," said Lorimer. "You see how easy it is, don't you? You shouldn't have put that jealous husband idea into my head, dear."

Loretta stared at him. She was trembling—a thing she had never done all the time they were playing this act.

They slid quickly down the ropes, landed on the sawdust to the well-timed accompaniment of two crashes on the tympani in the band, bowed and salaamed and kissed their hands in all directions, and ran out of the ring.

In the wings Anton was waiting, after watching their act.

"You cut things a little close then, didn't you, Lorimer?" he said.

"I'll say he did," said Loretta. "He seems to think I can hang about in mid-air for a quarter of an hour while he puts his blessed beret straight."

The girl ran off to her dressing-tent.

"Lorimer…"

"Yes?"

"Be careful with that last turn of yours. You don't want anything to happen to Loretta, do you?"

"Why should it worry you?"

"She's a nice girl. I wouldn't like to see her break every bone in her body."

"No…I can understand that."

"I'll see you tonight—about what we were talking about this afternoon. Twelve o'clock—slip out of Dodo's party. I'll be round behind the cats' cage. Don't forget—I want to see you…alone."

"You needn't worry," said Lorimer. "I'll be there all right. I want to see you, too, Anton…."

He went slowly back to his own tent and changed into ordinary clothes. He lit a cigarette, and then unlocked a suit-case lying on the floor-boards of the tent. After rummaging about in the clothes lying inside the case, he brought out a service revolver and stowed it away in his hip-pocket. Then he strapped on his wrist-watch, and made sure that it was keeping correct time. He did not wish to be late for his appointment with Anton.

Chapter Six

Robert Minto did not greatly enjoy Dodo's supper-party. He could not help wondering what the Reverend Father M'Veagh would say if he saw his second-in-command enjoying beer and bangers in such company. Everyone was most pleasant and friendly, of course; the sausages were well-cooked and plentiful, and Mr. Carey's second funny story was undoubtedly a scream…though Robert wondered if he hadn't left out a bit in the middle, for it seemed a little pointless. However, he laughed heartily and only stopped when he was told that it was his turn now to tell one. On the whole, however, Father Robert Minto would have been much happier tucked up in his little bed instead of being a guest at the party. This was due chiefly to the fact that he had been made to sit beside Horace at the supper-table.

When Dodo threw a party, he did his throwing in the grand manner and invited everyone who was anyone in the circus. He usually held an overflow meeting in a smaller tent of the very important nobodies in the circus—the attendants, programme sellers, cleaners, and so on. Among the anybodies invited to this party was Lars Peterson, and Lars Peterson had said that he would be delighted to come, on one condition. He must be allowed to bring Horace with him. Mr. Peterson would no more think of going to a part without Horace than of entering the ring without his trousers. Horace was very touchy and easily offended, and if he got to hear that Mr. Peterson had been enjoying himself at parties without even asking him there would be the very devil to pay. The chances of getting Horace to balance three tennis balls, a parasol, five tumblers, and a bucket of water on the tip of his snout would be hopeless if the sea-lion got to know about it. Dodo, having listened to all this, said that by all means Horace must come to the party, and went out and bought a ton of fish.

Horace, then, was brought along and sat down at the table and behaved himself a great deal better than most of the guests, and—after a few unsuccessful efforts—balanced a banger on the point of his nose, at the same time applauding his feat by clapping his flappers together.

All very amusing—except to Father Robert Minto who had never sat next to a sea-lion in his life and who did not know exactly how to take it. It was no use ignoring the beast, for Horace had an awkward habit of turning towards Robert and blowing wetly into his ear if he thought he was being neglected. Nor was it any use being friendly to him, for that merely set him off barking in a lusty baritone and put an end to all conversation. Robert was at a loss to know what line to take with Horace; he grew hotter and pinker and more uncomfortable, and was perfectly conscious that he was an object of amusement to all the other people at the party. The sight of a Roman Catholic priest sitting down to supper cheek by jowl with a performing sea-lion has, after all, its funny side. Robert heaved a sigh and brought out his handkerchief as Horace's whiskers and snout fondled his ear.

"Don't you mind him, sir," said Lars Peterson. "It's just him being friendly. Wants to kiss you. He's taken quite a fancy to you, sir."

The rest of the party laughed loudly. Robert did not think it at all funny, and not very sanitary into the bargain.

The big dressing-tent had been rigged out for Dodo's supper-party with two long trestle tables, and a strong scent of sausages hung over the place, mixed—rather disturbingly—with a smell of horse from the stables near by. Mr. Minto, Claire, and Claire's young man sat at the top of one of the tables, beside the host and Joe Carey. Robert, poor soul, had been separated from them in some way, and was hemmed in between Horace and Miss St. Clair at the far end of the other table. Miss St. Clair had never had supper with a clergyman before, and was determined to make the most of the experience. Between her questions and Horace's friendliness, Robert had not a happy evening.

The rest of the company, however, appeared to be in the best of spirits. It was a tradition in Carey's that, whenever anyone threw a party, all who came were to come dressed in their circus garb, and not in the drab, ordinary costume of everyday life. So Dodo, in the host's place at the head of the table, still wore his harlequinade suit of yellow-and-red checked silk and his ridiculous little bowler hat, and had not taken off his make-up—the pure white face, with the nose and lips showing up in enormous blotches of brilliant crimson. Mr. Carey was in the glory of full evening-dress with two diamond studs in his shirt which seemed a little too large and a little too brilliant to be diamonds—but which were. Lorimer and Loretta, still in their neat white tights, were probably the only comfortable people in the heat of that July night; and poor Miss St. Clair, buttoned up tightly in the uniform of the French Legionnaires which she wore in the ring, was perspiring freely. Beside these people, Mr.

Minto and his guests looked dull and commonplace in their ordinary clothes…though Father Robert might easily have been mistaken for one of the clowns.

The bangers arrived, heaped high on two enormous ashets. Claire had not believed there were so many sausages in captivity, and said so. Mr. Carey made a bad joke about missing links, and laughed for a long time at it. Young Mr. Briggs even grew conversational, and when asked if he were enjoying the bangers, replied, "They're grand." Mr. Minto could hardly believe his ears, having expected the sausages to be described as "not bad".

The conversation whirled round to Anton, Mr. Minto having asked why he was not present at the party.

"Er…Anton?" said Dodo. "He's a bit shaky tonight. The tigers haven't been behaving themselves lately."

"I didn't notice anything," said Claire. "He seemed to have them under his thumb all right tonight."

"That's how it looks to you, miss. You don't know exactly how far they're supposed to go, and how much is performance and how much the real thing. This afternoon it was more real thing than performance; tonight it was about half and half…and even half and half isn't comfortable with seven tigers. I expect he's gone straight back to the hotel. He wouldn't feel like a party."

"Did you ask him, Dodo?" said Lorimer.

"No," said the clown, and left it at that.

Mr. Carey smiled and began to pick his teeth.

"I'll tell you why Anton isn't here," said a loud voice down the table. "Stuck-up, that's what he is. Thinks he's a damned sight too good for the rest of us. That lad's head is swollen that much it's a wonder he can get it inside the cage. He's heading for a fall one of these days—and it mayn't be them cats that does it."

The man who had spoken was so vehement about it that there was a fairly lengthy pause after his remarks, ended by Dodo calling for more bangers and a further supply of beer all round.

"That fellow who spoke just now is Miller," said Dodo. "He hates the very sight of Anton."

"Why?"

"He used to be with him—in the act. When they joined the circus there were two of them. Anton and Leon. Miller was Leon. They went into the cage together, and the big thing about their act was that one of them would be doing one trick with half the animals at the same time as the other one was doing something else with the rest of them. And that takes a bit of doing, I can tell you. Anton was always the star, mind you, and after a while this fellow Miller began to lift the elbow a bit too much."

"Not a thing one would advise in an animal trainer, eh?"

"No. Anton stuck it for a couple of months and then pitched him out. He didn't want the fellow to go to the dogs, so he got round Joe here to give him a job in the circus."

"Soft—that's me," said Mr. Carey. "It'll be the ruin of me yet."

"Now Miller's one of the ringside men—hoists the nets and ropes, clears the ring, holds up the hoops, and all that sort of thing. A bit of a come-down from being part of a top-of-the-bill turn, but he's lucky to be doing anything."

"If it wasn't for me 'e'd be walking the streets," said Mr. Carey. "Proper soft-'earted, that's what I am."

"He's never forgiven Anton for turning him out—especially as Anton improved the act a lot after he left, and it's better now than ever it was."

Mr. Minto drained his tankard and peered down the table to see what the man Miller looked like. But, having shot his bolt, the man had gone. Mr. Minto got no more than a glimpse of his back as he pushed aside the flap of the tent door and went out.

Joe Carey brought out his watch with a flourish—a massive gold watch, with an inscription on the back which said something about the watch being a small token of appreciation for long years of faithful service. Mr. Carey had been meaning to get the name on the inscription altered for years now, for the long years of faithful service were not his. He had, in fact, picked up the watch second-hand for a few shillings at a travelling fair. He made a brief calculation, and said: "I'll be back in a minute, Dodo. Got a bit o' business to attend to. 'Scuse me, all—keep some beer for me."

Dodo, watching him go, smiled and went on with his sausage. Mr. Minto was more interested in Lorimer, who was in the middle of a long anecdote about an occasion in Budapest when Loretta had let him down badly—"but we used a net in those days, so it was all right"—when Joe Carey left the tent. Lorimer also watched him go, and brought his story to a quick conclusion. Less than five minutes after the proprietor had gone, Lorimer had muttered an excuse and followed him through the flap of the tent. At the head of the table, Dodo looked puzzled and drew his hand thoughtfully across his face. The red of his lips smeared and turned his mouth into a shapeless outline.

At the foot of the other table, Miss St. Clair was discussing marriage with Robert.

"I was married in the tent. The first time, that is. We got a sky-pilot—a proper one, just like you. The whole circus turned out, animals and all. And just when I was going to say 'I do', or 'Oke', or whatever it is, one of the elephants got fed up with the ceremony and ran amok. My dear, you should have seen it! Took us a quarter of an hour to get him quietened down and—Lars, darling…I wish you'd take that beast of yours away…he keeps on slobbering over the priest here whenever I'm telling him anything."

"It's all right. He said he didn't mind it."

"Who—the priest? Did you say you didn't mind it, Father?"

"Well, I suppose it's just the animal's little—"

"Okay. Where was I? Oh, yes. Took us a quarter of an hour to get the elephant quietened down, and by that time he'd smashed up the bandstand and sat down on the altar we'd rigged up. Horace, let him alone, will you? Go and lick someone else."

"It's just his good nature," said Mr. Peterson from the other side of the table. "Isn't it, Horace? There you are, you see…kissing him, to show how much he likes him. Taken quite a fancy to you, sir."

"So I notice," said Robert, drying his ear.

"*And,*" said Miss St. Clair, "when we did get the elephant quietened down, we found that the sky-pilot had gone off home. So I don't really know to this day whether I was properly knotted or not."

"Most embarrassing," said Robert, pushing Horace's snout off his shoulder.

"It wasn't, really. It came in very useful later on. I found out he had some very awkward habits—the man I married, I mean, not the elephant—and I told him that as the marriage hadn't been finished I could leave him just when I liked."

"And did you?"

"I certainly did. Lars, give it some fish and stop it fussing like this, will you? I certainly did, mister. And then I met Musclo. He was a strong man with a travelling show. Bent me double, just like he did his iron bars. We got married at a registrar's office, without elephants. Sometimes I feel it was a mistake not having elephants. Because, a few months after that hitch-up…"

Claire Minto, at the other end of the tent, was discussing trapeze work with Loretta.

"How did you start?" asked Claire. "Did you begin by doing a few easy tricks on the bars of your cot?"

"I hadn't a cot," said Loretta. "I was born just outside a circus tent—between performances. My mother had sense enough for that. I was carried about on her back until I could walk. I started by breaking my leg when I was five, and I've never done anything else but trapeze stuff ever since."

"Ronnie and I are going to take it up, you know. Oh, this is Ronnie…my fiancé. We made up our minds as soon as we saw your act tonight. It'll give us something to do in the long winter evenings…and I'd love to see Ronnie in the sort of tights your husband wears."

Mr. Briggs did his clucking noises again.

"One of these days," said Claire solemnly, "you'll lay something—and that'll give you a shock all right.…Can you learn it by a correspondence course, Loretta? Or Dodo, could you—"

But Claire, turning to ask Dodo if there was any chance of her fiancé and herself being allowed to join the circus, found that her host had vanished. On the other side of the empty seat, Mr. Minto was talking horses to a foreign gentleman who made twenty-five Arab steeds stand on their hind legs and beg for sugar lumps.

"Ought we to be going?" said Claire. "Everyone seems to be disappearing—including mine host."

"They'll be back," said Loretta. "They keep on drifting in and out, but these parties usually go on till four in the morning. Good lord!"

Loretta's "Good lord!" was caused by a roar, or series of roars, so loud that they seemed to Claire to come from immediately behind her seat. Father Robert, on hearing the noise, leaped off his seat and began to look for his hat. Horace started to bark huskily. Everyone laughed.

"That's the tigers," said Loretta. "Anton's tigers. Their cage is just behind this tent. It's queer—they're usually as good as gold at nights. Never make a sound. But they're certainly letting us know they're awake tonight. Just listen to them…"

The party stopped chattering and listened. The roars increased in volume. Peter had started the din on his own; now it was taken up by the other six, in various degrees of strength according to their ages. Nor was it the usual roaring, either the demand for food or the snarl of rebellion which came from them whenever they entered the ring. This was the real thing…angry and furious.

"I know what it is," said Miss St. Clair. "They're peeved because they haven't been asked to the party. Couldn't we have them in to finish up the sausages?"

Robert, appalled at the idea of having to sit beside seven tigers as well as an intelligent but slobbering sea-lion, did his best to catch Claire's eye and signal to her that it was high time they were getting home.

"They're probably planning what they're going to do to Anton tomorrow," said the man who trained the Arab steeds. "They've been getting a little difficult lately—maybe you noticed it tonight? I think Anton is getting rather—"

The flap of the tent door flew open. Dodo stood in the doorway. He said two words only.

"Oh, God…"

The tenseness of the moment was heightened by the fact that Dodo could show no expression on his face. The white mask, the two scarlet patches of nose and mouth, gave away nothing at all.

"What's happened? What's the matter?"

"They've got him…the tigers…"

The party rushed out of the tent and over the grass to the tigers' cage. A table was overturned in the scramble to get through the tent's narrow opening. Robert cantered after the others, some lengths behind, and left the tent occupied only by Horace the sea-lion, who climbed down from his seat and flopped on his belly and barked and barked. Horace, being an intelligent beast, knew perfectly well what had happened without having to rush about wildly like these other people.

The crowd ran round to the cage and stopped suddenly. The night was moonlit; every detail of the unpleasant scene was shown up clearly. Peter, the largest of the tigers, was crouched in the far corner of the cage, his throat raised to heaven and roaring as only Peter could roar. The two other older beasts stood in front of him, helping him nobly with the din. The cubs paced up and down along the side of the cage furthest from the crowd. They were scared and trembling.

On the floor of the cage lay the body of a man, red with blood. The legs of his trousers were ripped into tatters; the blood oozed out from a wound in the right leg.

"Anton…" said Loretta. "They got him at last…."

Chapter Seven

It seemed to Mr. Minto a little hard. If an overworked Det.-Insp. (for that abbreviation was the official way of describing Mr. Minto) couldn't take a week's holiday from Scotland Yard in order to get his only sister safely married—if he couldn't do that without being confronted by a corpse—then Mr. Minto didn't know what things were coming to. His first thought was to have nothing to do with the business at all. He would murmur his sympathies and regrets to all concerned, take Claire's arm and lead her and her fiancé and Robert away from the scene of Anton's death, and forget the entire affair. Mr. Minto, however, had a nose for blood. He thrived on it, and when a particularly bloody corpse was placed invitingly in front of him, it would have taken several discharges of dynamite to remove him from the spot marked with the cross—without first looking into the matter. Mr. Minto, still staring at the unpleasant sight of Anton lying in the cage, could not help remembering what Dodo had said at breakfast that morning.

"Carey's is a hot-bed of crime…"

The fact that Anton had been set upon and mauled by his tigers had, of course, nothing to do with that statement.

Or had it? Mr. Minto heard a confused babel of orders being given all around him, and realized that some unfortunate person was being handed out the job of removing Anton's body from the cage. It was not a job that he himself would have volunteered for right away. The surprising thing was that it was accomplished with the greatest of ease. The door of the cage was opened gingerly, while two attendants stood by with revolvers raised. A modern Daniel (with the exception that it was a tigers' den, and not a lions' den, that he was entering) stepped cautiously inside the cage, put his hands under Anton's shoulders and dragged him slowly out. He laid the body on the grass and wiped blood from his hands with a dirty handkerchief.

This piece of work had been carried through in complete silence. The group of Dodo's supper-guests stood some little distance away from the cage, with mouths wide open and standing very still. They made a grotesque picture in the moonlight…the acrobats, the bare-back riders, the clowns still in their circus costumes…a few, like Claire and Mr. Minto, in evening-dress…Robert, a study in black and white, with clerical garb and a very pale face…and a crowd of the circus attendants and workmen in shirt-sleeves, or half-naked, having tumbled out of bed and pulled on their trousers on hearing the rumpus.

It was the silence that impressed Mr. Minto. The chattering of the human beings had died away while Anton was being lifted out of the cage and laid on the grass, and the seven tigers watched the body of their trainer being dragged inch by inch away from them without uttering the smallest snarl of protest. Even Horace, left behind in the tent where the party was being held, had given up his barking…having found a supply of fish which had up to then been kept a secret.

Mr. Minto had watched the tigers very carefully as Anton's body was being taken out of the cage. The cubs were obviously scared. They crouched back against the bars at the far side of the cage, and their bodies trembled. What seemed much more interesting to Mr. Minto was the fact that the three older beasts were also frightened. Mr. Minto had had little or no experience of tiger-mauling, but he imagined that any tiger who had half-mauled a man would be worked up into a state of considerable excitement over it. It didn't seem right to Mr. Minto that Peter, for example, who had probably done most of the damage, should have nothing to say when the door of the cage opened and a comparative stranger crept in and dragged away the body lying on the floor. If all the stories which were told about Peter were true, he ought to have had something to say about it, instead of being so very relieved (or so it seemed to Mr. Minto) when Anton's body was out of the cage and the door clanged between it and the tigers. Queer, thought Mr. Minto. But then he knew very little of the ways of tigers.

The body was still lying on the grass, with the little crowd staring stupidly at it. Mr. Minto thought it high time that someone did something, and suggested sending for either a doctor or a policeman, or both. His suggestions were at once downed on all sides. There was no need to send outside for a doctor, it seemed. Carey's Circus, complete with all modern conveniences, toured with its own medical adviser, and Dr. Blair was quite capable of dealing with this business. If sober. Mr. Minto agreed meekly, at the same time mentioning that it might be a good thing to get hold of Dr. Blair as quickly as possible, instead of standing around like a collection of stuffed fish. The stuffed fish scattered in all directions in which Dr. Blair might be found, going first to his caravan (for the Doctor slept on the field) and subsequently on a round of all the places in the town where drinks were in the habit of being served after hours.

"Not that there's any hurry," said Miss St. Clair. "I mean, he can't do anything for him, can he? I mean, he's dead all right, isn't he?"

"I never saw anyone deader," said Mr. Minto. "What about telling the police?"

The crowd, or what was left of it, seemed even more reluctant to bring the police in than they had been to introduce a doctor. There was nothing the police could do, they said. It wasn't as if it had been a crime, they said. It was just an accident, they said. And, in any case, you wouldn't be likely to find a policeman at this time of night, and no one knew where the police-station was. Mr. Minto murmured something about the possibility of an inquest, and added that the police would have to be told sooner or later. All very well to talk like that, he was told, but they couldn't do anything without Mr. Carey's permission. He was the one to do anything, he was.

"Well, then," said Mr. Minto, exasperated, "where is Mr. Carey?"

No one knew. They'd gone to his caravan to report the tragedy, but it had been in darkness and the door had been locked. Possibly he was out visiting friends in the town. Possibly not. They would just have to wait.

"And are you going to leave this lying here all night?"

Oh no. The body of Anton was lifted carefully and carried away to an empty caravan in a corner of the field. The remnants of the crowd broke up. Mr. Peterson went back to the tent to collect Horace and put him in his tank. Horace had finished the fish by this time and was barking hoarsely. Dodo said that he'd better go and change, as the night air was a little chilly for going about in these clothes. Loretta, who had not spoken a word since the discovery of the tragedy, walked slowly away to the gate at the other side of the field, and Mr. Minto was interested in the remarks which went round as she left. Loretta, it seemed, would miss Anton a lot. Loretta had been very fond of Anton; and what exactly had Lorimer been doing since leaving the supper-party? And where was he now?

Mr. Minto decided that it was time to shepherd his guests to their homes. He put his arm round his sister's waist, and snapped his brother out of a shocked stupor.

"Come on," he said. "Where's that young man of yours, Claire?"

Young Mr. Briggs was not to be found. He had been standing beside Claire when they came out of the tent to see what had happened; after that he had not been seen.

"Perhaps he went to help find the doctor," said Claire. "I'd better go and see."

"You're going home," said Mr. Minto. "He can look after himself all right."

He arranged his sister's wrap over her shoulders, and the three set off across the field.

"A dreadful business," said Robert. "Poor fellow...what a terrible end...."

"What on earth would he be doing inside the cage at that time of night?" asked Claire.

Mr. Minto took some time to answer.

"That's a moot point," he said. "A very moot point. Not knowing the habits of tigers, I can't tell you. They may have to be fed at one in the morning, for all I know."

"And didn't you think it a little odd that everyone—I mean, Carey and the others—left us high and dry with the bangers about half an hour before it happened?"

"Very odd, Claire."

"You might almost think that they knew it was going to happen."

Mr. Minto stopped in his tracks.

"I won't have you trying to make a case out of this," he said. "I'm down here to see you married to that young man of yours, and I'm not getting mixed up in any work in my spare time. It's a most unfortunate accident, and nothing more. As far as I'm concerned, the thing's over and done with. We might send a wreath to the funeral between us, but apart from that I'm having nothing to do with the business."

Having got that off his chest, Mr. Minto arrived at his hotel, and said good night to his brother and sister. He then spun through the revolving doors into the entrance hall of the hotel, waited for perhaps two or three minutes, spun out through the doors again, and went as fast as his legs could carry him back to Martin's Field. The light was not good enough to be certain that his nose was twitching, but he was enjoying that pleasant sensation which always came to him when confronted with something that demanded looking into.

There was still a great deal of excitement going on when he got back to the circus ground. Mr. Carey had returned and seemed mostly concerned with what was going to happen to the circus minus its star act. Loretta and Dodo were walking up and down in front of the tigers' cage, talking earnestly. The tigers were not asleep; they sat still, crowded in one corner of their cage, staring out at each person who passed by.

What concerned Mr. Minto more than anything else was the fact that Dr. Blair had been routed out from a back-parlour behind one of the town's public-houses, and had made a preliminary examination of Anton's body. Mr. Minto, without waiting to be asked, went straight to the caravan where the body had been placed. He found Dr. Blair with a sponge in one hand and a double whisky in the other.

"Hullo," said the Doctor, greeting him as an old friend. "Come in. Sit down. We cater for sensation-mongers. The more the merrier. Want a close-up? Not exactly pleasant, but you can have a look."

Mr. Minto had a look. A long and careful examination, in fact. What seemed so very strange to Dr. Blair was the fact that Mr. Minto looked longest and most carefully at those parts of Anton's body which had been untouched by the tigers. He seemed most interested in the chest and right shoulder, where there was not a single scratch. Dr. Blair came to the conclusion that the man, whoever he was, had been drinking.

"How did he die?" asked Mr. Minto.

The Doctor did not appear to have heard correctly.

"What's that?"

"How did he die?"

"He was mauled, you silly ass. By those cats. Always said they'd get him. Nasty brutes. Worse than women. Much worse. He was mauled to death. Poor fellow."

Mr. Minto had another look.

"Are you a qualified doctor?"

"Edinburgh—1897. F.R.C.S. into the bargain. And what the hell has that got to do with you?"

"Nothing. Nothing at all."

"Let me tell you, whoever you are—"

Mr. Minto produced his card.

"Never heard of you," said the Doctor, reading the card upside-down. "Let me tell you, sir, that in my day I had a practice so big that the panel patients used to queue up the night before they wanted to see me. The night before. Like they do at Covent Garden."

"And what are you doing in a circus, if it isn't a rude question?"

"It is a rude question. It's a very rude question. I refuse to answer it," said the Doctor, going on to answer it at some length. "I was forced to give up my practice owing to a breakdown in health."

"Whose health?" asked Mr. Minto. "Yours, or your patients'?"

"Mine. I joined the circus because I've always wanted to join a circus. And I may tell you, sir, that I've operated on a baby elephant with great success. And that's more than any other doctor can say. And I don't know who the hell you are, or what you're doing barging in here and asking questions. Questions, I may say, which I refuse to answer."

"I'm a policeman," said Mr. Minto.

"I don't believe you," said the Doctor. "If you're a policeman, why don't you arrest me for being tight?"

"I'm not interested in you being tight."

"Who says I'm tight?"

At this stage of the proceedings the door of the caravan opened and Mr. Carey came in, followed by Dodo, now changed into his drab, ordinary clothes. Mr. Carey was in a bombastic mood.

"Now, then, Minto, time you were getting off 'ome," he said. "Nothing you can do 'ere. We want to get the place locked up and everyone off to bed."

"I'll see Mr. Minto back to the hotel," said the clown. "He's staying where I am—at the Station Hotel."

"You know," said Mr. Minto, "I do think you ought to call in the police. Right away, I mean."

"What the blazes can the police do about it?" demanded Mr. Carey.

"I thought you said you were a policeman," said the Doctor.

"I am. A sort of policeman. I'm from Scotland Yard."

The Doctor dropped his glass on the floor of the caravan. Mr. Carey seemed shaken. Only the clown remained calm.

"Didn't I tell you, Carey?" he said. "Minto's a detective. He's up here on a holiday—not on business."

"I had hoped it was going to be a holiday," said Mr. Minto. "It looks as though business were beginning to shove its nose into things, though."

"What do you mean?"

"Anton's death, of course."

"That isn't a job for Scotland Yard—when a man gets mauled by a tiger."

Mr. Minto took another look at the body of Anton before replying.

"It all depends," he said. "If the man is mauled *after* his death, it may quite easily be a job for Scotland Yard."

"Eh?" said Mr. Carey.

The Doctor poured himself out another whisky with a hand that shook.

"I'm afraid you're talking in riddles, Minto," said Dodo.

"I'm talking about riddles. This unfortunate young man's body is riddled…as well as mauled. In fact, I wouldn't go so far as to say that he had been mauled at all. Certainly he wasn't a pretty sight when we found him lying in the cage. The tigers had scratched him a bit, and there was a good deal of blood about his body. But mauled—no. Look at him, will you?"

The three men looked down at the body of Anton.

"Our friend the Doctor has sponged most of the blood away. I wouldn't say that he's made a very good job of it, but perhaps he isn't seeing things very well tonight. However… look at these. He's been given three quite nasty scratches, and that's all. I wouldn't call that being mauled, gentlemen. It's not my idea of mauling at all. That's the peculiar part about Anton's death…why *didn't* the tigers maul him? Now, I don't know a great deal about tigers, but even I could see that those beasts were frightened. They were scared stiff. They had a chance to maul Anton, and they didn't take it. Why? Because I honestly believe that those tigers had a sneaking fondness for their trainer, however little they showed it in the ring. And because I believe that, at that moment, they very much wanted to maul someone else."

"Who?" said Mr. Carey.

"The man who threw Anton's body inside their cage," said Mr. Minto.

"What on earth are you talking about?" asked the clown.

Mr. Minto pulled back the torn shirt which Anton wore.

"Come a little closer, gentlemen," he said. "You see? There…there…and there. Three punctures."

"Punctures?"

"If there aren't three bullets inside that young man's body at this moment, I'll willingly eat my best Sunday Homburg. We'll soon find that out definitely…if you'll do as I suggest and send for the police—and a doctor who is capable of doing his job."

"See here, you," said the presumably incapable Doctor.

"Shut up, Blair!" said Mr. Carey. "What are you getting at, Minto?"

"Anton was shot. Murdered. I believe he was placed inside the cage after he had been killed, so that the tigers would complete the job and destroy all trace of the crime. Whoever did it knew the frame of mind the tigers had been in lately, and knew that Anton and the tigers weren't seeing eye to eye in their act. They thought they could rely on the beasts putting Amen to this young fellow who made them leap through hoops and all that sort of thing. They thought the tigers would maul him beyond recognition, and that everyone would say 'What a terrible accident!'…and leave it at that. Unfortunately—or maybe fortunately—these tigers appear to have a conscience. Or perhaps they were frightened of smashing their teeth on those three bullets. I don't know. All I do know is that Anton was shot. And now, if you're not going to call in the police, I'll do it myself. Because I very much want to get to bed."

Mr. Carey stepped slowly out of the caravan and down on to the grass.

"By the way, Dodo," said Mr. Minto, "you haven't taken off all the grease-paint from round your mouth."

The clown put up his hand to his lips and wiped them.

"Oh," said Mr. Minto. "My mistake. It isn't grease-paint. It's a scratch. Quite a nasty one, too. Well, well…"

Chapter Eight

"Come across to my caravan, Mr. Minto," said Joe Carey. "I'd like a word with you."

Mr. Minto followed the circus proprietor over to his green-and-white super-caravan, reflecting that he had never expected to be up and doing at four o'clock in the morning. Mr. Minto came to the conclusion that he was a bad advertisement for any respectable town or village. However well-behaved a place might have been before his arrival, Mr. Minto, it seemed, had only to put his foot in it for a crime of some sort to be committed. It was another case of Mary and her little lamb: wherever Mr. Minto went, crime was sure to go.

On his way to the caravan he passed the tigers' cage. The beasts had quietened down now, though they were not yet asleep. The four cubs lay huddled together in one corner, staring through the bars of the cage with eyes that never flickered. Peter still paced silently backwards and forwards along the full length of the cage. Mr. Minto, looking at them and trying to analyse their thoughts, made a mental note to visit the town's Public Library first thing in the morning. He wanted to look up the habits and characteristics of tigers in a Natural History Encyclopaedia. If there were such a thing as a Natural History Encyclopaedia in the town's Public Library, that is. If, again, there were such a thing as a Public Library in the town. (Mr. Minto found out in the morning that there was not. He was directed to the local branch of a circulating library, where the nearest he could get to the subject in which he was interested was a novel by a Roberta M. Pottersleigh entitled *Claws of Desire*.)

Mr. Carey had gone ahead, making for his caravan. Mr. Minto, to use a favourite expression of his, did a little nosing around in the neighbourhood of the tigers' cage. There was no need to strike matches or produce a torch: the moon still shone obligingly. Perhaps that was the reason why the tigers were not sleeping, but Mr. Minto did not think so. He was quite certain that each of the seven beasts knew what had happened that night, and were still brooding over it. A nice heart-to-heart chat with these seven tigers was what he wanted. Mr. Minto thought it a great pity that Anton had not trained a troupe of performing dogs, instead of Bengal tigers. Dogs were so much more approachable. Greatly daring, Mr. Minto put his hand through the bars of the cage and scratched the posterior of one of the cubs. Peter stopped his pacing at once and gave him a look. It was not a friendly look. Mr. Minto withdrew his hand. Peter went on pacing.

On the grass under the cage, a piece of brightly coloured cloth caught Mr. Minto's eye. He picked it up, inspected it carefully, and stowed it away between two five-pound notes and his tailor's account rendered in his pocket-book. Mr. Carey's voice boomed out from across the field, asking if he were going to stand there all night.

"No," said Mr. Minto. "I'm just coming."

Inside the caravan, the proprietor motioned him to a seat, shut and locked the door, pressed a convenient button and asked him if he could go a little something. Mr. Minto said that while he was not in the habit of going little somethings at four in the morning, he would not, under the very special circumstances, object to a small whisky-and-soda. Mr. Carey poured out the largest whisky in Mr. Minto's history, and added a teaspoonful of soda-water.

"I've got a proposition to make to you," said Mr. Carey.

"As long as you don't want me to take Anton's place in the circus…"

"No. If I call in the local police and outside doctors and all that, it'll bust up the show. They'll keep us 'ere until they've solved this business, and God knows 'ow long that'll be. I've got to get this circus to Norwich on Monday, York a week come Monday, Middlesbrough, Durham, Newcastle, after that, right on to the end of the season. I can't let a thing like this upset the whole tour."

"What's all that got to do with me?"

"Why don't you look into this business on your own?"

Mr. Minto took a sip of his drink, recovered his breath, and asked for a little more soda.

"I'm sorry," he said; "I'm here on pleasure. If you can call a wedding pleasure, that is. In any case, you're apt to get yourself into a whole packet of trouble if you don't call in the police on this. You'll have to do it sooner or later. You'd much better do it sooner."

"But you're the police, aren't you?"

"I admit it," said Mr. Minto gravely. "It's a dreadful thing to say of anybody, but I admit it."

"Well, then—you take on this job yourself. I can't afford to 'ave the whole show 'eld up while the local bobbies go round taking everybody's fingerprints. The show must go on."

"Where have I heard that before?" said Mr. Minto.

"Anton's dead—but 'e doesn't come out of the bill. No, sir. Anton and 'is ruddy tigers will be in the programme tomorrow, matinée, same as if nothing 'ad 'appened."

"How do you propose to do that?" asked Mr. Minto. "Resurrection or substitution?"

"I'll get a new man," said Mr. Carey, who had no great love for long words. "One bloke in a loin-cloth looks very much like another bloke in a loin-cloth. From tomorrow onwards Miller's name will be changed to Anton. I don't say as 'ow 'is salary will be changed to Anton's salary—but 'e's going to do the act."

"Miller? Is that the fellow who made the outburst in the middle of the party?"

"That's the bloke. 'E used to work with Anton. 'E knows the act backside foremost. Couldn't do it same as Anton could, of course, but if 'e keeps off the liquor 'e'll put it across all right. Liquor, Mr. Minto, is the curse of the circus business."

Mr. Carey drained his glass, and refilled it.

"It's the curse of any business," said Mr. Minto, "except the brewers and distillers."

"I can shove Miller into Anton's place, if this thing isn't given publicity. Now, listen....If you 'adn't been invited to Dodo's party, you wouldn't 'ave known nothing about this business, would you?"

"I'd have read it in the newspapers tomorrow morning."

"Not on your life, you wouldn't. You wouldn't 'ave known nothing about it, and the police wouldn't 'ave known nothing about it. There'd just 'ave been an accident, Mr. Minto, and the whole circus staff would 'ave been told pretty plain that if they'd opened their mouths about it they'd 'ave been booted out of the show. We can 'ush these things up all right, Mr. Minto. Now, see 'ere. You're in town till the end of the week, aren't you?"

"Saturday night. Sunday morning, if the wedding reception is a good one."

"Right. Take over this job on your own until then. I'll give you the run of the circus. You can go where you like, do what you like, ask what questions you like. I'll do everything I can to 'elp you. I'm just as anxious as anyone to get this business settled up."

"But not anxious enough to call in the local police?"

"You know what these local police are—all feet and no 'eads. If you 'aven't got anywhere by the end of the week, I'll go and put the whole thing before the proper police."

Mr. Minto drained his glass and put it down on the table.

"Are you suggesting that I'm an improper policeman?" he asked.

"You know what I mean. What d'you say?"

"Right," said Mr. Minto. "I'll do it. You understand that, as soon as I do find out anything, I'll have to report to the proper quarters? And that I can hold you here as long as I like—just as much as these proper police can?"

"If you're going to find out anything, find it before the end of the week. We open in Norwich on Monday. I'll do everything I can to 'elp you, Minto. Any 'elp you want, just you come to me. I want to get this cleared up. I don't want any murderers slinking about in my circus. I—"

"Where were you when Anton was murdered?"

"Eh?"

"I'm sorry. Perhaps I ought to have warned you. I've started, you see. My nose is twitching, and I'm on the trail. Where were you when Anton was murdered? You left the supper-party about a quarter to twelve. Where did you go? What did you do? And why?"

"Good God!" said Mr. Carey, wondering if it would not have been as well to have invited the local police to investigate. "I was in the town—with some pals of mine."

"In the town, with some pals. Doing what?"

"Nothing. Just a friendly call."

"Rather bad manners, don't you think? Walking out on Dodo's bangers, just to pay a friendly call on some pals in the town. Couldn't it have waited until the morning?"

"No. It couldn't."

"Right. Name and address of pals in the town, please."

"What the 'ell for?"

"My dear man, you've put me in charge of this confounded business. Against my wishes. At your own special request. Now you've got to help me, or I'll get peevish and refuse to play."

"But…I'm not under suspicion, am I?"

"Good heavens, yes." Mr. Minto laughed heartily at the idea of anyone imagining himself free from suspicion. "Of course you're under suspicion. Clark Gable is under suspicion. So is President Roosevelt. So is the Emir of Transjordania, *and* the Secretary of State for Foreign Affairs."

Mr. Carey said he didn't see what these persons had to do with it.

"They weren't at Dodo's party. The only people who *aren't* under suspicion at the moment are the people who were at Dodo's party, and who stayed at the party until the tragedy was discovered."

"Why?"

"Because Anton was killed during the party."

"How d'you know that?"

Mr. Minto sighed.

"Because his turn was half-way through the bill—about nine-thirty. And after his turn was over, he went back to his hotel. I've been to the hotel, and asked the hall-porter. He stayed in his room until shortly before midnight, and then went out. For a walk, he said. A very long walk, as it turned out."

"Well!" said Mr. Carey. "Looks as if you'd taken on this case before I asked you to, doesn't it?"

"Not at all. I merely wanted to find out whether Anton had been back to the hotel. Now, then…Anton was murdered while the party was going on—"

"Just a minute. You're sure this is murder, are you?"

"Of that there is no possible doubt," said Mr. Minto, "no possible, probable, shadow of doubt—no possible doubt whatever."

Mr. Carey, who was not in the habit of patronizing the Savoy Operas, was impressed. He said, "Oh, well, if you're as sure about it as all that, of course."

"Anton was murdered between twelve and one-thirty—"

"Couldn't 'ave been suicide, I suppose?"

"I wish you wouldn't interrupt," said Mr. Minto. "Why should it have been suicide?"

"Well—'e was getting pretty down with them tigers, you know. 'E'd 'ad a bad day with 'em—at the afternoon show in particular. Maybe 'e got it into 'is 'ead that 'e was losing 'is nerve, and—"

"And shot himself three times, afterwards dragging what was left of himself inside the tiger's cage, shutting and locking the door, lying down on the floor and passing gracefully out?"

"Not necessarily. 'E might 'ave done it once 'e was in the cage."

Mr. Minto pondered.

"M'm…an odd place to commit suicide, isn't it? But quite possible. In which case, what became of the revolver? Did the tigers eat that?"

"Maybe it's lying about somewhere—on the grass round about the cage."

"It's not. I looked. I found something else, but I didn't find a revolver."

"What did you find?" asked Mr. Carey. He seemed a little worried about this.

"Never mind. And stop asking me questions. It's most disconcerting. I've lost the place now—where were we? Oh yes. Anton, for the third and last time, was killed during the party—probably between midnight and one-thirty. So that anyone who wasn't at the party at that time is under suspicion. Clark Gable, for instance. The Emir of Transjordania, for example. Or the Secretary of State for Foreign Affairs. Or you.…You left the party about half past twelve, didn't you? You'd any amount of time to do it. Much more time than Mr. Gable or the Emir of Transjordania. In fact, I think we can safely wipe them out. I'm not so sure about the Secretary of State for Foreign Affairs. He might have been addressing a meeting in the district, and nipped over and done it. I can't see why, but we'll have to check up on him. But, at present, we'll check up on you. Where were you from the time you deserted those excellent bangers until Anton was found dead?"

Mr. Carey poured out another drink.

"I was with some people called Winter. 288, Bank Street. Above a pawnshop."

"Why?"

"I don't know. If they want to live above a pawnshop, it's none of my business, is it?"

"I didn't mean that. Why did you go to see them?"

"I told you—a social call. Nothing more."

"At one in the morning?"

"At one in the morning."

Mr. Minto fumbled in his pocket-book and produced his tailor's account rendered. The small piece of cloth which he had picked up from the grass beside the cage fell on to the floor of the caravan. Mr. Carey picked it up.

"Where did you get that?" he asked.

"It's a pattern for a new suit of plus-fours I'm having made," said Mr. Minto. "Rather nice, don't you think?

Guaranteed to add at least six strokes to your opponent's handicap."

"Don't kid me. It's a bit of Dodo's clown costume, that is."

"Correct," said Mr. Minto. "Have you a pencil?"

Mr. Carey produced a pencil. After studying the details of the tailor's bill and deciding that, if they continued to write "Please" at the foot, he would really have to pay it one of these months, Mr. Minto wrote on the back of the account:

Carey, social call on Winter, 288, Bank Street, above pawnshop.

"Now, let's think," he said. "Who else left the party? This man Miller, after his little outburst. And Lorimer—he went out shortly after you, didn't he? And Dodo…he was out for twenty minutes or so."

"It was Dodo who found out what had happened, wasn't it?"

"It was. Is there any reason why Dodo should kill Anton?"

"Eh? Oh—no; not that I know of."

"Any reason why you should kill Anton?"

Mr. Carey laughed heartily. A small china ornament fell off one of the caravan walls as a result.

"Do you think I'd smash up the best drawing turn in the circus?"

"Any reason why Miller should kill Anton?"

"Well…yes, I suppose there is."

"Tell me."

"You 'eard what 'e said at the supper-party. 'E 'ated Anton like poison. Anton chucked 'im out of the act, and 'e's never forgotten it. And…well, I suppose 'e knew that if anything 'appened to Anton 'e stood a good chance of getting back in the show in 'is place."

"That's interesting. Any reason why Lorimer should kill Anton?"

"Yes…"

"Again? Tell me."

"Loretta—Lorimer's wife...and Anton. They were... you know."

"Oh, dear. If there's one thing I hate, it's when Love gets mixed up in a case. People do the daftest things, and the poor detective keeps on trying to find reasons for them. When, of course, there aren't any reasons. It's Love, Mr. Carey, that makes a detective's head go round. However..."

Mr. Minto made some more notes on the back of his bill.

"If what you say is true—and it may be—"

"Thanks very much," said Mr. Carey.

"If what you say is true, two out of these four people had reasons for seeing Anton dead. Miller and Lorimer. Of course, it may not be any of these four, may it? It might, as I said before, be the Emir of Transjordania. Though at the moment I can't see the connection. But out of these four, two had reasons. Which probably means that, if Anton's murderer is among these four, it was either Dodo or yourself who killed him."

Mr. Carey looked peeved.

"Why?" he demanded.

"Because you haven't any reasons for wanting him dead," said Mr. Minto. "Don't you ever read detective novels?"

"Never. Have another drink?" said Mr. Carey, thinking that his visitor had already had more than enough.

"No, thanks. I must be going. I'm probably locked out of the hotel as it is. I'll have to wake the night porter, and that'll take some doing. Was that a whistle?"

"I didn't hear anything," said Mr. Carey.

"I thought I—yes—there it is again. I didn't know you had the nightingale in these parts."

"It isn't the nightingale. It's someone at the door."

Mr. Carey went to the door of his caravan and opened it a few inches. Mr. Minto could not see the whistler, who was shielded by Carey's back. He heard only one side of the conversation.

"What d'you want?" asked Carey.

A mumble.

"I've no time to see you just now."

A mutter.

"Get out. You can't pester me at this time o' night. Go on—clear out!"

Another mumble.

"Get out!"

Mr. Carey banged the door.

"Someone touting for money," he said. "I'm always getting 'em. They know I've got a soft 'eart, and they just take advantage of me."

"Yes…" said Mr. Minto, and collected his hat. "Well, good night, Mr. Carey. Thank you for all the information you've given me—intentionally and otherwise. I'll see you in the morning."

Mr. Minto walked unsteadily down the caravan steps and landed safely on the grass. The door of the caravan shut with a bang. He was perfectly conscious of the fact that the green curtain in the caravan window had been drawn aside, and that Joseph Carey was watching him as he walked across the field. It was only when he reached the gate leading out into the town that Mr. Minto looked back and saw that the curtain had been pulled along again. Then he turned and ran quietly across the field to the other exit, by which Carey's whistling visitor had left. He caught sight of the man some two hundred yards outside the field, and followed him, keeping always a convenient corner between the stranger and himself. There was something about the man's back which seemed vaguely familiar, and once when he passed under a street-lamp Mr. Minto could have sworn (and did, in fact, swear) that he had seen him before. If anyone had asked him why he was following the unknown gentleman at this time of the morning, Mr. Minto would have been completely stumped for an answer. He was simply nosing around.

The man walked on through the shopping centre and into the poorer districts of the town. He turned a corner into a long, dirty street made up largely of fish-and-chip restaurants and second-hand clothes shops. An electric light standard was still lit at the corner, and Mr. Minto was able to read the name of the street on the enamel plate fixed on the wall. He was now in Bank Street. He lit a cigarette, watching the whistler out of the corner of his eye. Again he was sure that he had seen the man before. He had some difficulty in shielding his match in the breeze, and by the time he had got his cigarette going the man had disappeared down a side-entrance some distance along the street. Mr. Minto followed him briskly and noted the number above the entrance. It was, as he had imagined, 288.

Mr. Minto then did a very rash thing. He hopped inside a telephone kiosk and rang up the local Superintendent of Police. To ring up a police superintendent at five in the morning is simply asking for trouble. Like the Guardsman who dropped his rifle and the man who lit his cigar before the loyal toast, it is a fit subject for one of Mr. H. M. Bateman's cartoons.

The Superintendent was sleeping the sleep of the just, and the constable on night duty, when roused, was not at all inclined to wake him up. He knew his Superintendent, and nothing short of murder would persuade him to cut short his senior officer's beauty sleep. Mr. Minto said that this happened to be murder, and would he mind getting a move on. The constable then asked who was speaking and, when told, refused to believe it. Certainly he'd heard of Detective-Inspector Minto of Scotland Yard, but how was he to know that the gentleman who was speaking was Detective-Inspector Minto of Scotland Yard? Mr. Minto said, somewhat snappily, that until television came along he had no way of identifying himself over the telephone, but that if he didn't wake up the Superintendent right away there would be an outsize tornado at the police-station in the early hours of the morning.

The constable vanished, in fear and trembling; the Superintendent arrived after an interval, swearing lucidly. Mr. Minto re-introduced himself and explained the position.

"If I hadn't hit on this business by a fluke, you wouldn't have heard anything about it. Now that I'm in on it, they want me to carry on with the case. I think it's as well to let them think that I'm doing that—if you've no objections."

The Superintendent was too sleepy to have objections.

"I'll report to Scotland Yard and get their authority. It's your case, really, and you've got to do the work without letting the circus people know that the local police know anything about it."

"All right—good night, sir."

"Just a minute. I'm not finished yet. I want you to find out all you can about some people called Winter, living at 288 Bank Street. I want you to put a man on to shadow Mr. Joseph Carey, proprietor of Carey's Circus, whenever he leaves the circus ground. And I want you to put a man—or a couple of men—to watch the ground, and report on any visitors Carey has late at night, after the circus show is over."

"What—now?" asked the Superintendent.

"Oh no," said Mr. Minto. "First thing in the morning will do very nicely, thank you."

"What do you think this is? It's a quarter past five now."

"I appreciate the point," said Mr. Minto, and rang off.

Getting back to the hotel, Mr. Minto roused the night porter and asked if the gentleman who did the tricks with the tigers—Anton, he thought the name was—had come in during the night. He had: arriving about ten-fifteen and leaving again shortly before midnight. Mr. Minto was glad to hear it, for he had been exaggerating slightly when he told Joe Carey that he had already checked up on Anton's movements.

"He hasn't come in again, as far as I know, sir," said the night porter.

"I don't think he'll be in," said Mr. Minto. "He's staying down at the circus. His animals have been a little troublesome, I understand."

Mr. Minto then asked the night porter politely for the key of his room, 210, the number was. At a quarter to six in the morning night porters are rarely at their brightest and best. It is the witching hour when they stop snoozing illegally and prepare to go to bed for a spot of honest sleep. The porter handed over the key willingly, ignoring the fact that he had already given Mr. Minto one key that night, and that Mr. Minto was down in the register as occupying room number 224. Mr. Minto walked upstairs and opened the door of Anton's room.

Anton had not expected death, at any rate. His room was untidy, and a half-finished letter lay on the dressing-table. It was written in German, and Mr. Minto's knowledge of that language was restricted to a single sentence asking for another glass of beer, please—and even then he was not sure whether beer was masculine or feminine in Germany. He opened some of the drawers of the dressing-table, and out of one produced a sheet of foolscap. It was the only interesting find in the room. It was a document—not very properly drawn up, but still perfectly legal—giving over the ownership and management of Carey's Circus to one

Ludwig Kranz, otherwise known as Anton. It was signed by Joseph Carey, but the space for Anton's own signature was still blank.

Mr. Minto put the document away in his pocket and went to bed.

Chapter Nine

Father Robert Minto ate a hurried breakfast, for he had much to do. The date of his sister's marriage, like her courtship and engagement, had come on him with a rush and left him rather short of breath and considerably short of time. Claire was like that: if she made up her mind to do a thing, it was usually done before one had time to find out when it was going to take place. Saturday, the twenty-third of July, which last week had seemed so far ahead, now presented itself in front of Robert as an urgent affair which demanded his immediate attention.

There now seemed no chance of persuading Claire to drop the idea of marrying her young man; if anyone could have done it, it was the third member of the Minto family, and Detective-Inspector Minto, however good he was at solving crimes, had failed miserably in this. Claire and her vacuum-cleaning fiancé were scheduled to be married at two o'clock on the following Saturday, and nothing could be done about it now. Except to make the various arrangements for the ceremony, and the celebrations which followed it. And, having come to this conclusion, Robert realized that there was still a tremendous amount of things to be done.

The job of the delegates to the League of Nations Assembly was, in Father Minto's opinion, mere child's play compared with the number of things he had to deal with before two o'clock on the following Saturday. The League of Nations people could, at any rate, adjourn their tasks *sine die*, and frequently did so; but Robert was tethered down to Saturday, the twenty-third of July, and the million and one things which Claire had told him to do had somehow to be done before that date.

Claire, businesslike as ever, had written out three lists of Things to Buy; one for herself, one for her fiancé, and one (the largest, it seemed) for Robert. The priest had lost his list and did not like to ask his sister for a copy. The only thing he could remember being on the list was socks, for Claire had said that he hadn't a decent pair of socks to his feet, and that she refused to be married by a priest whose toes were sticking out through his hose. Robert finished his breakfast, and dashed out to buy socks.

Armed with the socks (an unusual thing to be armed with), Father Minto made his way to the church to keep an appointment with the organist. He had to tell the man exactly what was required of him during the wedding service. Claire had given him very definite instructions about this, for she knew the organist of old, and had been at a number of weddings in the church when the ceremony had developed into an organ recital, with much throbbing and a great many twiddly bits on the *vox humana*.

Robert found the organist enjoying himself in an empty church with a spot of Wagner. It should have taken the priest no longer than two minutes to tell the man what he was to play, when he was to play it, get him to repeat his instructions to make sure that they had sunk in, and hop off on some other errand. (Robert had just remembered another item on his list: Order Buttonholes from Florist's—and he was impatient to dash off and do this before he forgot.)

The organist, however, was a chatty soul. Robert listened to him attentively for an hour and three-quarters. After brushing aside all Claire's instructions with an airy "Just you leave all that to me, Father", the organist launched forth on a favourite theme of his, the gist of which was that Beethoven, if he had not been blind, would never have written the magnificent music he did write. If Beethoven had not been blind, according to the organist, his imaginative powers would never have been developed to the extent that they were. He would have done all his composing by hard theory and cut and dried rules, instead of allowing his genius to have full play. If Beethoven had not been blind...But here Robert, remembering that he had to meet Claire and Mr. Minto for lunch, got a word in edgeways and reminded the organist that Beethoven hadn't been blind at all. Deaf, quite likely; blind, definitely no. The organist said that it must have been Milton he was thinking about, but that it all came to the same thing in the end. The priest, harking back to the subject of music for the wedding service, was assured that everything would go all right if it was just left to the organist.

Robert left him, and he began at once to play a movement from the "Pastoral" symphony in rather a vicious manner, as though piqued at the idea of the composer having been deaf instead of blind.

On his way out of the church, the priest was stopped by a man.

"Father M'Veagh?" the man asked.

"No. I am Father Minto."

"You're a priest here, though? In this church?"

"That is so."

"You're the priest who was at the circus-party last night?"

Robert, who was doing his best to forget the evening he had spent with the intelligent sea-lion, admitted this.

"I thought I recognized you."

The priest looked at him closely, and remembered the face.

"Can I do anything for you?" he asked.

"I...I've come to confess."

"Come this way, will you?"

He led the stranger to a little panelled room off the choir stalls. It was his custom to have a heart-to-heart talk with those who came to him in circumstances such as these.

"Sit down," he said. "You can talk freely to me here. Then I will take you back to the church. If you wish, you can talk to your God there."

The man sat down and played nervously with his hat.

"Are you a member of the Church?" Robert asked.

"I'm a Catholic, Father, and as good a Catholic as I can be. It's the first time I've been inside a church in three years. I'm with the circus—I can't get to services. We're always on the move on Sundays."

Robert smiled.

"You have an excuse, at any rate," he said. "Many who have no excuse still do not come. Well...what has brought you here?"

"Maybe you know what happened last night. There was a man found dead in one of the cages. Anton—the man who trains the tigers."

"I know. I saw him. Most distressing."

"I killed him."

Robert looked for a long time at the oak tablet on the wall, on which were printed in gold lettering the names of the priests in charge of the church since its inception. He found himself unable to take his eyes away from the tablet and fix them on the man seated in front of him. There was a long silence. Then the man spoke, very quietly.

"I shot him. Three shots, high in the chest. One grazed his shoulder, the other two went into his chest. I was mad...I didn't know what I was doing. It was out in the field—just behind the tigers' cage. They were making a bit of a noise at the time...so were the people in the tent where the party was going on...it drowned the sounds of the shots. I opened the door of the cage and threw him in. The tigers leapt on him right away...it was horrible. They think he was mauled by them. He wasn't. He was shot...I killed him, Father... God help me."

The priest stood up. He was very pale.

"Come into the church," he said.

An hour later, Father Minto joined his brother and sister at lunch at the Station Hotel. Claire's fiancé, who was to have been present, had telephoned at the last minute saying that he could not come. A big deal in the vacuum-cleaner world was, it seemed, imminent. Mr. Minto was in good form. Although he would have been the last to admit it, there was nothing which put Mr. Minto into such high spirits as a curious case. The more curious the case, the better he liked it.

"Hullo, Robert," said Claire. "You're late, darling. I'm interviewing Detective-Inspector Minto—he's nosing about again. Did you see about the buttonholes?"

Robert said that he hadn't had time to see about the buttonholes but had bought socks.

"I don't see what that has to do with it," said Claire. "You can't wear socks in your buttonholes, can you? Sit down, dear, and let me get on with the interview. Now, Inspector, may I tell my readers that an arrest is considered imminent?"

"My lips," said Mr. Minto, "are sealed."

"That's what Mr. Baldwin always says before his long speeches. Oh—you don't know, Robert, do you? The most thrilling thing has happened. You know the man who was found in the cage last night? Well, he hadn't been mauled at all. At least, he had, but that was after. He'd been shot. Murdered, I mean."

"Yes, I know," said Robert.

"How did you know?" asked Mr. Minto.

"I...heard something about it this morning."

"Well, Detective-Inspector Minto is on the job. Don't be at all surprised if he turns up at my wedding on Saturday surrounded by bloodhounds. Or arrests one of the ushers. Look at him, Robert—the the long arm of the law."

Mr. Minto reached out the long arm of the law and poured out another glass of Sauterne.

"Well, carry on, Inspector," said Claire. "As you were saying..."

"As I was saying," said Mr. Minto, "there are four definite suspects at the time of going to Press. Quite probably it's none of these four, but they're enough to be going on with. I think it's fair to assume that the man who murdered Anton is connected with the circus."

"Why?" asked Claire.

"Because he evidently didn't think twice about opening the door of the tiger's cage and heaving the body inside. I wouldn't have done that, and neither would you. Whoever did do it was used to tigers. Which brings us to Suspect Number One."

Mr. Minto sat back as the aged waiter came up to the table, and waited patiently until the question of fruit salad, steamed ginger pudding, tapioca and figs, and/or prunes and custard was satisfactorily settled by all concerned. All concerned wisely decided to overlook the sweet course and have biscuits and cheese.

"The four suspects are the four people who left Dodo's supper-party last night at various times before the thing was discovered. First of all, that man Miller. At present things aren't looking any too well for Comrade Miller. The outlook's distinctly unsettled, as far as he's concerned. He had a very definite grudge against Anton—he gave himself away at the party by saying what he thought of Anton—and he's been heard to say many times that he wouldn't break down and cry if Anton was torn into little pieces by his tigers. Mr. Miller is Suspect Number One."

The priest looked serious. He cut himself a small portion of a Gorgonzola which looked about the same age as the waiter, and reflected that his brother and Mr. Baldwin were not the only persons going about with their lips sealed.

"Next on the list, in order of suspicion, is Lorimer. The trapeze chap."

"Oh no!" said Claire. "He looked such a nice young man. In fact, if I hadn't met Ronnie first, I could quite easily have fallen for Lorimer. If he hadn't met Loretta first, that is. She's a very charming girl."

"That's just the point," said Mr. Minto. "Loretta, it seems, has been charming to more than her husband. I don't believe half I hear, but—believing only one-half of what I've heard last night and this morning—Loretta had been enjoying a little affair with another man. The other man was Anton."

"Poor girl…"

"Dodo—the clown—overheard Lorimer making a date with Anton for after the show last night. He says that Lorimer didn't seem to be on the best of terms with the tiger gentleman. He also says that Lorimer had just discovered that Loretta was having an affair with Anton. I've had a chat with Loretta, but I got nothing out of her. She gave one of the finest impersonations of an oyster I've ever seen outside the West End."

"Why not have a chat with Lorimer?" said Claire.

"For the very good reason that Lorimer has disappeared."

"Disappeared?"

Robert said this in such an unexpected, high-pitched voice that both his brother and sister turned and stared at him. The little priest stirred his coffee nervously.

"He didn't sleep at the hotel last night. He hasn't been seen at the circus ground this morning. In fact, after he walked out of Dodo's party, he seems to have vanished altogether. A stupid thing to do, if he killed Anton. And an even more stupid thing to do, if he didn't. Lorimer, then, is Suspect Number Two."

"And Number Three?"

"The clown—Dodo."

"Darling, you couldn't accuse Dodo of doing it. Not after that lovely supper. And he's such a mild little man. He reminds me of my Ronnie."

"Your Ronnie—" said Mr. Minto.

"Don't go any further. I know you're going to say something rude about him, so you needn't bother. It couldn't be Dodo, in any case. It was Dodo who found Anton lying inside the cage."

"If I committed a murder," said Mr. Minto—"and such a thing is not unlikely with people like your Ronnie running about wild—if I committed a murder, I should make a point of being the first person to discover the crime. The first person to find a dead body is the last person the police think of suspecting."

"The first shall be last, and the last shall be first," said Robert.

"Exactly. With the common run of policemen, that is. I, of course, am different. Pass the cheese."

Robert passed the cheese.

"But you can't suspect Dodo just because he happened to find the tragedy," said Claire. "Or just because he'd left the party before it happened. You have to have something more than that to go on. Or haven't you? You policemen seem to go on very little nowadays."

"I have something more," said Mr. Minto. "This…"

He took out his pocket-wallet and laid the piece of brightly coloured silk on his plate.

"That is part of Dodo's clown costume. The one he was wearing at the party last night. It's been ripped off the costume, not cut off. There's a little dried blood on the edges. It's just possible that this piece of cloth was torn from the costume by…claws."

"A nasty thought," said Claire.

Robert dropped his bombshell.

"That's purely guess-work, isn't it?"

Claire stared at the priest in amazement. It was the first time that she had heard Robert say anything of the kind to his brother. The detective Mr. Minto generally overawed and subdued the priest Mr. Minto. If anyone had suggested that Robert would have accused Mr. Minto of pure guess-work, she would have laughed for a considerable time. Perhaps, after all, she had misjudged Robert. The man who dared to accuse Mr. Minto of guess-work obviously had something in him. Unless it was only the Sauterne, of which, Claire noticed, Robert had had two glasses.

"Guess-work?" said Mr. Minto, snorting. "Of course it's guess-work, Robert. But what makes it worth looking into is the fact that this piece of cloth was picked up just beside the tigers' cage. By me, in fact. I'd very much like to see Dodo sun-bathing."

"Why?"

"Because I think he'll have quite a nasty scratch just above the right hip, where this piece was torn out of the costume. He had a small scratch on his lip when he came back to the tent last night. However, as you say, that is purely guess-work. All the same, Dodo goes down as Suspect Number Three."

"And the last on the list?"

"Joe Carey, the proprietor. And don't ask me why I suspect him, because I can't give you any valid reason at all. I don't like him. I think he's a nasty piece of work, and I don't hold with the kind of visitor who comes to his caravan at four in the morning and gives peculiar whistles—but that's all I have against the gentleman."

"Have you asked Dodo anything?"

"Yes. I asked him what he did after he left the party. He says he went across and had a drink in Carey's caravan, with Carey. He says that beer doesn't agree with his inside, and he had a quiet lime-juice, which was most acceptable. Carey bears him out in that. On his way back to the tent where we were, Dodo passed the tigers' cage and saw—what we all saw later. Then he dashed back to us and spilled the beans."

"And what about the costume?"

"I couldn't ask him to let me see it—having only guess-work to go on," said Mr. Minto, with a twinkle in his eye in the priest's direction. "Perhaps I'll get a chance to see it later. I shouldn't be surprised if it's at the laundry just now. There, now…that's the position. I think Anton was killed by one of those four. Maybe I'm wrong. I was once."

"In 1887, wasn't it?" said Claire.

"The year before. We don't know that he was killed by one of those four, but they're enough to be going on with. I'd like to find the revolver that killed him, as well as the person. Joe Carey has a revolver, but no ammunition—so he says. Dodo never possessed a revolver in his life—scared stiff of the things, so *he* says. Miller used a revolver every day. At least, he stood outside the ring with a loaded revolver while Anton was doing his act with the tigers—just in case anything went wrong. That's an argument in Miller's favour, if anything. If Miller wanted to kill Anton, he had every opportunity to do it when the tigers were being frisky yesterday afternoon, and then make out that he'd misfired and shot Anton instead of the beasts. In any case, Miller's revolver is handed up to the ring-master and locked away at the end of each performance.

"Whether Lorimer owns a gun or not I don't know. He's cleared out, and until he turns up we can't get very far, I'm afraid. I hate a case with a lot of suspects. I'd much rather start where it was a physical impossibility for anyone to have done the dirty deed. However, one can't complain. It's a case, and it'll pass the time away until you get married to the vacuum on Saturday."

"And after that?"

"After that I'll hand the whole thing over to the locals, and get back to the peace and quiet of London."

"Of course, you'll have solved the thing long before Saturday…"

"I expect so. If only we could lay hands on Lorimer, we might get somewhere."

Lorimer, taking his cue neatly, came into the dining-hall and ordered an *omelette aux champignons*, with a black coffee to follow.

"Well!" said Mr. Minto.

"Well!" said Claire.

Robert took advantage of the silence to get the thing that had been worrying him off his chest.

"I…I'd like to tell you something about this case," he said.

"Carry on," said Mr. Minto. "All help gratefully received. What's on your mind, Robert?"

"I know who killed Anton."

"I beg your pardon?"

"Robert…on two glasses of Sauterne…"

"I'm quite serious. I know who killed Anton. He came to the church this morning and confessed."

Mr. Minto stared at his brother. He had not yet realized the position. If one had a brother who was a priest, and if murderers made a habit of confessing to the priest, then it saved a great deal of trouble. He waited for Robert to tell him the name of the confessee.

"You understand, of course, that I can tell you no more than that," said the priest. "I only told you that in case the matter became…um…embarrassing for both of us. The man confessed—through me—to his God. It concerns only the man and his God. I know you will understand the position I am in.…"

"Quite," said Mr. Minto. "Quite, Robert. Perfectly. Of course."

Mr. Minto went to lie down.

Mr. Minto enjoyed the unusual, but this was a bit too much. To try and solve a murder case, and at the same time to be rubbing shoulders with a man who knew the murderer's name, was a new sensation for him. Robert, of course, was perfectly right: if that was his religion, he must abide by it. There must be no pumping of Father Robert Minto—no attempt to catch him off his guard and get him to give away this very important piece of information. Mr. Minto had solved a good many murder cases without having to call in his brother's help as a father-confessor, and he was not going to start now.

There was, of course, no reason why he should not use the information that Robert had already given him—however unknowingly. The murderer was a man…which cut out Miss St. Clair, the stout lady who handed the Indian clubs to the jugglers, and Miss Mae West. The murderer was also a Catholic, and that narrowed down the field a great deal further. Mr. Minto sat up suddenly on his bed, and went out to ask people questions.

As a result of these questions, Mr. Minto found that Lorimer was a Catholic, having joined the Catholic Church on marrying Loretta.

Mr. Minto also discovered that the man Miller was a Catholic, coming of good Irish stock from Dublin, where he had once broken a beer-bottle over a man's skull to clinch a religious argument.

Mr. Minto found, too, that Joe Carey was a Catholic, and had—somewhat surprisingly—attended Mass that very morning.

And, finally, Mr. Minto found that Dodo was a Catholic.

Mr. Minto went back to lie down.

Chapter Ten

Mr. Minto watched the afternoon performance of the circus from the draughty alleyway, and found it—in addition to being draughty—extremely exciting.

Joe Carey had taken the whole morning to persuade Miller to change his name to Anton, put on Anton's abbreviated tiger-skin pants, and go into the big cage with Peter and the rest of the troupe. Miller, who had been so keen to get back into the act, appeared to have changed his mind about it now that the chance had actually come. He was having none of it: he admitted frankly that he was scared. If the cats tore up Anton, what the devil would they do to him?

"But they didn't," said Carey. "They never touched 'im. 'E was dead as a door-nail before ever they went near 'im."

"I don't care," said Miller. "I'm not doing Anton's act— not with the beasts in that mood, thank you."

Mr. Carey coaxed, wheedled, bullied, cajoled, and threatened. Until half an hour before the matinée performance was due to begin, Miller was still having nothing to do with the proposition. Mr. Carey promised him Anton's salary. It nearly broke his heart to do it, but it seemed to be the only thing. Miller wavered. Mr. Carey said that, of course, they would not expect him to go into the ring unarmed, as Anton had done, and that there would be plenty of people standing round the ring in case anything did happen—not that there was the slightest chance of anything happening. Miller wavered a little more. Mr. Carey then made rather a *faux pas* by saying that, if anything did go wrong, he would make himself personally responsible for Miller's wife and family—they would be looked after and cared for in the event of Miller's death. On hearing this, Miller stopped wavering at once and said that he wouldn't go inside the cage with the tigers for all the gold in Christendom.

Mr. Carey gave up trying to be diplomatic and persuasive, and played his trump card. If Miller didn't do the act that afternoon, he could pack his grip and clear out of the circus right away.

Miller, sweating, said, "All right…I'll do it."

The six hundred school-children and fifty-odd adults who saw the matinée performance will not easily forget it. Mr. Minto, standing in the wings beside a group of silent performers, was as frightened as he had ever been in his life.

The cage was set up at the record speed for which Carey's was famed; the long tunnel leading from the tigers' own cage into the ring was placed in position; the band gave the cue, and was drowned by the roaring of the tigers as they slouched down from their cage, along the tunnel, and into the ring. They were in no mood to be played with…certainly in no mood to be put through hoops of fire. Mr. Minto, staring at them before Miller entered the ring, wished that he was on speaking terms with these tigers. Here was a murder case in which no fewer than eight living beings—seven tigers and a Roman Catholic priest—knew the name of the murderer, and would probably have been only too glad to have passed on that name if they could have done so…and Mr. Minto had to try and solve the thing on his own, surrounded by these eight know-alls. It was very trying.

The tigers were jumpy and excited. Even the cubs were wide awake, and two of them staged a fairly vicious fight between themselves before Miller entered the ring. The new trainer threw off his dressing-gown beside Mr. Minto, and Mr. Minto wished him luck. He was very pale and trembling a little. Mr. Minto didn't like the look of it at all. Why should this man Miller be so scared of doing the act, when—only the night before—he had boasted that he could do it far better than Anton himself?

Mr. Minto started to think. These seven tigers knew who had thrown the body of Anton into their cage last night. They hadn't actually mauled him; they had raised their necks to heaven and roared the place down. There must have been a certain bond of attachment between the tigers and their trainer—though it certainly had not seemed a very strong bond at yesterday's performances. It was quite likely that these tigers, more than any of the humans in Carey's Circus, could solve the mystery of Anton's death. If the man who placed Anton's body in their cage were put before them, wouldn't they show their feelings in no uncertain manner? Suppose that man had been Miller—at this moment opening the door and stepping slowly into the ring....Mr. Minto watched closely.

Five of the seven tigers had their backs to Miller as he stepped into the ring. The sudden roar of the other two and the clang of the door as it shut made the five swing round to face their new trainer. The band brought its introductory music to a close with a roll on the drums, and there was silence in the tent for a moment. Only for a moment. Peter, facing Miller, stood motionless. If only, thought Mr. Minto, if only one could tell what Peter was thinking at this moment. Was he, by any chance, thinking: "...This is the man who threw the body inside the cage last night…this is the man who killed Anton…this is the man whom we want to kill…?" Peter gave one roar, and sprang.

Miller lashed out with his whip, hitting the tiger across the face. The beast stopped, a yard away from him, and gave a second roar, of pain. The other two older tigers and the cubs were closing in on the trainer. The six men stationed at various points outside the ring stood still, their hands round the revolvers concealed in their uniforms. One of the cubs broke away from the rest and slunk round the wall of the cage, coming up behind Miller on his right side. Miller saw it out of the corner of his eye and slashed out again with the whip.…The cub winced and slouched back into the centre of the ring, but in that moment Peter saw his chance, and sprang again. Miller leapt aside, lost his balance and fell on the sawdust.

Peter was on him in an instant. A great paw thrashed across his naked body, from the neck down to the waist. Blood poured out suddenly. The women in the audience screamed; the children kept a frightened silence; every person in the tent, without knowing it, had left their seats and stood up, staring at the unpleasant sight in the ring. The men outside the cage whipped out their revolvers, and two of them fired high into the roof of the tent. It was impossible to fire direct at Peter in case of hitting Miller. Impossible at first: as soon as it was realized that Miller would probably prefer to be shot than to die the death which he was being dealt out at present, three more shots cracked out simultaneously. Peter leapt back and sank down on the sawdust beside Miller. He had two bullets in the throat, and lay pawing the ground feebly. The cubs, unhurt but terrified, raced round to the far side of the cage. One of the other beasts had taken a bullet in one of its paws, and limped round the ring in fury.

"Play, damn you!" shouted Joe Carey. The band struck up "Tiger Rag". No one could blame them for seeming so callous about it; this was the next piece of music on their programme, and they had not thought of changing it to a more suitable tune while Miller was being torn to pieces.

Mr. Minto could not gather what happened after that. There was a tremendous amount of excitement and yelling and running; somehow the tigers were shoved out of the ring, up the tunnel, and into their cage; somehow the body of Miller was carried past him and out to the nearest tent. He heard Joe Carey roaring for Dr. Blair, with a great many unnecessary but understandable adjectives thrown in. He caught sight of Dodo, in a brand-new clown's costume, standing in the wings with no expression on his painted face. He realized that Miss St. Clair, who was next on the bill, had fainted untidily right at his feet, but before he could do anything about it she was lifted up and carried off to the same tent in which Miller was lying. It was not, Mr. Minto thought, the ideal spot for a lady to recover from a fainting fit.

He looked back through the flap into the tent: the audience was still in pandemonium, and Peter, the biggest of the seven tigers, still lay motionless in the middle of the ring. But once again Mr. Minto was forced to marvel at the organization of Carey's Circus, for here was Joe Carey in person entering the ring, stepping over Peter, making a short speech, telling everyone to keep calm, assuring them that no serious damage had been done and that Anton (he nearly said Miller, but checked himself in time) was only slightly hurt.

Here, too, was a small squad of men carrying the heavy, limp body of Peter out of the ring, and a larger squad taking down the huge cage. Dodo was in the ring now, playing the fool, doing double somersaults and ending up with a brilliant timing in a large pot of whitewash.

The children slowly forgot how scared they had been, and began to snigger at the clown. The sniggers grew to laughs, the laughs to roars…much more pleasant roars than the last that had been heard in that tent. The band changed its tune. Miss St. Clair, revived with a large brandy, appeared with her Educated Ponies. The show went on….

"*Is* he only slightly hurt?" asked Mr. Minto, as Carey came out of the tent.

"What d'you think?" said the proprietor. "'E's dying—or dead."

"I've got to see him, then," said Mr. Minto.

He ran across the grass to the tent where Miller had been carried with Carey following him, puffing freely. Miller was lying on a trestle table. He was not a nice sight. Dr. Blair was fortifying himself with a double whisky…two cases of this sort within two days was a little too much for him.

"Is he dead?" asked Mr. Minto.

"No. Not yet. I can't do anything for him, though."

"Not if you stand there drinking whisky," said Mr. Minto, and went across to lean over Miller's body.

The man's eyes were closed, but he was still breathing.

"Miller…" said Mr. Minto. "Miller…can you hear me?"

The eyes gave a flicker and the lips moved slightly.

"Miller…I want to ask you something. Take it easy—don't move. You'll be all right if you lie still. Last night—when you went away from Dodo's party—where did you go? What did you do?"

The eyes opened and stared up at Mr. Minto. Mr. Minto did not hold with putting a man through a shorter catechism in circumstances like this, but it had to be done. Miller had perhaps a quarter of an hour to live—perhaps less. And after that quarter of an hour had passed Mr. Minto could do very little in the solving of Anton's death where Miller was concerned.

"Where did you go, Miller? I've got to know."

"Outside…walked round the field…that's all.…"

"You know what happened last night, don't you? Anton was murdered—shot dead and then put inside the tigers' cage. Miller…listen to me, if you can. Did you go near that cage last night?"

"No.…"

"Did you see Anton at all last night—after the party, I mean?"

The man closed his eyes again and lay still.

"Did you?"

"I…saw…"

"Take it easy—don't move. You'll be all right."

"Joe Carey…caravan…"

"What's that?"

Mr. Minto could hardly hear him. It was going to be considerably less than the quarter of an hour he had given him.

"Miller…did you kill Anton?"

No answer.

"Did you kill Anton?"

The man raised his head a few inches. His lips opened but no words came. The head sank back on the trestle table. The eyes closed and he moved no more.

"Blair! Come here, damn you—do something!"

The Doctor crossed to the table and made a brief examination.

"We'd better get a priest," said Mr. Minto. "He's a Catholic."

"He's dead," said the Doctor, and sounded relieved.

"And a hell of a lot you did to keep him alive," said Mr. Minto, and walked angrily from the tent.

One of the four suspects gone. Mr. Minto was in more of a quandary than ever. Did that mean that the case was finished so far as this world was concerned? Or did it mean that he had still to go on, on the chance that Miller had not been Anton's murderer? He could do a certain amount of nosing around before deciding on that point, at any rate. Mr. Minto went straight to the ring-master, and found that gentleman steadying his nerves with a cup of strong tea. He spoke with a Yorkshire accent as strong as the tea, which came as rather a surprise to Mr. Minto: apparently the immaculate English with which he announced the turns was confined to his appearances in the ring and could be dropped at will.

"Miller's dead, poor chap," said Mr. Minto. "It's just possible that he was the man who killed Anton last night. I've got to check up on one or two things before I can be sure about that. Now, I want your help."

"Ay," said the ring-master. "Owt I can do, I'll do it."

"Miller had a revolver, hadn't he? Up till today, I mean— when he was on the attendant's job during Anton's act?"

"Ay, that's right."

"Where was the revolver kept?"

"In here. In case, over yonder."

"Is it there now?"

"'Course it's there now. Never been taken out. He didn't need it today, seeing he was doing act himself. Eh, poor fellow…been a heap better if he'd had goon, wouldn't it?"

"Let's have a look at it."

"All right. All goons are handed in to me after performance. It's a right strict rule in circus, it is. Miller's was kept in here beside rest of them. Eh, now! What do you know about that?"

"Nothing," said Mr. Minto. "What do you mean—isn't it there?"

"No. Goon's vanished."

"Just as I thought. Who could have taken it? Was that case locked?"

"No. There was a key once, but I don't know where it is now."

"So that anyone could have walked in here and helped themselves?"

"They'd have me to reckon with, lad."

"You're in the ring a good deal, aren't you?"

"I am that."

"Anyone could have come in here and taken that revolver while you were away doing your stuff in the ring?"

"Ay. I suppose so."

"Thanks very much," said Mr. Minto. "I'd buy a key for that case. It might save a lot of trouble. Good afternoon."

Mr. Minto went out and walked across the field towards the tigers' cage. The noise of the band and of applause and the laughter of children came over to him from the big tent where the matinée performance was still going on. Mr. Minto reflected how quickly a tragedy is forgotten. He watched the tigers for a moment, and got the impression that they were now content. It was probably all imagination, of course, but it seemed to Mr. Minto that the beasts had now settled down after doing something they had been wanting to do. He walked round to the door of the cage and—not for the first time—cursed himself for not attending to the matter of fingerprints on the bars of the cage as soon as the tragedy was discovered. The bars were now covered with fingerprints—probably everyone in the circus had touched them between the finding of Anton's body and the present moment. And one out of all those prints would very likely be the print of the murderer's hand. Mr. Minto began supposing….

Suppose that Miller *had* killed Anton. Suppose that he had met him after leaving Dodo's party? He'd come out of the tent across there and walk over here. He might have met Anton just here, behind the tigers' cage, with the cage between them and the other tents and caravans. It was the most likely spot for any dirty work. Suppose he'd shot Anton and dragged the body up the steps of the cage and thrown him inside?

Mr. Minto examined the steps carefully. There was some mud and grass on them, otherwise nothing. Well, then…what after that? Surely, if he'd had any sense at all, he would have put the revolver back in the ring-master's tent? Wait a minute, though…would he? With three rounds fired, and no way of explaining away those three rounds? No—much more likely that Miller (supposing it to be Miller) would have disposed of the revolver altogether. How, then? By planting it in someone's tent, or in one of the caravans? Surely not. In any case, if it were such a strict rule in the circus that all revolvers were to be placed in the custody of the ring-master, surely it would have been found and handed over by now. No. Miller (or whoever it was) wouldn't have hidden the gun in that way. Mr. Minto then noticed, for the first time, the burn.

The burn ran through a corner of the field in which the circus had pitched its tents and caravans. It was less than thirty yards from the tigers' cage, and between it and the far exit from the field. It was a narrow, fast-running stream, perhaps two or three feet deep in places. What made it appeal to Mr. Minto was the fact that it was very dirty. The water was brown and muddy, and a number of miscellaneous objects, such as empty cigarette packets and tin cans, floated down on it. Mr. Minto scratched his head, lit a cigarette, removed his jacket, and got going.

There were quite a few of the circus people who, by this time, had come to look on Mr. Minto as—to put it politely—somewhat eccentric, and any of these persons who happened to see him during the next hour had their minds definitely made up. Eccentric was hardly the word for it: this man Minto was just plain daft. For Mr. Minto chose a spot about twenty yards above the tigers' cage, got down on his hands and knees, and started to build a dam.

After forty minutes of damming and a great deal of damning, Mr. Minto was filled with admiration for the men who make a habit of harnessing the waters of the Zambesi, Ganges, Nile, and other rivers. His own little stream was hardly in the same class as those, and yet the job of building a dam across even its narrowest part was far from simple. Mr. Minto, for one thing, had on his second-best suit: a pleasing thing of pale grey with a chalk stripe. No one should ever attempt to build a dam, however small, in a pale grey suit with a chalk stripe. Mr. Minto used, apart from bad language, mud and bricks and stones and divots. His dam reached more than three quarters of the way across the burn and was beginning to look really businesslike when the water took it into its head to come downstream at a greatly increased force, and Mr. Minto's handiwork was carried away as though it had been matchwood. Mr. Minto wiped a tear from his eye, introduced one or two new swears, and started the job again.

In just an hour the thing was done. Mr. Minto stood up, straightened his back—which was behaving exactly as backs behave in the advertisements of patent liniments before application—and held his breath. The dam also held. Mr. Minto, who was not often guilty of Americanisms, took off his hat and said, "Whoopee!"

The burn, rather taken aback at this new turn of events, dithered for a while before striking off on a new course. Mr. Minto noted with some alarm that it was now making straight for the big circus tent, and thought how very awkward it would be if a small river suddenly started to run bang through the middle of the ring and went on to undermine the one-and-threepenny seats. Fortunately the stream took a sudden twist just before reaching the tent, and made a new route for itself down towards the stables. It would probably come in quite useful there.

Mr. Minto was not really interested in the new course of the burn, however; it was the old in which he hoped to find something. He waited patiently while the level of the water fell inch by inch, until at last it was only a muddy bed with no more than a couple of inches of dirty water trickling along it. He lit another cigarette and walked slowly along the bank, falling in at intervals and putting any hope of getting the pale-grey suit dry-cleaned out of the question. And then, as he had hoped, he caught sight of something lying in the mud—not so very far from the tigers' cage. He put one foot on each bank, did a feat of contortion that would have gone down well in Carey's or any other circus, and took that something out of the mud. It was a revolver. He wiped most of the grime off it, and went back to the ring-master's tent.

"You haven't found that revolver, have you?" he asked.

"I have not, lad."

"Good. I have. At least, I think so. Is this it?"

The ring-master inspected the gun carefully.

"Ay, that's it all right. Where d'ye get it, lad?"

Mr. Minto had no time to answer that. He asked where Miller changed into his circus costume.

"In tent over yonder—next to blue caravan. Usually, that is. He'd use Anton's dressing-tent today, seeing he was doing his act, poor lad."

"And which one is that?"

The ring-master pointed out Anton's tent. Mr. Minto hopped happily over to it, still clutching the revolver. Miss St. Clair, seeing him running across the grass with a revolver in his hand, at once set a rumour flying around that the mad detective had run amok and was murdering practically everybody.

There was no one in the tent. Miller's everyday clothes lay scattered on a table and on the wooden floor-boards. A suit-case also lay on the table. Mr. Minto opened it and rummaged inside. A pair of flannel trousers, a sweater, and an old jacket were inside the case. The trousers and jacket were covered with mud, caked dry. They were the clothes which Miller had worn at the party last night. Mr. Minto compared the mud with the specimens on his own clothes… both were clay, and both appeared to be the same. That could be easily decided definitely by sending up samples of the mud on Miller's clothes and the mud on the banks of the stream for analysis. As it happened, such a step was not necessary. Mr. Minto felt through the pockets of Miller's jacket, and found a note-case, empty except for two pound notes and a single sheet of paper. Mr. Minto read what was written on the paper and sighed happily. It was a statement, to be revealed in the event of anything happening to him at the performance that afternoon. Miller must have guessed what was coming to him. It stated, in a minimum of words, how Miller had murdered Anton, and why.

Mr. Minto, humming softly, went back to his hotel to meet Claire and her young man. It was very nice to get the thing settled up so easily as this.

"I may be wrong," said Claire, "but I had the impression that you invited us here for five o'clock. It's now a quarter past six. Ronnie and I have discussed the kitchen linoleum, the disadvantages of twin beds, the kind of roses we're going to grow in the garden, and the Oxford Group Movement. Where the blazes have you been?"

"I've been to the circus," said Mr. Minto.

"What, again? Robert's gone there too. He got a summons to go along right away. Someone's dying or something. He said he'd look in here on his way back."

"Robert won't be of much use now," said Mr. Minto.

"What's been happening, sir?" asked Claire's fiancé. He seemed a little worried.

"I've had the unpleasant experience of seeing a man mauled by those tigers—and really mauled this time, mind you."

"Good heavens—who?"

Young Mr. Briggs had gone quite white at the mention of the word "mauled". Mr. Minto thought it was as well that he had not seen the actual mauling.

"Miller. He's dead now. And I've also found out who killed Anton."

"For the second time, good heavens! And who?"

"Miller."

"Tell us everything, Inspector," said Claire.

"Just a minute—here's tea. Wait until Lightning goes away, and then tell us all."

Mr. Minto waited patiently until the aged waiter had shuffled off. Then he took a cup of tea from Claire and stirred it thoughtfully.

"I didn't solve the crime," he said. "The tigers did it, by the way they behaved as soon as they saw who was to put them through their paces in the ring this afternoon. I'm glad you two weren't there…it wasn't exactly pleasant. They knew perfectly well who had killed Anton, those tigers; they were waiting for a chance to put the matter straight. Blood for blood, and all that. And they did it—most efficiently. They killed Miller."

"But you can't be sure that he murdered Anton, just because the tigers went for him."

"I'm not. I've been nosing around and I've found out quite a lot of things this afternoon. First of all I found the gun that was used to kill Anton. Miller's gun is kept by the ring-master; it had disappeared. I tried to think of a likely place where it might be—and I did a bit of damming."

"What?" said young Mr. Briggs.

"Quite all right—two 'm's'. There's a little burn running through the circus field, quite close to the tigers' cage. Very muddy water and two feet or more deep in places—just the ideal spot for parking an unwanted revolver. I dammed it—the burn, I mean."

"I was wondering what you'd been doing," said Claire. "You look as though you'd been digging a field of potatoes."

"Yes," said Mr. Minto. "A pity—I always liked this suit. However, I dammed the burn. I diverted its course and at this moment it's quite likely that it's running blithely down the High Street, or into Robert's church. At any rate, when the old course ran dry I found the revolver. Miller's revolver, with three rounds fired. Then I went to the tent where he changed into his circus costume and had a look through his personal belongings. The suit he wore at last night's party was there—with a great deal of mud on it. The same rich, clinging stuff that you see here. D'you think it'll come off, Claire?"

"Never," said Claire. "Go on—carry on with the story."

"That's about all. Miller was mad at Anton for pitching him out of the act. He killed him out of sheer jealousy, and planted his body in the cage, thinking that those tigers would destroy all trace of the crime. Unfortunately for him, Dodo found the body before the tigers had time to do any real destroying. The evidence was pretty strong against Miller from the start. I knew that Anton's murderer must have been someone who knew those animals fairly intimately. The ordinary man in the street would think twice about going inside a cage with seven tigers, especially when he was carrying another man over his shoulder. He may have had a little too much to drink at the party, and before it…."

"He went out after he'd said his little piece, you remember, and he must have seen Anton wandering about outside. He went to the ring-master's tent—the ring-master was at the party, of course—and he got his gun out. He met Anton behind the tigers' cage and he shot him. The noise of the shots wouldn't be heard in the tent where we were having supper: it's a fair distance away and we were all making a good deal of noise ourselves. In addition to which the tigers may have been saying their say and helped to drown the noise of the shots. He killed him, dragged the body inside the cage, and left it there. He threw the revolver into the burn, thinking it would be safe there—at any rate, until the circus moved on. He went to the tent where he usually changed for the performance, took off his clothes and put on another suit. Perhaps you didn't notice him in the crowd when we rushed out and saw what had happened to Anton. I did. He wasn't wearing the same suit as he wore at the party. For the very good reason that there was too much mud—and perhaps an odd spot or two of blood—on the clothes he wore when he killed Anton."

"Here's Robert," said Claire. "Come and sit down, darling. Were you in time?"

"No," said the priest. "The man was dead before I got there. This circus seems to be fated, doesn't it?"

"Have some tea and keep quiet, then," said Claire. "Detective-Inspector Minto has found out who killed Anton."

The priest looked at his brother.

"Who, then?" he asked.

"The man you were sent to see—Miller. He was mauled by those tigers this afternoon....He's paid the penalty for his sins all right."

Father Robert Minto selected a sandwich and munched it without replying.

"Well, go on, Inspector," said Claire. "Finish the recital."

"There's nothing more to say."

"But does that make it *certain*? I mean, can you definitely say that this man Miller did it, from what you've told us?"

"Not from what I've told you," said Mr. Minto, "because I haven't told you all I found this afternoon."

"Detectives are the most annoying people," said Claire. "Go on, then. Stop trying to be mysterious and tell us all."

"I found a confession."

The priest put down his tea-cup with a bang.

"Confession?" he said.

"Yes, Robert. As well as confessing to you—and to his God—this man Miller wrote down a confession for the benefit of the police. I wish every murderer were as considerate. It saves such a lot of trouble when you get the thing from the murderer himself. There are always any amount of people who don't believe the police, or the jury, or the judge, or the evidence—but when a murderer confesses himself, that puts an end to all discussion. I found a written confession in the pocket of the jacket which Miller had worn last night, written and signed by himself and admitting that he had killed Anton."

"Well!" said Claire. "That's that. I think the London police are simply marvellous. Or has somebody said that before?"

"I'm glad it's over," said Mr. Minto. "Now we can concentrate on the real business of the week. This blooming wedding on Saturday."

The priest dropped his head in his hands and said, "Oh, dear...."

"What's the matter, Robert?" asked Claire. "You needn't look so tragic whenever anyone starts to talk about the wedding."

"I...I don't know what to do," said the priest.

"What's worrying you, Robert?" asked Mr. Minto.

"Perhaps I ought not to tell you this...I don't know...."

"Well?"

"The man who came into the church this morning and confessed to having murdered Anton was…not Miller. I am afraid that you have not yet solved this terrible business. Miller did not murder Anton.…"

"Oh, hell!" said Mr. Minto.

Chapter Eleven

When Mr. Minto said "Oh, hell!" he meant it. To have rounded off what he thought was a neat, quick job of work, only to be stymied by this pink little priest who knew the name of Anton's murderer, was, to say the least of it, a little trying. Not for the first time did Mr. Minto wish that his brother had stuck to his original idea of becoming an engine-driver, instead of entering the Church. Mr. Minto, poor soul, had imagined that his interest in the circus and in Anton's death was now finished and that he could devote his time to preparations for the wedding of his sister Claire to Mr. Ronald Briggs on the following Saturday.

He had packed in a hurry when leaving London, and there were one or two things he would have to buy before he could appear in all his glory at the wedding ceremony. A quiet grey tie appeared to be indicated, for one thing; for Mr. Minto had discovered, through reading all the society papers in the hotel lounge, that cravats were no longer the Thing To Wear. His top-hat, which at present resembled a barbed-wire entanglement, had somehow to be transformed into a crowning glory before Saturday. Most important of all, Mr. Minto had his speech to prepare for the reception, and that would be a whole-day job in itself. Mr. Minto rarely spoke in public, except to give evidence in cases, but when he did so he liked to do the thing well. Neatly turned phrases, apt similes, and at least two brand-new jokes were essentials of the Minto speeches.

Up to now he had got no further than the somewhat hackneyed opening, "Ladies and gentlemen", though he had thought out the rough draft of a first sentence, saying what great pleasure it gave him to be present today on this happy and auspicious occasion. Sound stuff, as far as it went; but a great deal had still to be thought out. He had one very good joke, but was a little doubtful about how Robert would react to it. And now, just when he was thinking that he could lie back and concentrate on the speech and such matters, he was flung back into the middle of the Anton business by a single sentence from the priest.

Mr. Minto looked at his brother sadly, and wondered again what had possessed him to go through life wearing his collar that way round.

"Who did kill Anton, then?" he demanded.

The priest gave a worried smile.

Mr. Minto shrugged his shoulders, sighed, and walked away. He had not expected an answer, and ought not to have asked the question. The fact that Robert knew the solution of the circus mystery was no business of his, and any investigations he had to make must be made without pumping Robert. Mr. Minto, abandoning all thought of a quiet evening getting his top-hat into condition, stepped back into the fray and got busy once again.

Lorimer, to begin with. He had been trying to buttonhole Lorimer for a pleasant chat all day, but so far had not succeeded. Why had Lorimer disappeared last night? Where had he gone after the party, and what had he done? Mr. Minto went up to Lorimer's room, knocked, received no answer, came downstairs again and was told by the hall-porter that both Lorimer and Loretta had left for the evening performance of the circus.

"Arm in arm?" asked Mr. Minto.

"Beg pardon, sir?" said the hall-porter.

"I mean, did they appear friendly…or just like husband and wife?"

"They seemed to be getting on very well, sir. Joking-like, if you know what I mean, sir."

"Joking-like?" said Mr. Minto. "That's bad—very bad."

Mr. Minto put off his questioning of Lorimer until later in the evening, and rang up the local police-station to ask, politely enough, if anything had been done about his requests of the early hours of that morning. Mr. Minto didn't want to hurry them, and knew that he had no business butting in on a purely private murder, but if they were doing anything about what he asked, would they mind getting a move on? The local police-force got a move on at once: Superintendent Padgeham, in person, arrived at the Station Hotel and, in reply to a question of Mr. Minto's, said that he wouldn't say "no" to a small one. Even after the small one, the Superintendent kept on looking at Mr. Minto as if thinking how much better the world would be if Scotland Yard inspectors minded their own business. He passed on his report in a grudging baritone.

The occupants of No. 288, Bank Street, according to Superintendent Padgeham, were sober and respectable citizens of the name of Winter. They had lived above the pawnshop for sixteen years and—apart from what the Superintendent called "a bit of a to-do" about stolen milk-bottles away back in the spring of 1928—they had never had anything to do with the police. Mr. Winter was an elderly gentleman who lived on his old-age pension, a system of backing horses which rarely came off, and the earnings of his wife and daughter. The wife took in washing and, on occasions, lodgers. A lodger was believed to be living in the house just now, as well as an invalid sister of Mr. Winter.

The daughter (here the Superintendent became a little involved) was not actually a daughter of the Winters; it was believed that they had adopted the girl, though some unkind persons were inclined to think other things. In any case, the daughter looked after the pawnshop below, and received two pounds per week in wages from the gentleman who ran the business. The Winters were prominent members of the local Methodist Chapel, were understood to have voted for the National Government at the last General Election, and had won prizes for the excellent leeks which they grew in the small garden at the back of the pawnshop.

The Superintendent wound up his report on the Winter family with the remark that, if any Brilliant Brains from Scotland Yard thought they had hit on the headquarters of a gang of dangerous international crooks at No. 288, Bank Street, they had better think again.

"Thanks very much, Padgeham," said Mr. Minto, still polite. "Very good of you to go to all this trouble. Now, there's just one other thing. What about drugs?"

"Drugs?" said the Superintendent.

"Yes. I wonder—could you let me have a note of any known drug addicts, or cases in which drugs had been mixed up within the last few years?"

"Lord bless my soul!" said the Superintendent, slapping his stomach and laughing heartily. "Drugs, indeed! There hasn't been a case of drug-taking in this town, not as far back as I can remember."

"There may have been cases of drug-taking," said Mr. Minto, "without you knowing about it, of course...."

"Don't you waste your time about drugs in this town, sir. We'd soon get to hear about it, if that kind of thing was going on. Drugs, indeed! Ho-ho!"

"Ho-ho!" said Mr. Minto sadly. "Well, never mind. It's just as well. Drugs aren't nice things to have going round a town. Thanks very much, Superintendent. Good night."

Mr. Minto waited until the Superintendent had gone, and made his way at once to No. 288, Bank Street. For no sounder reason, it must be admitted, than that the Superintendent's report sounded far too good to be true. He took a look in the crowded windows of the pawnshop, climbed the stairs to the flat above, and beat a tattoo on the door.

Mrs. Winter (presumably) answered the door and said, "Well?"

"I'm the Housing Inspector," said Mr. Minto, never at a loss for words. "Overcrowding, you know. Did you get the form?"

No, Mrs. Winter had received no form.

"Dear, dear!" said Mr. Minto. "Slackness somewhere. However—it's just a formality, you know. Housing Act of 1935—I've got to look round and report any cases of overcrowding—see the number of rooms you have, and that sort of thing. May I step in? Thank you so much."

Mr. Minto stepped into the sitting-room. If he had been really an inspector of housing conditions, he would have found plenty of grounds for condemning at least this one room for overcrowding.

At a rough guess, two hundred and fifty china ornaments were busily gathering dust on a number of shelves, cupboards, mantelpieces, whatnots, and what not around the room. There was a great deal of furniture, mainly upholstered in green plush, as well as a bird-cage (empty) which stood in the middle of the room, like a policeman directing traffic on point duty. The room stank of stale tobacco smoke. Mr.

Winter (again presumably) lay on a sofa in his shirt-sleeves, reading the *Racing Chronicle*.

"Who's this bloke?" he asked.

"Someone from the housing people," said Mrs. Winter vaguely. "Wants to see through the house for overcrowding, or something."

"At this time of night?"

"I'm sorry," said Mr. Minto. "I won't take a minute."

"You won't find no overcrowding here, you won't," said the man. "There's five rooms in this house, and only the three of us and the wife's sister, what's staying here with us in the meantime. You can't turn us out for that, you can't."

"Of course not. It's just a formality. Don't you take in lodgers sometimes?"

"We do. We've got one with us now. There isn't any law against taking in lodgers, is there? If this country was worth living in, people wouldn't need to take in lodgers to make ends meet. You take me, now. Right through the War, I was—beginning to end, and a couple of wounds in that leg there what I could show you this very minute—and what has the country done for me, eh? Not a ruddy thing, it hasn't. And now they start all this monkey business about overcrowding—sending blooming inspectors nosing through people's houses, without so much as a beg-pardon or a by-your-leave. What things is coming to, I don't know. Inspectors for this, and inspectors for that, and inspectors for the other thing. And who pays for them?—that's what I'd like to know. The ratepayers, of course. You take Income Tax, now. All I have in this world is what we make off lodgers and odd jobs what I do, and they have the blooming nerve to make me fill up forms to pay Income Tax! I may tell you, mister, that I joined up in 1914 and I was right through the War until the end—and what have I got in return, eh? If a bloke what fights for his country isn't good enough to—"

"Oh, shut up!" said Mrs. Winter.

Mr. Minto murmured an agreement. The man whose one attitude towards the War is one of personal grumbling was not one of Mr. Minto's favourite types. He crossed the room, circumnavigated the bird-cage, and opened the bedroom door.

"That's the lodger's room," said Mrs. Winter. "He's out now. He works at the circus."

"Oh? What's his name?"

"Miller. He usually comes back here between his shows, but he's doing someone else's turn today. I expect he's staying down at the field."

"I expect so," said Mr. Minto, and walked to another door.

"That's where we sleep. You can't go in there just now."

"Why not?"

"My sister's in there. She's an invalid. You can't disturb her."

"I won't hurt her. I've just got to see the size of the room—regulations, you know."

"You're not going into that room, you aren't!" said Mr. Winter, bobbing up to the surface again over the top of the *Racing Chronicle*. "I don't care who you are, or what you're after, but you can't come barging into people's houses and walking about as though you owned the place, you can't. She's very ill, she is. And nervous. The least thing upsets her. God knows what a blooming Inspector would do to her, barging in without so much as a—"

Mr. Minto barged in. He stayed in the doorway rather longer than he had intended. The woman lying on the bed interested him.

"What's the matter with her?" he asked, as he shut the door.

"It's a sort of paralysis."

"Dear me. Poor soul. Where does this stair lead to?"

"Down to the shop below. We never use it."

"Never?"

"Never. It hasn't been used for years."

"And have you a cover to your cistern to prevent mice, insects, and dust from gaining access to the water contained therein?"

Mr. Minto was not at all interested in the Winters's cistern, but he remembered that this was one of the points on which the Housing Act of 1935 was particularly hot, and—like Pooh-Bah—he was anxious to add verisimilitude to an otherwise bald and unconvincing narrative.

Mrs. Winter said that she didn't know about the cistern, but from the colour of the water in the tap she felt pretty sure that mice, insects, and dust could fall in it just as they felt inclined.

Mr. Minto said it really didn't matter and that, as long as Mrs. Winter had no more than five children within the next three years, there was no danger of the premises being condemned for overcrowding until 1940. Mrs. Winter threw out her chest and hooted loudly at the idea of having five children between then and 1940, jerking her thumb back over her shoulder and in the direction of Mr. Winter to emphasize the folly of Mr. Minto's remark. Mr. Minto raised his hat, apologized for troubling everyone, and went downstairs to pawn his watch in the shop below.

The shop was being looked after by a young girl—a very charming young girl, Mr. Minto thought. Well-spoken, quiet, good-looking, and a little shy. He had a preliminary skirmish about the value of his watch, and was invited into a back room to complete the deal. While this was being done he heard a scuffle immediately above his head. Mr. Minto looked up and realized that the stairs leading to the house above—the stairs which had not been used for years—formed part of the roof of the back room. They were being used now. Someone large and heavy was coming down.

Reaching the bottom step, the owner of the feet which had made such a commotion on the stairs called out, "Hoi!"

The charming young girl excused herself and ran out into the shop. Mr. Minto, wiping the dust from a window-pane and peering through, saw a man in a checked suit hand a small parcel to the girl, pat her cheek, and pass on out of the shop. It was not Mr. Winter. It was, in fact, Joseph Carey, proprietor of Carey's Circus.

The girl returned, gave Mr. Minto his ticket, and shepherded him back into the main shop and towards the door. The collection of articles scattered across the counter intrigued Mr. Minto, and he paused to admire a blunder-buss, two pairs of corduroy pants, a crucifix, an edition of Robbie Burns' poems, and a pipe-rack executed in compli-cated fretwork.

"What queer things people leave in a pawnshop," he said.

"Yes, sir," said the girl. "You'd be surprised, sir."

She had a very soft, refined voice. Mr. Minto took quite a fancy to her.

"That, for instance," he said, holding up a brightly coloured garment. "Now who on earth would ever wear a thing like that?"

"It's a fancy-dress costume, I suppose, sir," said the girl. "A gentleman popped it last night. A very nice, quiet gen-tleman, too. You wouldn't ever have thought that he would have been the sort what would have needed for to have done anything like that, sir."

Mr. Minto parsed this sentence inwardly and inspected the garment more carefully.

"It's a little torn, isn't it?" he asked.

"Is it, sir? So it is. Still, that's easily put right if you've got a piece to match."

Mr. Minto took out his note-case and put his pawn-ticket away beside the piece of Dodo's clown costume.

"And…isn't that a spot of blood on it?"

"So it is, sir. Some of the things what we get popped here are in a terrible state, sir. Messy isn't the name for them, sir. Tomato soup and everything all over them, sir."

Mr. Minto put his note-case away, resisting the temptation of handing the girl the piece of torn material and telling her to mend the garment lying on the counter. It would have done the job very well, for the garment was Dodo's clown costume.

He changed his tactics.

"Who was that gentleman who came down the stairs just now?" he asked.

"Just a friend of mine, sir," said the charming girl, in a softer and more polite voice than ever.

"And what was the parcel he gave you?" asked Mr. Minto. "A present for a beautiful young lady, eh?"

"Listen, you…" said the girl, in quite a different kind of voice. "You keep your nose out of this, Mr. Ruddy Detective! Think you're a smart guy, do you? You get this, son—with feet like yours, you couldn't ever disguise yourself as anything but a 'tec. There's your watch, mister. Now scram!"

Mr. Minto scrammed.

Chapter Twelve

The evening performance of the circus was nearly over before Mr. Minto reached Martin's Field. The audience was bigger than ever; news of the afternoon's tragedy having got round, they rolled up in their thousands—people who would have written strong letters to the newspapers condemning bull-fighting as a cruel sport—in the hope of more blood. They did not get blood; instead, they were themselves bled.

The tiger act did not appear at all, owing to a strange reluctance on the part of everyone in the circus to take the place of Anton and Miller; but Joseph Carey, with an eye always open for business, made a neat little speech towards the close of the performance, regretting that the tigers were not able to appear in the ring, and inviting the audience to view these dangerous man-eating animals in their cage at the conclusion of the show. A small charge would be involved for the privilege of seeing the beasts—sixpence per head, children half-price. The attendants would pass among the members of the audience, and Mr. Carey advised all to purchase tickets in advance, and on no account to miss a sight that only came once in a lifetime.

The audience flocked to gape at the tigers, and Joe Carey found himself nearly fifty pounds richer as a result. It was, he decided, an ill wind that blew nobody any good.

Mr. Minto cornered Lorimer at last, two turns before he went on.

"I've been wanting to see you all day," he said. "I'd like to ask you a few questions."

The trapeze artist smiled.

"I've been expecting you," he said. "Loretta, stay here—in case he arrests me."

"Well, now...where did you go after you left Dodo's party?"

"I went to keep an appointment."

"With whom?" asked Mr. Minto, remembering his prepositions.

"With Anton."

Mr. Minto rubbed his chin.

"And did you keep the appointment?"

"I did."

"What happened?"

"We talked for a quarter of an hour or so. Then I left him, and went across to my own dressing-tent."

"Why?"

"To get a revolver."

"What for?" asked Mr. Minto, forgetting his prepositions this time.

Lorimer lit a cigarette before answering.

"To kill Anton," he said.

Loretta, sitting on a table and staring at her husband, did not move. Mr. Minto scratched his head. He did not like these people who were so commendably frank and who told you everything.

"You realize what you're saying, Lorimer, don't you?" he asked. "I could arrest you for the murder of Anton."

"You could," said Lorimer. "You'd be a damned fool if you did, though. I said I got a revolver to kill Anton. I didn't say that I killed him. I didn't kill him, if you want to know—I was beaten to it."

"Really?" said Mr. Minto. "Very interesting. Come on, now. Wouldn't it be better to tell me the whole story?"

Lorimer looked across at his wife.

"Tell the man, Lorrie," said Loretta. "He'll find it out in any case, so you might as well tell him."

Mr. Minto bowed an acknowledgment of this compliment.

"Right," said Lorimer. "I'll start at the beginning."

"A very sensible place to start," said Mr. Minto.

"Loretta—my wife—and I haven't been hitting it off very well lately. Maybe it's been my fault—I don't know. I'm pretty well wrapped up in the circus and in our act. I don't think of much else. I suppose I've rather neglected her."

"No—it's my fault," said Loretta, "you're not taking the blame for any of it, Lorrie. It's all my fault, and I know it."

"Darling—"

"It doesn't really matter to me whose fault it is," said Mr. Minto. "Suppose you draw lots as to who is to tell the story, and let us get on?"

"Carry on, Lorrie," said Loretta.

"Well, I began to see that Loretta was—seeing too much of other men. Carey in particular. I thought Carey was getting fresh with her, and I went and played hell with him about it. He—"

"You didn't play hell the first time," said Loretta. "That was the second time. The first time you—"

"All right. I'm coming to that later."

"But I thought you said you were starting at the beginning?" said Mr. Minto.

"I am. This happened before the beginning."

"What he means is—"

Mr. Minto took out a small slab of chocolate which he had bought from one of the circus attendants. He was hungry, and this looked like being an all-night session. He never enjoyed these cross-talk acts. They wasted your time and told you nothing.

"I went to see Carey about it and he told me not to be such a damned fool. We had a bit of an argument, and finally he said I was wasting my time worrying about him and Loretta—and that if I looked in another direction I might find plenty to worry about. Well, I looked in the other direction, and I found it. Plenty. Loretta was...well, she was living with Anton."

Mr. Minto munched his chocolate. The girl continued to swing her legs over the edge of the table.

"It's all right now," she said. "I mean, it's all over and done with now."

"Naturally," said Mr. Minto, as drily as possible with his mouth full of chocolate. "Anton's dead. Naturally it's all over and done with."

"Yes—but it wasn't that that put an end to it," said Lorimer. "It was the fact that I was ready to kill him for it. When Loretta knew that, it ended it."

"Not the fact that you did kill him?"

"I've already told you," said Lorimer. "I didn't kill him."

"All right. Carry on."

"I met Anton about midnight—behind the tigers' cage, as I'd arranged. I told him what I'd found out, and he didn't deny it. I lost my temper and we had a hell of a row. I ran away and went off to my dressing-tent. To get a gun. I keep a gun there—"

"Because once when we were with another circus a lion escaped and if it hadn't been for Lorrie's gun—"

"And ever since then I've carried one about with me. I got out the gun and walked back to where I'd left Anton.

He wasn't there. I walked back round the tent where the rest of you were having supper—I looked in—"

"No one saw him—"

"—but Anton wasn't there, either. I went across to Carey's caravan to see if he were there. I didn't go in—I just listened outside the door. He didn't seem to be there. I don't know where I went next—out of the field, I think, and into the town a bit. I meant murder…I didn't know what I was doing. After a while I came back to the field and I saw the crowd of you gathered round the tigers' cage. I kept out of sight—no one saw me, I'm sure. Then I saw them go into the cage and carry Anton's body out…dead. I got the wind up—I don't know why. I was still carrying the gun about with me…I couldn't get it out of my head that I had meant to kill him… and that now he was dead. I began to think that I *must* have killed him. I thought I was going cuckoo. I slipped back to my tent again and put the gun back. Then I went out and walked about the town a bit. Later on—about two in the morning—I came back and found out what actually had happened…that Anton had been shot—not mauled. That settled it. I got panicky. I knew I'd be suspected. Plenty of people in the circus knew what was going on between Loretta and Anton…and a good few of them knew that I'd just found out. I went out and walked the streets until morning. Then I realized what a damned fool I was being and came back to the hotel. That's all."

"So you see—" said Loretta.

"Just a minute. You didn't know Anton had been shot until you came back to the circus ground about two in the morning?"

"That's right."

"You thought he'd been mauled when you saw him being lifted out of the cage?"

"Yes."

"And yet you got the wind up right away…got it into your head that you might have killed him?"

"So I might. I was going to. I tell you that—quite frankly. I would have killed him, if I'd been able to find the man."

"M'm. Why did you make that appointment with Anton? To get this business about your wife and him straight—or was it for some other reason?"

"It was something else."

"What? Tell me."

"Well—the night before—the night we arrived here—Loretta and I had a bit of a row—"

"Nothing serious, you know. Only Lorrie kept on trying to make out that I—"

"All right. One at a time, if you don't mind."

"Loretta and I had a row, and I went out for a walk."

"You seem to have been doing a lot of walking recently, don't you?"

"Yes. It's very good for the muscles."

"It might be very bad for the neck," said Mr. Minto. "Go on."

"I came down to the field here pretty late at night. I was going to see Carey about the way he was playing around with Loretta. I got to the field and was going up to Carey's caravan when two men came across from the other side of the field. I couldn't make out who they were—strangers to me, I think—they weren't circus people. They went straight to the caravan and gave a whistle."

"A whistle?"

"A funny sort of whistle," said Loretta. "Like this…wasn't that how it went, Lorrie?"

"No; more like this…."

Mr. Minto listened for a minute or two to a whistling duet that would have put any pair of mating nightingales to shame.

"All right," he said. "They whistled. Like that. Or like that. And then what happened?"

"The door of the caravan opened an inch or two and the men stood very close up to it. They didn't speak—at any rate, I didn't hear a word. Then the door was closed and the men went away."

"Empty-handed?"

"I don't know. I couldn't see. They couldn't have been given anything bulky, or I would have noticed it."

"And after that?"

"I waited until the men had cleared out, and then went right up to the caravan. Carey wasn't alone inside. There was a bit of an argument going on. After a few minutes the door opened again and someone came down the steps. Pretty quickly down the steps, too. Carey said something about 'minding his own business', and slammed the door. I tried to keep out of sight, but the man saw me. It was Anton. He said, 'Good God—are you another of them?' and walked away."

"Now what d'you think he meant by that?" asked Loretta.

"I haven't the slightest idea. Don't you know, Lorimer?" said Mr. Minto.

"I don't know yet what the man was talking about. I thought of following him to find out, but I changed my mind. I was just going to have another shot at getting in to see Carey when the same thing happened. A man came up to the door of the caravan, whistled, and went away. I could see who it was this time, though. Dodo—the clown."

"And then you went away?"

"I did not. I went up to the caravan myself and whistled."

"Like this," said Loretta, and blew shrilly.

"Not exactly. Like this.…The door opened—Carey stepped out, took a look at me, and planted a Grade 'A' sock on my jaw. I don't think I came round for an hour. It was past four when I got back to the hotel."

"And a pretty noise you made getting into bed."

"Didn't you bring the matter up with Carey, then?" asked Mr. Minto.

"Yes. He says I was never near his blessed caravan. Tries to make out I was tight. There's something very funny going on in that caravan, Mr. Minto."

"It's nothing funny. It's very tragic."

"D'you know what it is?"

"I've a pretty good idea. Is that the end of your story?"

"Yes. Apart from the fact that I tackled Anton about what he'd said to me. I asked him what he'd been getting at when he said, 'Are you another of them?' He said I knew damned well what he meant. After a while he realized that I didn't, and we fixed up this appointment last night. He was going to tell me all about it. Unfortunately I started off on another line—Loretta, I mean—and I never got the truth about Joe Carey's whistling visitors."

Mr. Minto rubbed his chin thoughtfully.

"Anton was going to tell you what happened in Carey's caravan," he said. "And before he could do so, he was killed. It must have been pretty damning, mustn't it?"

"You don't think that Anton's death was mixed up with the Carey business?"

"I'm sure of it."

"But—isn't it as clear as daylight? Didn't Miller do it?"

"No. That's the annoying thing. He didn't."

"Then who did?"

"I haven't the slightest idea," said Mr. Minto. "That's what I'm trying to find out. At the start of this business— which has nothing to do with me, and is just an infernal nuisance—I made out a list of four suspects. The four people who left the supper-party at various times before Anton was discovered in the tigers' cage…and who didn't come back until after the discovery. Miller, Dodo, Carey, and yourself. Miller is dead, and I know he didn't do it. That leaves three. If you're speaking the truth, it leaves two—Dodo and Carey."

"He's speaking the truth all right," said Loretta.

"My dear girl, you're his wife. You're the last person to judge whether he's speaking the truth or not. You must admit, Lorimer, that it looks pretty black against you. You had the best possible motive for killing Anton. You admit that you met him. You even admit that you had a row with him and went to get a revolver to kill him. And after that you've no one to check up your movements. You've no one even to check up your movements on the previous night, since Carey says you were never near his caravan. There's just one thing in your favour."

"And what's that?" asked Lorimer.

"No one but a congenital idiot would have told me as much as you've done about your doings last night," said Mr. Minto. "And congenital idiots rarely commit murder."

"That's a relief, certainly," said Lorimer.

The ring-master popped his head suddenly through the flap of the tent and said that that was Lorimer and Loretta's entrance. The two trapeze artists wrapped dressing-gowns around them and got ready for their act.

"By the way," said Mr. Minto, "when you were looking for Anton last night—after you'd got your revolver—you said you went across to Carey's caravan."

"That's right."

"Was there anyone inside it?"

"I don't think so."

"Were the lights on?"

"No."

"Right. Thanks very much…."

Mr. Minto went back to the big tent and watched Lorimer and Loretta go through their act. He felt himself at a dead end, and wished that he had never agreed to have anything to do with this case. There were far too many loose ends lying about for his liking—far too many unexplained and unconnected happenings. Why was Anton killed, in the first place? Revenge or jealousy? Perhaps…though with Miller out of the running there seemed no one else who would have gone the length of murder with that sort of motive. The eternal triangle?…Yet Mr. Minto believed at least a great deal of what Lorimer had told him. His experience was that the people who have difficulty in proving an alibi, or in checking their movements, are usually innocent; those who have a ready answer for every question, and can prove conclusively that they were miles away and in the company of four other people all ready to swear to the fact…those are more often than not the ones who end up by watching a square of black silk being placed on a judge's head.

For what other reason might Anton have been murdered? To keep his mouth shut: a most excellent reason. Lorimer had said that Anton had paid a visit to Carey's caravan on the night before his death; that the two men had been quarrelling and that Carey's last remark, on showing Anton to the door, had been something on the lines of mouths being kept shut. Anton had intended to pass on whatever he knew to Lorimer, and before he could do so he had been silenced… permanently so. Mr. Minto decided to concentrate on Joseph Carey for the next day or so. He might even make it an excuse for skipping the wedding. The speech was beginning to prey on his mind; he had tried out the joke on his brother, and it had not gone down at all well. And, as yet, he had not heard any to take its place.

There were several other things to be cleared up, however. The whistlers, for example. The charming girl in the pawnshop, and the grumpy folk who lived above it. Were they connected in any way with the circus, apart from taking in lodgers? If they weren't, why did Joe Carey visit them in the early hours of the morning—and why did he use the stairs which, according to Mrs. Winter, had not been used for years? What was Dodo's costume doing lying on the counter of the pawnshop? Was Lorimer telling the truth, after all? Why did the tigers waste so little time in going for Miller, if Miller had nothing to do with the death of Anton? Was Father Robert Minto telling the truth?

"Gosh!" said Mr. Minto, and stood up for the National Anthem.

He let the audience file out, and made his way back to the artists' quarters, where he sought out Dodo.

"Congratulations," said Mr. Minto.

"On what?" asked the clown.

"You've got through a whole performance without a single fatality."

"Oh yes. Quite a record, isn't it? People will be demanding their money back if we go on like this."

"Going back to the hotel now?"

The clown hesitated.

"I'll walk home with you, if you don't mind," said Mr. Minto.

"Delighted. Just wait until I get my make-up off and change. There's *Seven Pillars* to read—I won't be ten minutes."

"If you're only going to be ten minutes, I don't think I'll start the book. I'd hate to get to the last chapter and then have to leave it...."

The clown sat down in front of his mirror and smeared cream over his face. The black of his eyebrows, the red of his nose and lips, and the white of his face became mixed and made him even more grotesque and unreal to look at.

"Why didn't you wear your nice harlequin costume tonight?" Mr. Minto asked the question casually, playing with Dodo's sticks of grease-paint.

"It's being cleaned. All our stuff gets laundered twice a week. We've got our own laundry here—all the modern conveniences in Carey's, you know.'

Mr. Minto smiled and waited in silence until the clown was back once more in his sober suit of dark grey. Then he got up and led the way out of the tent.

"Let's go this way," said Dodo. "It's shorter."

Mr. Minto, after a brief argument with some tent-pegs and ropes, headed south in the direction of the tigers' cage.

"A terrible business that this afternoon," he said. "Poor Miller…not a pleasant way to die."

"I shouldn't choose it," said Dodo.

"Hanging is preferable," said Mr. Minto.

"Infinitely so," said the clown.

They came up to the cage. The tigers, which had been sullen and silent ever since their affray with Miller, jerked up their heads and started to roar. They roared as they had done during the supper-party, when Anton's body lay beside them. Mr. Minto was intrigued. He stopped and watched the animals.

"What happened to Peter?" he yelled through the din.

"They had him put down after the show. He was badly wounded, anyway."

The roaring increased. Mr. Minto took a step forward to the bars of the cage.

"Don't go any nearer," said Dodo, and walked on past the cage.

Mr. Minto followed him, satisfied. He had wanted to find out whether he or Dodo was the cause of the tigers' anger. It would have been most annoying to have discovered that he was the one who was unpopular, or that the tigers roared like this when anyone passed their cage. But the few steps which Dodo had taken away from the cage settled this point quite conclusively. The tigers, ignoring Mr. Minto, followed the clown as far as they could to the corner of the cage, still roaring their loudest. Two great paws reached out through the bars in a vain effort to touch the little man. The tigers did not like Dodo.

Mr. Minto overtook the clown and the two men walked on for a while in silence. At last Mr. Minto took the plunge.

"Why did you pawn your harlequin costume?" he asked.

"I beg your pardon?"

"Why did you pawn the costume you were wearing last night?"

"I'm afraid you're mistaken. I've never been inside a pawnshop in my life."

"That's rum, because your costume is lying on the counter of a pawnshop at 288, Bank Street at this moment. Unless someone's taken a fancy to it, that is. It's got a piece torn out of it…and some dried blood on it."

"Just what are you getting at, Mr. Minto?"

"The murderer of Anton. And I think you can help me…."

"I wish I could. I don't know what you're talking about."

"Why did you tell me that costume was being cleaned—when you knew very well it wasn't?"

"Oh—*that* costume. My dear man, I have over twenty costumes. I didn't know you were talking about that one. That one may quite well be in a pawnshop for all I know. I gave it away after last night."

"To whom?"

"To one of the other clowns. They don't get very good pay, and I thought he might be able to use it. I had no further use for it."

"I can imagine that. It had some pretty damning evidence on it."

"It had a piece torn out of it, if that's what you mean."

"That's what I mean. I found the piece. Lying beside the tigers' cage—just after we'd found Anton."

"It's very likely. Are you suspecting me of murdering Anton?"

"At the moment—yes."

"Then you mustn't waste any more time doing so, Mr. Minto. I'll tell you exactly what happened. After I left Carey's caravan, I made my way back to the tent where we had the supper. I had to pass the tigers' cage on the way. I saw Anton, lying in the cage—apparently dead. I tried to pull him towards the door of the cage. Peter—the big tiger—sprang at me. I just got my arm free in time. As it was, I got a scratch across the face—the scratch you noticed last night. It was as near as I ever wish to be to a tiger. He made another jab at me through the bars—standing over Anton's body—and tore the costume I was wearing. His claws went right through the silk and opened up another scratch across my hip. If you like, I'll show it to you. After that I dashed back and told the rest of you what had happened. The costume was no use to me any more…I gave it to this man this morning. It's quite possible that he pawned it as soon as he got it. In fact, knowing the man, I should have been surprised if he hadn't pawned it. Does that satisfy you, Mr. Minto?"

Mr. Minto agreed, grudgingly, that it satisfied him.

"Which clown was it that you gave the costume to?"

"Ginger. The one who rides the comic bicycle."

Mr. Minto lit a pipe in an attempt to soothe his feelings. It was really very trying. Everybody had such excellent explanations for everything.

Chapter Thirteen

Whenever Mr. Minto found himself up a *cul-de-sac*, he resorted to pen and paper. It was, he found, a great help to put the facts of the case down in black and white in the form of a *questionnaire* and go away to a quiet corner to brood over it. Things which in real life seemed a mere muddle very often cleared themselves up quite a lot with the aid of a fountain-pen.

Mr. Minto, therefore, after getting back to the hotel and saying good night to Dodo, went into the lounge and helped himself to a large quantity of the hotel's note-paper. Then he went up to his room, pausing only to order a "John Collins" at the bar (for the night was even warmer than at the beginning of the week), and settled down to put his observations on paper.

"Death of Anton," Mr. Minto wrote, and underlined it neatly three times. He then took a lengthy sip of his "John Collins", said, "Ah…!" and got down to business. Thus:

Q. Who killed Anton?

A. That's what we're trying to find out, and up to now we don't seem to be doing any too well.

Q. Taking the evidence collected so far, everything would appear to point to the fact that Miller had killed Anton. He had an excellent motive; he had the opportunity for doing the deed after leaving the supper-party; he left the note confessing to the crime; and the tigers themselves wasted no time in recognizing him as a person with whom they wished to settle an account. Against all this evidence there is only the fact that Robert (who is a confounded nuisance) says that he is not the man who confessed to the crime. Which are we to believe—the evidence or Robert?

A. Robert. It was all against the principles of his religion to pass on a matter which was sacred to him. It isn't likely that he would have done so unless it had been a question of saving an innocent man's life. (*Mem:* Good thing that Robert intervened before Miller himself died; otherwise the priest might have thought it wise to keep silent.)

Q. If Miller did not kill Anton, why did he leave a confession behind saying that he did?

A. He didn't, you fool! That confession was planted in Miller's jacket by someone who wished to throw the guilt on to Miller.

Q. Who, then?

A. Now you're asking!

Q. What about Lorimer? Is it likely that a sensible young man like Lorimer would invite suspicion by behaving as he did on the night of the crime—i.e. by spending the whole night walking the streets?

A. No. But you never know.

Q. What have we against Lorimer?

A. He had an equally strong motive for killing Anton—the affair, rumoured or true, that his wife was enjoying with the animal trainer. There is no one to check his movements after he left the supper-party. He says he came back to the field and saw the rest of us standing round the tigers' cage—yet no one appears to have seen him. He admits that he owns a revolver, that he keeps it in his own tent (against the rules of the circus), and that he had it out on the night of the tragedy. In addition to which, through spending the night walking the streets, he was not able to put his shoes outside his bedroom door and get them cleaned—and his shoes are fairly thickly coated with what looks like the same species of mud as is found along the banks of the stream.

Q. And what in favour of Lorimer?

A. The fact that no one but a nit-wit would pass on such a lot of damning evidence and information to a detective. And Lorimer, whatever one may think of the things he does on his trapeze, is no nit-wit.

Q. Pass on to Dodo, then. If Dodo killed Anton—which is possible considering that he left the supper-party some time before the thing was discovered—is it likely that he would dispose of such a vital piece of evidence as the torn costume in so open a manner as he did?

A. No. Which seems to point to the fact that the costume isn't a vital piece of evidence at all, and that Dodo's story about trying to get Anton's body out of the cage is true.

Q. Does that clear Dodo, then?

A. Not on your life!

Q. Is there any evidence at all to suggest that Carey committed the murder?

A. None whatever. On the contrary, it seems most unlikely that he would put out of circulation the biggest money-maker in his circus.

Q. Does that mean that he did it?

A. Judging from the standards of the average mystery novel, yes. Going by ordinary standards of detection, no.

Q. If Carey was on the point of selling his interest in the circus to Anton (as seems likely from the document found in Anton's room), would this be a possible motive for someone making sure that the deal did not go through by murdering Anton before it was completed?

A. Yes. But for heaven's sake don't ask who would be likely to want the deal stopped.

Q. What is the connection, if any, between the circus and the pawnshop, or the house above the pawnshop?

A. Ask us another.

Q. Why do people come to Carey's caravan at all hours of the night and morning and whistle in a peculiar manner?

A. See answer to previous question.

Q. Why should I bother with this confounded case,
   when it is really none of my business?

A. Because you're a damned fool!

Mr. Minto, having drunk his drink and studied this
catechism, realized that the idea of putting down the facts
on paper had not worked quite so well this time. There
were still an annoyingly large number of things which
were as muddled as ever. The confession was one of them;
the costume in the pawnshop another. The confession had
been found in the jacket of the suit which Miller wore at
the supper-party—not in the clothes he had worn before
entering the ring to meet the tigers for the last time. That
seemed to indicate that the confession had been planted by
someone else, and that whoever had done the planting had
made a mistake. If Miller had written that note himself,
confessing to the crime before he went into the ring, and
in case anything happened to him in the ring, it was much
more likely that he would have placed it in the suit he had
been wearing at the time.

The clown's costume…it was possible to get that cleared
up right away. Mr. Minto looked at his watch and found
that it was ten past twelve. According to the rules, things
ought to be just beginning to happen down at Martin's Field.
Probably at this minute a choir of whistlers were advancing,
like the Dawn Chorus, on Joe Carey's caravan. He put on
his hat and went down to the field.

One or two of the circus people were still wandering
about. He asked an attendant if the clown known as "Ginger"
slept on the field or in lodgings in the town.

"On the ground, sir. That caravan over there." Mr. Minto
went to interview Ginger, and found him aggressively drunk.

"Did Dodo give you one of his clown costumes yesterday?"

"What do I care?" said Ginger. "Come in and sit down and have a drink."

"Did he?"

"Did he what?"

"Did he give you one of his costumes—a red-and-yellow checked costume?"

"Who said it was red and yellow, eh? It was red and black. With blue spots. And knobs on."

Mr. Minto took a breath and began again, pausing between each word to let it sink in.

"Did—he—give—you—a—costume?"

"What's it got to do with you?"

"Never mind what it's got to do with me. *Did he?*"

"I don't know what you're talking about. Did he what?"

Mr. Minto sighed deeply and started all over again.

"The trouble with you," said Ginger, "is that you've had a drop too much. That's the trouble with you, my lad."

Mr. Minto, for the sake of peace, admitted that he'd been drinking steadily since the pubs opened that afternoon.

"Who are you, anyway? Coming in here and asking stupid questions about Dodo's costumes at this time of night. You take more water with it next time, that's my advice. What have I got to do with Dodo's costumes, eh? None of my business. No concern of mine. Why don't you go and see Dodo himself, eh? He'll tell you. Nothing to do with me. Don't know what you're talking about. Have a drink."

"Listen—did Dodo give you—"

"Yes."

"Well, why couldn't you say that at first?"

"Why didn't you ask me at first?"

Mr. Minto groaned.

"What did you do with it?"

"What did I do with it?"

"That's what I said."

"What did you say?"

Mr. Minto ran his fingers feverishly through his hair.

"What did you do with the costume?"

"What costume?"

"*Dodo's costume.*"

"What would I be doing with Dodo's costume, eh? I've got costumes of my own. Dodo's got costumes of his own. I don't wear Dodo's costumes. He doesn't wear mine. Who are you, anyway? Never mind—I don't care who you are. Have a drink...."

Mr. Minto slackened the knot of his tie and felt round the inside of his collar. He appeared to be in danger of having some sort of seizure.

"Listen..." he said. "You've just told me that Dodo gave you one of his costumes yesterday. What did you do with it? And if you say 'With what?' I'll crown you...."

"I pawned it," said Ginger.

"Where?"

"In a pawnshop. Where d'you think—in a fish-and-chip restaurant? You're tight, you know, old man. Tight as a garter."

Mr. Minto had not heard the expression before.

"Was it the pawnshop in Bank Street—at No. 288?"

"If you know, why are you asking?"

"Was it?"

"Was it what?"

Mr. Minto gave a hollow little groan.

"Was it the pawnshop at 288, Bank Street?"

"Yes. 'Course it was. I told you that hours ago."

"Thanks very much," said Mr. Minto. "Good night."

"What d'you mean—good night?"

Mr. Minto left the caravan hurriedly. A cross-talk act like that might make quite a lot of money on the music-hall stage, but it seemed to him quite out of place in a circus. He had, at any rate, put one of the loose ends in its place. Dodo had been telling the truth when he said that he had given away his torn costume. The pawnshop, perhaps, was a perfectly innocent pawnshop. Perhaps…

Mr. Minto walked over to the other side of the field, where Joe Carey's green-and-white caravan stood in what Lord Beaverbrook would call splendid isolation. The lights were on inside the caravan; there were no signs of whistling visitors. Mr. Minto knocked on the door and stepped in. Joe Carey shut a drawer quickly and turned round to beam on his visitor.

"'Ullo, Minto," he said. "Come right in. Glad to see you. 'Ow's things, eh? Found the murderer yet?"

"No, not yet."

"Why are you so damn' sure it wasn't Miller, eh? Didn't 'e leave a note be'ind saying that 'e did it?"

"How did you know that?"

"Dodo told me."

Mr. Minto stroked his chin.

"That's quite right," he said. "He left a note behind, saying that he had killed Anton."

"Well—what more d'you want than that?"

"Plenty, Mr. Carey. For one thing, a person only leaves a note like that lying around when he's going to commit suicide. And Miller didn't intend to do that—unless he knew that it was suicide to go in beside those tigers. That's not the point, though. I know Miller didn't do it. The murderer of Anton is a Catholic."

"Well—Miller was a Catholic, wasn't he?"

"He was. But he wasn't the man who went to the Catholic Church in this town yesterday morning and confessed to the priest there that he'd murdered Anton."

Joe Carey sat down heavily.

"How d'you know that?"

"Never mind. I know—that's the main thing."

"You know…who did confess?"

"No. I only know that someone confessed, and that that someone was naturally a Catholic. You're a Catholic yourself, aren't you, Carey?"

Mr. Carey moistened his lips and appeared to have some difficulty in answering.

"Yes—I'm a Catholic. So's half the circus. What are you trying to get at, Minto?"

"I'm trying to get at the man who killed Anton. I'm getting a little tired of this case, and unless I get it finished tomorrow, I'm chucking the whole thing up. I've got a wedding to attend at the end of this week, and I never allow business to interfere with pleasure. If you can call a wedding pleasure, that is. I've never chucked up a case yet, though… in other words, I'm going to have this one settled up tomorrow. Tonight, maybe."

"I…I hope you do," said Carey. "'Ave a drink?"

"This is a most hospitable circus. That's the second drink I've been offered in the last ten minutes. No, thank you—none for me."

Mr. Carey poured himself out his usual outsize whisky.

"Carey…why did Anton come to see you the night before he died?"

"Did 'e?"

"He did. He was here—in the caravan—round about midnight. You were quarrelling. Your last remark when you showed him out—or threw him out—was 'keep your nose out of my affairs'. Or something like that. Just what are your affairs, Carey?"

"Running a circus. Would you like to try it?"

"Not this one. You're not thinking of giving up the circus, are you?"

"Why the 'ell should I? I make a pretty good thing out of it."

"I had an idea you might be selling out—to Anton."

Joe Carey produced a gold tooth-pick and did a little excavation before replying.

"You've been busy, 'aven't you?" he said.

"Fairly busy—yes."

"'Ow did you know I was thinking of selling to Anton, eh?"

"I found the agreement you'd drawn up—signed by you, and not by Anton."

"You did, did you? Yes…I was going to sell out. I'm not so young as I used to be—this moving about from one place to another doesn't suit me. Anton's always been crazy to 'ave a circus of 'is own. 'E's saved for years to buy one. We'd 'ad a talk or two about it, and drawn up the preliminary agreement. It was all fixed up—just needed 'is signature. And now it's all off."

"Very unfortunate."

"Very. There aren't many that would give the price Anton was giving for it."

"You haven't any other interests—outside the circus, I mean?"

"Yes. I own some pawnshops. Quite a few, in fact. It's a grand paying line. I've one in this town—288, Bank Street. You seem to 'ave got a bit suspicious of it, Minto. Been paying it visits, 'aven't you? You're just wasting your time, I'm afraid. It's as respectable a business as a pawnshop can be."

"I see. What had Anton been doing that he was told to keep his nose out of your affairs?"

"Talking. A dangerous 'abit, Mr. Minto."

"What had he been talking about?"

"If I wasn't a perfect gent—and if you weren't a detective—I'd give you the same advice as I gave to Anton. To mind your own business. You being a detective and me being a perfect gent, I'll tell you. 'E'd been talking about me and Loretta. There was a lot of silly gossip going round, and Anton 'ad 'eard things. 'E was sweet on the girl 'imself, and 'e got it into 'is 'ead that I felt the same way about 'er."

"That was what you were quarrelling about?"

"That's right."

"Lorimer seemed to think it was something more important," said Mr. Minto.

"Lorimer? What the 'ell 'as Lorimer got to do with it?"

"He overheard you having your quarrel. He met Anton after he left your caravan. Anton was going to tell him something very important—and before he could do so he was killed."

"What d'you mean by that?"

"Anton knew too much about someone—or something. Before he could pass on his knowledge he was murdered. Now who was it that Anton knew too much about?"

"'Ow should I know?"

"I just thought you might. You were the last person to have an argument with him."

"It'd just be this business about Loretta—just a lot of gossip. Don't you worry your head about that, Minto."

"All right," said Mr. Minto, "I won't. Well…time I was getting a little sleep. Good night, Carey."

"Good night."

Mr. Minto left the caravan and walked smartly across the field to the gate leading out to the town. Once again he was conscious of the fact that Joe Carey was watching him leave. He shut the gate carefully behind him, walked fifty yards or so up the street, lit a cigarette, turned and made his way back to the field. The curtains in the green-and-white caravan were drawn. Mr. Minto, scorning the idea of catching a chill, sat down on the damp grass to await developments. It would be most annoying if no developments developed, of course, but that did not seem likely in a circus such as Carey's.

After half an hour, when Mr. Minto was beginning to feel definitely moist in the seat of his trousers, a development duly arrived in the shape of a man making his way towards Carey's caravan from the opposite side of the field. Although it was moonlight, Mr. Minto was too far away to make out the arrival clearly, but he had a strange feeling that he knew him quite well.

He watched him go up the steps of the caravan, heard him give the short, peculiar whistle, and saw the door open an inch or two. The man stood motionless on the top step; the door shut and the visitor left without a word having been spoken. Mr. Minto then got rather worried, for the visitor, instead of leaving the field by the way he had entered it, carried straight on and seemed likely to pass within a few yards of where Mr. Minto was sitting. Mr. Minto had no desire to be found sitting in the middle of a damp field at two in the morning: it would have been so very difficult to explain the reasons for such behaviour. He hopped behind a convenient pile of timber props and lay low. The man passed uncomfortably close to him. Mr. Minto was able to get an excellent view of him, and in doing so he got by far the biggest shock of the week. He had been perfectly correct: he knew Joe Carey's latest visitor very well indeed.

Mr. Minto allowed the man to get out of the field, recovered his breath, nipped his damp seat to make sure that he wasn't dreaming, and went off at the double to visit his brother Robert.

The priest was not in the habit of receiving visitors at two in the morning, and it took Mr. Minto some little time to get an answer to his knocks and ringings. Claire eventually opened the door, clad in a negligée which made her look rather like the Principal Girl of a pantomime.

"Good lord!" said Claire. "What's the matter with you? Sleep-walking?"

"I've got to see Robert," said Mr. Minto.

"He's in bed, and snoring. What's happened? Sensational developments?"

"Sensational isn't the word for it," said Mr. Minto, and took the stairs two at a time. "You go back to bed, Claire. I'll let myself out."

"Can't I hear what's happened?"

"Sorry. This isn't for little girls."

"Pig!" said Claire, and went off to her own room.

Mr. Minto sat down heavily on the edge of his brother's bed and spent a busy five minutes rousing the priest and getting him into a fit state to answer questions. Once he was in that state, Mr. Minto wasted no time in asking the questions.

"Robert…what do you know about this fellow Claire's going to marry?"

"Very little. He seems an upright young man."

"What's his job?"

"Some kind of canvassing, I believe. Vacuum-cleaners."

"Do vacuum-cleaner canvassers earn a lot of money, Robert?"

"I've no idea."

"Young Mr. Briggs seems to be well supplied with the world's necessities, doesn't he?"

"He's in a position to keep Claire, if that's what you mean. I made a point of asking him as soon as he—"

"I'm not worrying about that—just now. Is he a Catholic?"

"Yes, he is."

"Does he do this vacuum-cleaner job all over the place—or just in this district?"

"I understand he covers a considerable area. He's doing this district this week, and of course they intend to make their home here. But he seems to go all over the country. He was in Leicester last week."

"Leicester....You don't know where he was the week before that, do you?"

"I couldn't say really. If you ask Claire she'll tell you."

"No—I don't want her in on this just now. You don't know any of the other places he's been to recently?"

"No. Well—I know Claire mentioned that he was in Scotland at the beginning of the month—a week in Edinburgh and then a week in Glasgow. Then he came down south... to Hereford, I believe, before Leicester. Why on earth do you want to know this?"

"He's not the man who confessed to killing Anton, is he?"

The priest sat up in bed and stared at Mr. Minto. He did not answer.

"Well...is he?"

"You must not ask me anything more about that," said Robert. "I've had it on my conscience ever since I told you....I only told you because it seemed likely that an innocent man was going to be punished. I could tell you who confessed that day, but you know that I must not. And you must not ask me, or try to get me to tell you...."

"That's all right, Robert. I wouldn't think of doing such a thing. It—it wasn't young Briggs, then?"

"Good gracious, no! You're not suggesting that Claire's fiancé is involved in this circus business, are you?"

"Yes," said Mr. Minto, "I am."

The priest shot two skinny legs over the edge of his bed and showed his brother politely but firmly out.

"I am afraid you have been drinking," he said. "In the morning, when you are more yourself, I will have a word with you. Just now I think you had better go to bed."

Mr. Minto went to bed. But not before adding a further question and answer to his questionnaire:

Q. Why is young Briggs on Joe Carey's visiting-list and what the devil has he to do with this business?

A. Search me!

Chapter Fourteen

Mr. Minto took up work on the case again at five minutes to eight on the following morning, when he paid a visit to Lorimer and Loretta, who were still in their beds.

"Lord, it's the sleuth!" said Lorimer.

"He's come to arrest you," said Loretta, sitting up in bed to see who it was and immediately lying down again and closing her eyes.

"Good morning," said Mr. Minto. "May I come in?"

"You're in, aren't you?" said Lorimer.

"Yes, so I am. Lorimer, would you like to do something to help me?"

"He doesn't get his salary until Friday," said Loretta, still with her eyes shut.

"And even then I don't get it," said Lorimer. "She does. So I'm afraid it's no use...."

"I didn't mean money. It's this Anton business. I want to use you as bait."

"Bait?"

"Bait. I think I've narrowed it down to two people—possibly to one person. If you're willing to help me, I might be able to say definitely who the one person is."

"Carry on. Bait me."

"I want to tell Joe Carey that you've found out something about this case, and that you're going to pass it on to me."

"That's all right. Have I found out something?"

"No. That's the bait. You're sure you don't object?"

"Why should I?"

Mr. Minto sat down on the edge of the bed. He felt it only fair to make the position perfectly clear. Lorimer, after all, was but half awake.

"Well...Anton found out something. Anton was going to pass it on to you. Before he could do so he was stopped. Murdered...."

Lorimer sat up in bed. He seemed quite wide awake now. "You mean...?"

"Yes. I want you to take Anton's place. I want you to allow me to tell Carey that you've got hold of something and that you're going to spill the beans to me—say between the matinée and evening shows today. If Carey is the man who murdered Anton, he'll do the same to you as he did to him. Shut you up, I mean."

Loretta sat up in bed.

"Hoi!" she said. "Bump him off, do you mean?"

"Probably," said Mr. Minto. "It'll be a great help to me. I'll be most obliged to you, Lorimer. It'll prove definitely that Carey is our man."

Lorimer made an attempt at sarcasm.

"Of course," he said, "anything to assist a policeman in the execution of his duty. What's a little thing like an extra corpse if it helps you to solve the mystery? Only too happy to oblige, Mr. Minto. You'll probably get promotion—over my dead body!"

"And think of the insurance," said Loretta.

"Shut up!" said Lorimer, and disappeared below the sheets.

"Listen," said Mr. Minto. "You can look after yourself all right. All you've got to do is to keep your eyes skinned and be careful. There may not be any actual violence… Carey might try and keep your mouth shut with £ s. d. for all I know. It doesn't matter. To me, at any rate. As long as I know he's trying to shut you up, that's enough for me. I'll stick around—I'll be there if there's any trouble. And here… you can take this with you."

"This" was tossed lightly on to the counterpane of Lorimer's bed. It was an efficient-looking revolver.

"Use it if anything happens," said Mr. Minto. "You'll know how to. It's your own."

"Mine?"

"Yes. I pinched it from your dressing-tent. I went to make sure you'd put it back."

"Does this mean that I'm no longer a suspect?"

Mr. Minto looked shocked.

"Good gracious, no!" he said. "Of course you're a suspect. In fact, I'm almost sure you did it. Well, what about it? Will you let me tell Carey that you've found out something and that you're going to pass it on to me?"

"No damned fear!"

"What a pity," said Mr. Minto, getting up off the bed. "Because I've already told him.…"

"What?"

"So be careful today, won't you? If Carey *has* a dirty secret, it's a hundred to one he'll try and keep your mouth shut in one way or another. I don't know how he'll do it, but he will. And if anything serious happens to you," said Mr. Minto cheerfully, "I'll assume full responsibility."

"Will you take Lorimer's place in the act?" asked Loretta.

"Certainly," said Mr. Minto.

"Look here—" said Lorimer.

"Good morning," said Mr. Minto. "And the very best of luck."

Mr. Minto's next move was breakfast, and again he found himself the sole occupant of the dining-hall. As he had done each morning since his arrival in the hotel, he removed the floral decorations, folded his newspaper, had a brief sparring-match with the aged waiter over the respective claims of lean and streaky bacon, and began to squirt grape-fruit juice over the wallpaper. Dodo came in when he was half-way through his meal, and sat down at his table.

"The very man I wanted to see," said Mr. Minto. "Dodo, you were a great friend of Anton's, weren't you?"

"A very great friend," said the clown. "He was an interesting man. Cultured—very cultured. You don't meet many like him in the circus."

"What happened to his belongings?"

"Eh?"

"His belongings. His goods and chattels. His clothes and papers and personal effects and all that. What was done with them, after he died?"

"I—as a matter of fact, I took charge of them. As far as we know he had no relatives in this country. I've cabled his sister in Germany, telling her what happened. I merely said that poor Anton had been attacked and killed by the tigers. I thought it better not to worry her with the other business."

"Much better. And less expensive—on a cable."

"Quite. He was a fine fellow—Anton. There'll never be another animal-trainer like him in Carey's."

"I'd like to see his belongings," said Mr. Minto.

"Certainly. I should have told you right away that I had taken charge of them. I didn't really think that—"

"That's all right. As long as you didn't send them to the pawnshop."

The clown gave Mr. Minto a sad little smile.

"I'll take you up to my room and show you them after breakfast," he said.

"Doesn't matter," said Mr. Minto. "Any time today will do. I'm going back to London tonight."

"I thought you were staying for a wedding on Saturday?"

"No. It's off."

"Off?"

"Yes. The marriage will not take place."

"That's very distressing. Is your sister very upset?"

"She doesn't know yet," said Mr. Minto, and got up and folded his serviette. "By the way, I must have your autograph before I go away—to add to my collection. D'you mind?"

"Not at all. I'll give it you now, if you like."

"The back of the menu will do. Have you a pen?"

"No—it's up in my room."

"Never mind," said Mr. Minto. "Pencil will do. Here you are."

The clown wrote his signature and an appropriate message on the back of the menu and handed it to Mr. Minto.

"Thank you. 'In memory of an exciting week'…very apt."

"Have you a good collection?" asked Dodo.

"Almost every murderer except Crippen," said Mr. Minto, and went out of the dining-hall leaving Dodo a little worried by the remark.

Mr. Minto went straight to the reception-clerk's desk in the hotel *foyer*.

"218 please," he said.

The clerk brought the key out of its pigeon-hole and then gave Mr. Minto a suspicious look. His predecessor had lost his job handing over the key of a rich American's suite to a professional burglar.

"I think you've made a mistake, sir. Your room number is 224, isn't it?"

"I know. I want 218, though. It's all right—I'm just getting some things out of a friend's room."

"I'm very sorry, sir. We're not allowed to give up keys to anyone else but the—"

"Manager," said Mr. Minto crisply. "Where's the manager?"

The manager was produced, wiping egg from the outskirts of his neat little moustache. Mr. Minto explained that he was trying to get the key of room number 218; that he was merely going into the room to get something for a friend; that he had the friend's permission to go into the room as often as he wished; that the suspicious attitude taken up by certain members of the hotel staff was one which he did not like at all; and that if he never came back to this rotten hotel it would still be considerably too soon. The manager, sympathetic up till this last remark, changed his tune and muttered something to the effect that you couldn't be too careful and that they had had a lot of suspicious-looking characters hanging about the place recently.

Mr. Minto then lifted the veil. "I'm from Scotland Yard," he said. "Detective-Inspector Minto of the C.I.D. I can't force you to let me into that room, but I'll get a search-warrant and burst the door open if you stand there clucking like an old hen."

The manager stopped clucking at once and rammed the key into Mr. Minto's hand. Mr. Minto bounded into the nearest lift, leaving the manager and reception-staff to discuss excitedly the possibilities of the quiet little man in 218 being a bigamist, co-respondent, or cat-burglar. Murder did not enter into their heads at that moment, though it had entered into Mr. Minto's.

He opened the door of 218 and locked it again behind him. It was going to be difficult to know which were Anton's things and which were Dodo's. A general investigation seemed to be indicated.

Dodo had been starting on the fish stage when he had left him in the dining-hall; he would have ten minutes at least for the investigation. Mr. Minto got to work. The wardrobe was filled with an overcoat, a waterproof, and a number of suits of a small size—all Dodo's own belongings. Three suit-cases were stacked in a corner of the room—two open and the third locked. Mr. Minto tried every key on his own bunch without success. He hunted through the drawers of the dressing-table and found a smaller bunch of keys. The first three were too small to turn the lock; the fourth and fifth too large even to go in the keyhole; the sixth opened the case. Mr. Minto flung the lid back. Anton's goods and chattels all right.

Two suits, a pocket-book, and a bundle of letters. Mr. Minto felt through the pockets of the suits and took a quick glance through the letters. They were written in German, and consequently were Double-Dutch to him. He was just going to close the suit-case when he noticed a fountain-pen stuck into the waistcoat pocket of one of the suits. Mr. Minto took the pen out and unscrewed the top. The hotel management provided note-paper and envelopes to each bedroom; Mr. Minto removed a sheet of note-paper from the holder and wrote a single sentence on it with the fountain-pen: "Now is the time," wrote Mr. Minto, "for all good men to come to the aid of the party."

Mr. Minto appeared to be satisfied with this. He looked at his watch, locked the suit-case, and fled. The lift, as usual, had just passed his floor on its journey down. Mr. Minto took the stairs two at a time and passed Dodo coming up.

"Off to make an arrest, Mr. Minto?" asked the clown.

"I have the handcuffs polished," said Mr. Minto.

It was the last remark he was heard to make for some considerable time. For Detective-Inspector Minto of the

C.I.D. disappeared from the scene of the crime shortly after passing Dodo on the stairs.

Of all concerned, Lorimer felt Mr. Minto's disappearance most keenly. When Mr. Minto bounded into his bedroom early that morning, Lorimer had been in that pleasant state of semi-coma which comes to all right-minded persons on realizing that it is high time they were out of bed but refusing to do anything about it. Mr. Minto's words came to Lorimer as through a mist darkly. He had gathered that Mr. Minto wished him to assist in something or other, but it had been far too early in the morning to take the thing in properly.

An hour or so later, while patting talcum powder on to his chin, the true import of Mr. Minto's conversation dawned on Lorimer. "Bait" was the word that Mr. Minto had used, and it was to that word that Lorimer took objection. The more he thought about it, the less he liked it. Anton had not died a nice death, either one way or the other. Anton had been on the point of passing on information, and—according to this fellow Minto—he had been silenced. Lorimer, it seemed, was now due for a spot of silencing himself. He had no desire to go the same way as Anton so early in life. There were many things Lorimer wanted to do before he died—appearing in New York and owning a villa on the Mediterranean were two of the most pleasant—and he was dashed if he could see why the idea of a detective using him as bait should upset these plans. No; Lorimer was having none of the bait business. He dressed quickly and went off to tell Mr. Minto that he would have to find another minnow.

Mr. Minto had vanished. He had had breakfast with Dodo, but had left before the clown had finished. Dodo had seen him running downstairs, probably leaving the hotel. The manager and reception-clerk could give no information of Mr. Minto's movements, and at the same time managed rather cleverly to convey the impression that they knew a great deal more than they cared to tell, but that their lips had been hermetically sealed by Scotland Yard.

As the morning wore on and Mr. Minto failed to materialize, Lorimer grew hotter and hotter. He had left the revolver in his bedroom (where it had given a chambermaid what she described as a "proper turn"), but now he planted it in his right-hand jacket pocket and kept his right hand in the pocket beside it. If he couldn't get out of being used as bait, he would at least be ready for action. When Joe Carey walked suddenly into the hotel *foyer* on a friendly visit to Dodo, Lorimer leapt in the air like a shot rabbit and locked himself in the nearest cloak-room. They were after him. To keep his mouth shut. In the same way that Anton's mouth had been kept shut. Lorimer took out the revolver and looked it over carefully. The inspection did not do much to cheer him. Mr. Minto had removed all ammunition from the gun.

At one o'clock Lorimer went down to the field to prepare for the afternoon performance. He still carried the revolver, and he was rather worried at the thought that he would not be able to take it with him into the ring when he went on to do his act. A pair of white, skin-tight trunks have little or no facilities for the concealment of odd revolvers. The costumes which Lorimer and Loretta wore in their act did not even allow them to carry loose change about with them. He undressed and stepped into his trunks, slipped a dressing-gown on and went out to watch the rest of the show from the wings. A new trainer had been recruited from a Paris circus to take over Anton's act; he had flown across that morning, and was going on without a rehearsal. He was supposed to be good, if not in Anton's class; the important thing was that the tigers seemed to have taken to him. Lorimer wanted to see how the act went; he stood in the wings and peered through the plush curtains.

On the other side of the curtain stood Mr. Joseph Carey, resplendent in slightly soiled evening-dress. Mr. Carey would don a new boiled shirt for this evening's show; for a matinée performance with attendances down owing to the bad business of Miller, the slightly soiled shirt would do the turn. He was talking in a low voice to someone standing beside him. Lorimer could not see who his companion was; he was afraid to move the curtain in case of being seen. He heard Carey's conversation, or as much of it as he wanted to hear. The other man did not speak.

"He's on to something," Carey was saying. "He knows Miller didn't do it. He's narrowed it down to three—Lorimer, you, me. God knows how he did it, but he has. I've left a note at his hotel asking him to come and see me tonight. We can keep him quiet for a week or so. After that Carey's circus will probably be up for sale. I shan't be sorry. It's a damned expensive way of running things, anyway."

Lorimer walked back from the plush curtains and thought this out. Carey was talking of Mr. Minto, that was evident. Mr. Minto, it seemed, was in danger of being used as a spot of bait himself. He ran back to his tent and scribbled a note:

Come and see me before going to Carey.—Lorimer.

He walked out and looked round for someone who could spare the time to deliver the message. One of the boys who sold cigarettes and chocolates was wandering aimlessly round the tigers' cage. The circus patrons did not buy a great deal of cigarettes and practically no chocolates, and the boy had evidently given up all idea of making a sale until the interval came along. Lorimer whistled him across and gave him the note.

"Do you know where the Station Hotel is?"

"Sure."

"Take that note along. Right away. I'll give you half a dollar when you get back."

"What about His Nibs?"

"I'll look after His Nibs for you," said Lorimer.

The boy disentangled himself from his tray and went to park it in a caravan. Lorimer ran back to the wings; it was getting near the cue for his act. He watched Miss St. Clair putting her Educated Ponies through their paces, and Loretta came up and joined him.

"How's the bait?" asked Loretta.

"Shut up!" said Lorimer. "Don't tempt Providence."

The plush curtains parted and Dodo pushed his way through them and past Lorimer and Loretta. He seemed in a considerable hurry. He ran round the back of the tent and disappeared up the other alleyway—the entrance used by the animals.

"What's the matter with him?" asked Loretta.

"He's gagging before our act. The whole show's upside-down with this new fellow in. Come on—that's our cue."

The spotlights swivelled round to shine on Loretta and Lorimer as they entered the ring. There was a round of polite applause from an audience who felt slightly cheated by the fact that the show was more than half over and not a single performer had yet been mauled. The long rope-ladder was let down and Lorimer and Loretta shot up to the roof of the big tent. They landed on their little platform and took a further round of applause. The band changed its tune.

"I've heard something," said Lorimer. "That fellow Minto's right. There is something dirty going on. I heard Carey planning to keep Minto quiet—he's got the wind up."

"Why—did he kill Anton, do you think?"

"Don't know. Shouldn't be surprised. Carry on...."

Lorimer, hanging on to the trapeze, shoved himself off the platform with a kick of his heels and swung out over the ring. He gathered speed and swung backwards and forwards, and then let go of the trapeze and shot head downwards through the air to the lower trapeze. He shot out again over the heads of the cheap seats, and then back into the middle of the ring. He leapt again and reached out for the first trapeze, sent out to meet him by Loretta.

Loretta, watching his face as it came up through the air towards her, gave a little gasp. She knew that Lorimer was not going to catch the first trapeze as he usually caught it. He very nearly failed to catch it at all; only a last throw of the body shot him towards it.... He clung desperately to the rung by his fingers and hoisted himself on to the platform. The trapeze swung back loosely into the air. The band crashed out a chord; the house applauded wildly.

"You were late in throwing that out," said Lorimer.

"I wasn't. There's something the matter with it—it's not the usual length."

"Rubbish! You were late, I tell you."

"I wasn't. There's something wrong with it."

"Never mind—get on...."

Lorimer, watching Loretta sail out on the trapeze, turned round on the platform and looked down to the edge of the ring below him. The ropes which raised or lowered the higher of the two trapezes stretched down to the spot at the ringside where they could be adjusted if necessary. Joe Carey was standing at that spot. He was staring up at Lorimer, high in the roof of the tent. Lorimer turned round to see Loretta half-way on her journey back to the platform. Instead of hanging to the trapeze by his ankles, he shot himself out, clinging by the hands, and stretching his body down as far as he could. Even so, Loretta only managed to grasp his ankles by a matter of inches. She clung on desperately, struggled to secure a better grip, and at last hoisted herself up on to the platform. Lorimer landed beside her, sweating.

"What's the idea?" said Loretta. "Why did you go out that way?"

"This trapeze has been heightened," said Lorimer. "You were right—it's six inches higher than usual. If I hadn't gone out that way you couldn't have caught me. You'd have been killed...."

"Who's done it?"

"Look—down there. Carey...."

"Come on—we'll end the act."

"We can't. They can't do anything now. We know they've changed it—we can't make a miss now. Carry on."

Loretta swung out again, turned her two somersaults in mid-air, connected with the other trapeze at the last possible moment, shot back again and passed Lorimer in mid-air. They passed again: Lorimer was back on the higher trapeze, Loretta swinging far out at the opposite side of the tent. It was here that Lorimer had to carry off his nonchalant business of putting his beret straight, dropping, and hanging on by the ankles to catch Loretta when it seemed too late for anything but a tragedy to happen. He found it difficult to bother about the beret...sitting, swinging his legs on the trapeze, he felt it being raised...three inches, no more. But enough—quite enough.

He dropped at once, holding tightly on by the ankles. He realized that it was hopeless. This was a trick that was timed to a fraction of a second and measured to a fraction of an inch. Three inches smashed the whole thing. He yelled out to Loretta:

"Don't jump!"

He saw Loretta rush through the air towards him—saw her let go of the other trapeze with one hand...threw himself towards her in an effort to save her. She did not need his saving; she had heard him, and hung grimly to the trapeze with one hand. The jerk which Lorimer had given towards her threw him off his balance. His ankles slipped from their hold round the rung of the trapeze. He gave a little scream and fell to the sawdust below him. There was a crack as his bones broke…an unpleasant sound. A woman near the ringside yelled and screamed hysterically.

Loretta, swinging on the other trapeze, looked down at the still body lying in the ring. No one was there. Carey had gone.

Chapter Fifteen

Mr. Minto, meanwhile, was learning a whole lot about the vacuum-cleaner business.

Vacuum-cleaner canvassing is not an easy job. Young Mr. Briggs, who was due to marry Claire Minto at two o'clock on the following Saturday, was forced, poor soul, to spend his last days of freedom ringing door-bells, giving demonstrations, and getting snubbed in various degrees of rudeness. His job, it seemed, allowed only the very minimum of time off for such unimportant matters as marriages, and a honeymoon was out of the question, at any rate for the time being. Young Mr. Briggs, who by all the rules of the game ought to have been in the middle of his first quarrel of married life round about the Monday after his wedding, had to be in Norwich that day, complete with sample vacuum; he was scheduled to open a crusade to make the housewives of that city vacuum-conscious at nine o'clock on the Monday morning.

Having cleaned up Norwich in the course of a week's canvassing, Mr. Briggs passed on to pastures new and worked his way north, calling at York, Middlesbrough, Durham, and Newcastle-on-Tyne in the order named.

Then he transported his vacuum to Wales, and after that did a round of the Lancashire towns. There was a sporting chance that, after he had thoroughly vacuumed Preston (which would take some considerable time), he would be allowed a fortnight's holiday in order to take a belated honeymoon. Until then Claire had to wait.

Mr. Minto squeezed all this information out of his sister, whom he visited immediately after passing Dodo on the stairs of the hotel. He did not approve of pumping his kith and kin; in fact, pumping in any form was not a thing of which Mr. Minto was particularly fond. He preferred to solve his cases slowly and by degrees rather than quickly and by third degree, but in this case a little pumping seemed unavoidable. Sister Claire had proved an apt pumpee—it was the first time that Mr. Minto had shown any interest at all in the young man whom she was about to marry, and Claire was only too eager to talk about him and his work. Had she known to what purpose Mr. Minto was going to use the information, she might not have allowed her tongue to wag quite so freely. But then, had she known more about young Briggs she might not have said "yes" quite so quickly and loudly on the evening when he proposed to her.

Mr. Minto, having pumped, left her abruptly and paid a visit to the circus advance publicity manager.

"Where do you go after this week?" he asked.

"Norwich, sir," said the publicity man. "A week in Norwich."

"Yes...I thought so," said Mr. Minto.

It might, of course, be a mere coincidence that Mr. Briggs was to canvass for his vacuums at the same time as the canvas of the circus tents went up in Norwich.

"And after Norwich?"

"York, sir. Another week in York. We only did three days

there last summer, but we did such good business that we're trying a week this year."

"And after that?"

"Middlesbrough. Three days in Middlesbrough and three in Durham—worse luck. My old woman lives in Durham. Then we have a week in Newcastle. Why, sir? You're thinking of staying with us that long, are you?"

"Heaven forbid!" said Mr. Minto. "I'm leaving you tomorrow—I hope. I've got other things to attend to. After Newcastle, I suppose you go down to Wales, do you?"

"As a matter of fact, sir, we do."

"And then Blackburn and Bolton and Preston and all those places?"

"That's right, sir. How did you know that?"

"A little bird told me," said Mr. Minto, and went off to look at the Norman ruins.

The Norman ruins were not particularly impressive, and what interest they had had been largely removed by the Office of Works, who had patched them up in odd places with red sandstone. To Mr. Minto they looked very like the inner-tubes of motor-car tyres with a number of new and pink spots attached to cover up the punctures. He was not really interested in the ruins. He had only visited them because he could sit down on what few portions the Office of Works had made sittable and think things out without being disturbed. Young Briggs, it was quite obvious, was connected in some way with Carey's Circus. He was no ordinary vacuum-cleaner canvasser. Was he connected in some way with the death of Anton? Mr. Minto devoutly hoped not. At the same time his mind was made up on one point...the marriage arranged between Claire Minto and Ronald Briggs, to take place at two o'clock on the following Saturday, would not take place. Not, at any rate, if he could help it.

It was at this point that Mr. Minto lit a pipe and, turning round to shield the match from the breeze, caught sight of a figure labouring up the hill towards the Norman ruins. A slim young man, carrying a case of peculiar shape. Mr. Minto could not believe that the gods, who up to now had been behaving so awkwardly, had suddenly decided to give him a break. The young man with the case was Mr. Briggs.

The houses around the hill on which the ruins were situated were large, solid affairs with a great deal of ivy and a greenhouse apiece. Mr. Minto imagined that the town's gentry lived in these parts, and thought to himself that young Briggs was wasting his time trying to secure a demonstration, let alone a sale, in a locality like this. It was only the people who could not afford expensive vacuum cleaners who bought them nowadays, according to Mr. Minto's experience; those who were able to afford a dozen vacuums preferred their houses to be cleaned by much elbow-grease and many maids.

He sat still on his piece of ruin and watched Mr. Briggs turn into one of the big houses, walk up the long drive, and ring the door-bell. And, what is more important, disappear at once inside the house. Sales-resistance was conspicuous by its absence: Mr. Briggs was received with open arms. It was the first time that Mr. Minto had known a vacuum-cleaner canvasser to be allowed inside a house without at least a preliminary skirmish on the door-step, and it intrigued him.

He waited until the salesman reappeared some ten minutes later, and prepared to watch him continue his assault on the other houses along the street. But young Briggs did nothing of the kind. He was evidently satisfied with the business he had done in his one call, and he set off at a brisk pace along the street. Mr. Minto jumped down from his ruin and followed him at a discreet distance.

He spent the whole morning following young Mr. Briggs. It was hot work, and Mr. Minto began to think things about the people who argued that a stiff collar was preferable to a soft collar in sultry weather. Young Briggs appeared to have a widely scattered constituency. From his call at the big house in the west end of the town he went right into the centre of the town and visited a block of solicitors' offices, where he stayed for two minutes only. Mr. Minto was not surprised at the shortness of his stay; what did surprise him was that young Briggs should think it worth his while to call on a solicitors' office at all. Did solicitors use vacuums in their offices? Mr. Minto had never heard of such a thing.

After a second call the young man, still complete with case, hopped on a bus and gave Mr. Minto a spot of bother by dashing away from him towards the poorer quarter of the town. Mr. Minto took a taxi, and asked the driver to follow the bus. The driver did not grasp his meaning; in any case, it was beneath his dignity to be seen following buses. He had spent almost his entire lifetime racing buses, cutting in past buses, and overtaking buses at corners contrary to Section 33 of the Highway Code, and he was not going to start lagging behind any blooming bus at his time of life. To Mr. Minto's annoyance the taxi shot past the bus at the first possible opportunity and the driver then asked: "Where to now, sir?"

Mr. Minto told him, rather tersely, a suitable destination, going on to explain that what he wanted the driver to do was to keep behind the bus they had just passed. The driver said that it seemed kind of queer to him, but if that was what was wanted, all they had to do was to turn left up this side-road, double back along this one-way street, turn right, get back on the main road. After which, according to the driver's arithmetic and sense of direction, they should be behind the bus once more as requested.

Mr. Minto agreed to this and told the driver to get a move on.

The taxi turned left, doubled back, turned right, and came out again on the main road. The thing worked splendidly; the taxi was now definitely behind the bus—so far behind it, in fact, that the bus was now almost a twopenny stage ahead and disappearing out of view round a corner. The driver turned, beamed on Mr. Minto, and asked him if he was satisfied. Mr. Minto stopped the taxi, got out, swore at and paid the driver, and began to run. He discarded his hat and undid his waistcoat buttons *en route*, and found himself presently in Bank Street.

Coming near the pawnshop, Mr. Minto applied the brakes and bought a *Daily Mail* from a convenient newsagent. He passed the pawnshop slowly, to all outward appearances immersed in the details of the several White Sales advertised on the front page of his newspaper. Out of the corner of his eye he saw young Mr. Briggs leaning across the pawnshop counter and chatting lightly to the charming girl who, only yesterday, had asked Mr. Minto to scram. He walked on, still deep in the details of the White Sales, until he hit a lamp-post. He then turned round cautiously and was just in time to see young Mr. Briggs leave the pawnshop. Minus, he noticed, his case.

Mr. Minto leaned against the lamp-post which had just struck him and pondered a while. Was it possible that the pawnshop people had been so impressed by Mr. Briggs' sales-talk that they had decided to buy a vacuum on the spot? Or had Mr. Briggs left his sample vacuum behind for a day or two in order that they might get to know the prowess of the model? Mr. Minto was inclined to think that there was more in the business than merely that kind of thing. He walked slowly back to the shop and lit a cigarette opposite its entrance. The shop was empty. The girl had disappeared, either to the back shop or upstairs to try out the vacuum on the carpets of the flat above.

Mr. Minto entered the shop on tiptoe. A Scotland Yard Detective-Inspector on tiptoe is a very rare sight indeed, and all who witnessed the phenomenon taking place in Bank Street must count themselves lucky. There was a sort of elephantine grace in Mr. Minto's movements, like the late Mr. G. K. Chesterton dancing a minuet. He got inside the shop without attracting any attention, however, and began to nose around. He found the case which Mr. Briggs had left lying on a shelf behind the counter.

The case was locked, but had two small keys thoughtfully attached to the handle by a piece of string. Mr. Minto turned the keys in their locks and opened the case with something like bated breath. He sat down on the floor of the shop, baffled and amazed. The vacuum-cleaner case contained—of all things—a vacuum-cleaner.

It was at this moment that Mr. Minto realized that he was no longer alone in the pawnshop. A customer had arrived and was stampeding up and down on the other side of the counter. Sooner or later, thought Mr. Minto, using those powers of deduction which had won him promotion on various occasions, sooner or later someone would come to attend to this customer. Very likely they would attend to him from the side of the counter where he himself was hiding. Mr. Minto removed himself, silently and just in time, to a deep alcove hung thickly with old clothes. They had an unpleasant tang, and Mr. Minto held his nose.

The girl came running down the stairs from the flat above. Mr. Minto heard her say: "Oh—it's you!" He then realized that the new arrival was Dodo. Forgetting the smell of the old clothes, he pushed himself further back into the alcove, leaving his best ear ready to pick up any interesting snatches of conversation.

"Where's that costume of mine?" said the clown.

"The one Ginger brought in?"

"Yes. Is it still here?"

"'Course it's still here. Why—do you want it?"

"Yes. That detective's getting a bit too inquisitive for my liking. I'm going to destroy it."

"What's the matter? There's nothing to get windy about, is there?"

"I'm not so sure. Hand it over, in any case."

"O-kay. It's hanging up here.…"

The girl walked round the counter to the alcove where Mr. Minto was buried deep in smelly clothes. Mr. Minto had a busy time holding both his nose and his breath as she ran her fingers through the various garments hanging in the alcove.

"That's funny," she said.

"What's the matter? Isn't it there?"

"No. I'm sure I hung it up there."

"You haven't let it out of the shop, have you?"

"No. No one would want a thing like that."

"Well, where is it?"

"I don't know. It'll be lying about somewhere. Old Winter may have shifted it. He's always messing things about. I'll go and ask him."

Mr. Minto sent up a brief but devout prayer to heaven that the girl would not be too long in finding old Winter. He knew of many more pleasant spots than this alcove in which to spend a hot summer morning.

The girl came back, followed by old Winter.

"He says he hasn't seen it."

"Well, find it. I've got to have it."

"I could have sworn it was hanging up there," said old Winter. "I'm sure it was there when we shut up last night. I remember saying to the missus, just as we were shutting up for the night—"

"Never mind all that," said Dodo. "Find the damned thing."

The girl and old Winter returned to the alcove and made a thorough inspection of the clothes hanging there. Mr. Minto had only once held his breath for as long a time; that was on the day during his summer holidays at Bournemouth, several years before, when he had got out of touch with his false teeth while swimming and had been forced to grope about the sea-bottom until he found the things. He had a particularly nasty moment when old Winter's hand reached in through the clothes and touched his own suit, feeling up and down the lapel of his jacket…until, satisfied that it was not the missing costume, the hand withdrew and fumbled through the garments hanging in the other side of the alcove.

"Beats me," said old Winter. "I could have sworn—"

Dodo, beating him to it, swore fluently. Mr. Minto was impressed. He had not thought the little clown capable of such a vocabulary.

"It's bound to be somewhere," said the girl helpfully.

"What did you want it for, anyway?" asked old Winter.

"Never mind. I want it. And I've got to have it. I haven't time to wait now while the pair of you moon about looking for it. You find that damned costume and send it round to the circus this afternoon—understand? If you don't find it, it'll be very awkward—for you, as well as for me."

The clown stamped out.

"Well…!" said the girl. "He's in a nice state and no mistake, isn't he?"

"I could have sworn I saw it lying up over there," said old Winter.

"We'll find it all right. It's a wonder you can lay your hands on anything in a place like this. I'll get it after dinner. Come on."

The girl started to go upstairs, with old Winter following. Mr. Minto was just on the point of pushing his way out of the old clothes when he heard Dodo coming back into the shop. He retreated carefully and resumed a tight grip on his nose.

"Here, you two!" said Dodo.

"What's up now?"

"I forgot to tell you—we can't get any stuff round to you today. That ruddy man Minto's got his eye on this place."

In the alcove the ruddy man Minto suppressed a tremendous desire to sneeze.

"How are we getting it, then?" asked old Winter.

"At the circus, this afternoon. You'd better send O'Donnell."

"Oh—all right."

Dodo then stopped using the English language and said something in what Mr. Minto took to be Double-Dutch.

"The one-and-threepenny attendant," said Dodo. "Ask for twenty Player's, cork-tipped."

"Twenty Player's, cork-tipped," repeated old Winter.

Mr. Minto, in his alcove, sighed. It was always a pity when lunacy became mixed up with a criminal investigation.

He waited until the clown had left the shop and the girl and old Winter had disappeared upstairs. Then Mr. Minto came out of the alcove and took a deep gulp of fresh air. He had never tasted anything sweeter in his life. Champagne in comparison was mere dish-water.

Two minutes later Detective-Inspector Minto again rose on his points—perhaps not so gracefully as Riabouchinska, but nevertheless with a pretty sense of balance—and tiptoed out of the pawnshop. He was carrying the case in which young Mr. Briggs trundled around his sample vacuum-cleaner. And inside the case was the red-and-yellow checked clown costume which Dodo had been so very anxious to find. It had, after all, been hanging in the alcove. Mr. Minto had noticed it in the nick of time and had removed it from its peg and stuffed it inside his jacket. He felt that it might be of interest in the case.

He then went back to his hotel and took the lift up to his bedroom. He laid the case on his bed and took out the vacuum-cleaner. Mr. Minto did not know a great deal about vacuum-cleaners except that the one which his housekeeper used in the early morning made an infernal noise and was the one thing calculated to get him out of his bed. This particular vacuum looked an excellent job, though Mr. Minto could not help feeling that it would have functioned much more satisfactorily if the bag which was meant to hold dust had held only dust.

He took out his penknife and split the bag open from top to bottom. To his relief, no dust fell out at all; it would have been very difficult to explain away a large heap of dust to the hotel chambermaid. What did fall out of the bag was a great deal more interesting than dust. Almost two dozen small white packages, neatly parcelled and carefully sealed. Mr. Minto bent down, picked one up and broke the seal. Inside was a tin box, perhaps an inch square. Mr. Minto punctured the lid of the box with the point of his penknife blade and cut a small round hole. He poured out a little of the white powder which filled the box into the palm of his hand, smelt it, and put some on the tip of his tongue. And spat it out at once, and crossed to the wash-basin to rinse out his mouth.

Light was beginning to dawn on Mr. Minto. There was enough opium hidden inside the bag of that vacuum-cleaner to bring tragedy into a hundred lives.

Chapter Sixteen

Mr. Minto went, for a change, to the afternoon performance of the circus and sat in the one-and-threepenny seats. He went to quite a lot of trouble to get inside the circus without being recognized by any of the staff or performers. Mr. Minto did not usually hold with disguises: they made him feel self-conscious and itchy. He had only once in his whole career lowered himself to donning a false moustache, and it had come unstuck at a very critical stage of the case which he was trying to clear up. Since then Mr. Minto had steered clear of moustaches, wigs, blue spectacles, and the like. As the girl in the pawnshop had reminded him, it was useless to try and disguise himself as anything but a policeman with feet like his.

On the occasion of his visit to the circus, however, Mr. Minto lifted a stray cap off a peg in the *foyer* and the Station Hotel and borrowed an oilskin from the hall-porter. The cap was of a good vintage and belonged to a fisherman; flies and portions of tackle stuck out from it at all angles and made it look more like a barbed-wire entanglement than a cap. The hall-porter seemed reluctant to part with his oilskin until half-a-crown was flourished before his eyes…after which he would gladly have loaned Mr. Minto his trousers if necessary.

The fact that it was a warm, sunny afternoon did not worry Mr. Minto; he buttoned up the oilskin, pulled the cap down over his eyes and caught his finger on a hook in doing so; and walked into the big tent of Carey's Circus without anyone recognizing him. He passed within a yard of Joe Carey and that gentleman paid no attention to him, beyond thinking what queer folk one met in the world. Once in his one-and-threepenny seat and surrounded by small children, all of whom appeared to be chewing gum, Mr. Minto peeled off his oilskin, removed the cap carefully, and sat down to enjoy the performance.

He found it a little boring. One of the great attractions of a circus is that it comes only once or twice a year, and Mr. Minto, who had seen the show four times that week, got rather restless quite early in the programme. It may, of course, have been the seating accommodation which, in the one-and-threepennies, consisted of a narrow board of extremely hard wood—Mr. Minto, from the hardness of the wood, took it to be mahogany. At any rate, even such high spots in the bill as Lars Peterson and his Intelligent Sea-Lion and the troupe of baby elephants left him more or less cold, while the ordinary run of acts like Miss St. Clair and her Educated Ponies bored him stiff. When the tigers came into the ring he sat up and took notice.

It was the tigers' first appearance in public with their new trainer, and Mr. Minto was interested to see how they behaved. The new man was an enormous German youth with blond hair and muscles which rippled up and down his back like waves breaking on a shore. He entered the ring without a whip, and Mr. Minto hoped that there was not going to be any more blood spilt. There was not. The tigers behaved themselves like the dux children of a Sunday School, and went through their tricks and manoeuvres without even a single roar of protest. The second largest of the animals, now promoted to Peter's place as leader of the troupe, went through the hoops of fire as though leaping through hoops of fire were its strongest weakness.

The act finished, the school-children around Mr. Minto said what they thought of it in no uncertain terms. There was a strong movement among the boys in the audience to go and demand their money back, on the grounds that no one had been mauled, attacked, or even scratched during the act.

Mr. Minto, unfortunately, leaned back to ponder over this change of attitude on the part of the tigers. Unfortunately, for one is not supposed to lean back in the one-and-threepenny seats, and a yawning chasm awaits all those who do so. Amid a good deal of excitement, Mr. Minto was rescued and replaced by a crowd of delighted youngsters, who thought this by far the best part of the performance and much better than any tigers. Once replaced in his seat, Mr. Minto went on with his pondering. Had the tigers forgotten all about the death of Anton by now? If Miller were still alive and went into the ring beside them, would they treat him as they had treated him earlier in the week…or would they be as well-behaved as they had been just now with the muscular German?

It was at this point that Mr. Minto noticed a well-known young man thread his way through the children and sit down in the one-and-threepennies, rather nearer the ring than where Mr. Minto was sitting. Young Mr. Briggs, to be exact. Mr. Minto remembered the strange conversation he had overheard in the pawnshop and wondered if young Mr. Briggs could possibly be the man O'Donnell. He was very nearly sure of it when the attendant, who had been shouting "Chocolates! Cigarettes!" in a shrill alto all afternoon, went up to young Briggs and took quite a long time over his sale. Mr. Briggs seemed to be getting in a fairly large stock of cigarettes. Mr. Minto waited until the deal was over and then, taking care not to be seen by young Briggs, beckoned the attendant across.

The attendant was neatly intercepted by a small boy who didn't know what he wanted, and Mr. Minto had to wait until the respective claims of plain, milk, or nut-milk chocolate were settled before he could get any attention. He waited until the attendant climbed up beside him, and then spoke in what he hoped was a suitably mysterious whisper:

"Twenty Player's," said Mr. Minto, "cork-tipped...."

He waited, expecting to be told that Player's cigarettes were not manufactured with cork-tips, and not to be such a damned fool. The attendant, however, did not answer. He looked hard at Mr. Minto for an instant, and Mr. Minto wished that he was still wearing his oilskin and hooky cap. The attendant then selected a packet of cigarettes from the back of his tray and handed it to Mr. Minto. Mr. Minto took them without a word and passed over half-a-crown. An expensive afternoon; he hoped that this was the correct procedure.

Apparently it was. The attendant took the half-crown, winked, and pushed his way off along the row. Apparently it was not the correct procedure to give change.

Mr. Minto did not pay very much attention to the next turn in the ring, which was a number of Cossack riders doing their best to kill themselves and their horses. He was very busy opening the packet of cigarettes under cover of the oilskin lying on his lap.

When he opened the flap of the packet he got the same sense of shock as he had got on opening up Mr. Briggs's vacuum-cleaner case. There had been, of all things, a vacuum-cleaner inside the vacuum-cleaner case; and there appeared to be cigarettes, again of all things, inside this packet of cigarettes. As he had done in the case of the vacuum-cleaner, however, Mr. Minto went a little further into the matter. He found, rummaging about with his fingers, that the cigarettes were dummies and extended only to about an inch from the top of the packet. In the space below, there was a neat square package. Mr. Minto did not bother to open the package. He had a good idea what it contained.

The next turn was Lorimer and Loretta. Mr. Minto was relieved to see that Lorimer had looked after himself during the day and was still in circulation. He prepared to enjoy this act, at any rate, but just as the two trapeze artists were running up the rope-ladders to the roof of the tent Mr. Minto caught sight of the attendant who had handed him his twenty cork-tipped Player's. He was talking to young Mr. Briggs and appeared to be agitated.

Mr. Minto tried to make himself as inconspicuous as possible, and even asked the small boy sitting next to him if he would like to sit on his knee in order to see the show better. He had no great wish to have the small boy on his knee, but he thought that some kind of screen might be useful. The small boy, however, told Mr. Minto rather snappily that only Cissies sat on people's knees, and Mr. Minto felt squashed. Squashed and also worried; for the attendant had left young Briggs and had gone to have a word with Joe Carey…and was at that moment pointing him out to the circus proprietor.

Lorimer and Loretta were in the middle of their second trick; Mr. Minto did his best to appear interested in Lorimer swinging across the roof of the tent, at the same time keeping an eye on young Briggs, Joe Carey, and the attendant. Difficult, and not a little sore; he felt he had quite a sporting chance of coming away from the circus with a permanent squint.

Lorimer arrived back safely on his platform; Mr. Minto applauded, and noticed that young Briggs had left his seat and was making his way towards Joe Carey by the back of the one-and-threepenny seats. Loretta was swinging out now, to be caught by Lorimer at the last possible moment. It seemed to Mr. Minto that the connection had been made a little later than usual, but he had no time to worry about that. Briggs was at the entrance to the tent, talking to Joe Carey. Carey looked up to where Mr. Minto was sitting; Mr. Minto appealed to the small boy to sit on his knee, and was choked off even more snappily than before. He looked down to where Carey was standing, and for an instant their eyes met. Lorimer and Loretta were back on their platform again, and the audience was applauding wildly.

Mr. Minto was beginning to feel that he had had enough of the circus…especially when he saw Joe Carey collect four of the ringside attendants and point up in his direction. The four attendants were by no means weaklings; they could have given Mr. Victor McLaglen a good run for his money. What Mr. Minto did not like was the fact that all four were edging towards him…two along the front of the cheap seats and two working their way along the back. Mr. Minto was a marked man. He wished he had left the oilskin at the hotel and brought an automatic instead.

He was saved at the last minute by one of the nastiest sounds he had ever heard—the crack of Lorimer's bones as he fell from the higher trapeze on to the middle of the ring. Chaos reigned around Mr. Minto and all over the tent. Women screamed, children yelled, everyone stood up in their seats and fell over their neighbours. Mr. Minto took a quick look round. Joe Carey had vanished. The four attendants had forgotten Mr. Minto for the moment and were dashing back to the main entrance. Mr. Minto dived through a sea of sticky children and crept out under the canvas side-walls of the tent. He was very sorry for poor Lorimer—very sorry indeed, but he was most grateful for the five minutes' grace which his accident had given him.

He ran across the field to the corner where Joe Carey's caravan was pitched, found the door locked, picked up a convenient pit-prop lying on the grass and burst his way through the door. He had five minutes, possibly less, in which to lay his hands on a great deal of damning evidence and finish up this business. In the first of those five minutes Mr. Minto had rather upset the normal tidiness of Joe Carey's caravan. Drawers were flung open, cases burst into, and a great heap of miscellaneous goods scattered across the floor.

Mr. Minto had not found what he was looking for, though. He tapped the walls. It was not a very conclusive test, for all four walls of the caravan were made of thin Beaverboard and gave out the same hollow sound when knocked on. Taking a shot in the dark, Mr. Minto gave the back wall of the caravan a hefty kick with his right foot. The inside back wall was vertical, whereas the outside of the caravan was gracefully curved.…Mr. Minto was curious to know what, if anything, was kept in the space between the inside and outside walls. Four more kicks told him, after which he found the little knob which would have opened up the back wall without causing quite so much damage. The space between the inside and outside walls was packed tightly with the same packages which he had found inside the bag of the vacuum-cleaner and inside the dummy packet of cigarettes. Even Mr. Minto was impressed. He had never imagined the business to be on quite such a large scale as this.

He left the caravan hurriedly, dodged his way across the field through the tents without being seen, and paid a couple of quick calls in the town. The first was a very pleasant visit, the second distinctly unpleasant. He went first to the local police-station, presented his compliments, and asked if he might have a word with Superintendent Padgeham.

The Superintendent was in a benign mood. It was the day of the weekly Magistrates' Court, and no less than fourteen motorists had been successfully prosecuted for hooting after eleven-thirty, leaving their cars parked in the High Street for five minutes longer than the time allowed, and travelling at thirty-one miles an hour through restricted areas. Superintendent Padgeham felt like a man returning from a day's fishing with a heavy basket, and even felt kindly disposed to nuisances from Scotland Yard who came snooping into affairs that were no business of theirs.

"Well, well, well!" said the Superintendent. "If it isn't Mr. Minto! How are you, sir? Come to hand over this circus business to us poor locals, eh?"

"Yes," said Mr. Minto. "I wash my hands of the whole thing. You can carry on, Padgeham."

"I had a feeling we'd get it in the end," said the Superintendent. "Well, I'm afraid there's not much any of us can do now. I've been making a few inquiries on my own, sir, and there seems no doubt that this fellow Anton was killed by the attendant Miller. Motive—jealousy. Shot the fellow and then threw him into the lions' cage to cover up the murder—"

"Incidentally, they were tigers."

"Tigers, then. And the tigers took the law into their own hands and finished him off. We can't do anything about Miller now, sir. He's dead."

"So is Queen Anne," said Mr. Minto.

"I don't see what she's got to do with it."

"Listen," said Mr. Minto. "Anton's murder isn't the most important thing in this case—not by a long chalk. This is one of the biggest and nastiest cases I've ever had anything to do with. I'm handing it over to you, Padgeham, on one condition."

"And what's that, sir?"

"You do exactly as I tell you from now until the end of the circus show tonight."

"I'm sorry, sir. That's impossible, sir. I've got my own ideas about this business, and—"

"All right. Go ahead. Use your own ideas—and get a severe kick in the pants from headquarters. Use mine, and you'll get promotion and your face on all the front pages. Local Superintendent Rounds Up Dangerous Gang of Criminals. Padgeham, my dear good ass, the case is finished—over and done with. I've solved it—otherwise I wouldn't be handing it over to you. Now that I'm sure you can't make a mess of it, I'm prepared to let you have all the honour and glory of the last round-up. It's my nature. Or, rather, it's because I've no right to be mixed up in the thing at all."

The Superintendent seemed impressed. The vision of his photographs on the front pages swam before him.

"What d'you want me to do, sir?" he asked.

"Put a guard round Martin's Field. Now—right away. A man on each of the two exits, and some more patrolling round the field. If Carey, the proprietor, attempts to leave, have him followed wherever he goes. Don't arrest him—just keep an eye on him. Do the same with the little clown— Dodo. Have your entire force—all four of 'em, or however many you have in this town—at the circus tonight. They can go to the show in plain clothes and enjoy themselves. I'll pay for the tickets and put it down in my expenses."

"Why?" asked Superintendent Padgeham. "What's the idea, sir?"

"There's going to be a mass arrest tonight," said Mr. Minto. "I'll tell you when to do it, and you step in and do your stuff. Have you a large supply of handcuffs?"

"You're not arresting the whole circus?"

"Very nearly," said Mr. Minto. "I've nothing against the sea-lion, and I think we'll let the baby elephants go. They'd be a nuisance in gaol, anyway. But I've got enough to keep you boys busy for one evening. Got a pencil and paper?"

The Superintendent produced a note-book and a stump of pencil.

"Just in case you get them mixed up, I'll tell you whom I want arrested. Ready? Write down numbers one to eight in your note-book, then."

"Eight?" said the Superintendent.

"That is all at present," said Mr. Minto. "There may be more."

The Superintendent sighed and wrote down his list at Mr. Minto's dictation. It made an impressive display.

1. Joseph Carey, alias Joseph Smythe, proprietor of Carey's Circus.

2. Ernest Mayhew, professionally known as Dodo, clown in the aforesaid Carey's Circus.

3. James Winter, occupation unknown, resident at 288, Bank Street, in this town.

4. Helen Winter, wife of the aforesaid James Winter, same address.

5. Janet Winter or Carey, illegitimate daughter of Helen Winter, same address.

6. Ronald Craig Briggs, alias Donald O'Donnell, so-called vacuum-cleaner salesman, permanent address unknown.

7. John Barker, cigarette and chocolate salesman in Carey's Circus.

8. Sebastian Rowley, Esq., independent means, of "The Cedars", Castle Terrace, in this town.

The Superintendent lasted well until the last name on the list. At that he jibbed.

"Mr. Rowley?" he said. "I can't arrest Mr. Rowley. He's a magistrate."

"All the more reason why you should arrest him," said Mr. Minto.

"And—if it's not asking too much—what are the charges?"

"I haven't the slightest idea," said Mr. Minto. "I'll let you know later."

He left the Superintendent in a dazed condition, and went off to make his second call.

For a quarter of an hour he walked up and down on the pavement outside his brother's flat, brooding on the unpleasantness of his visit. When at last he went in he found Claire and Robert busy with final preparations for the wedding. It was going to be awkward enough for Mr. Minto to break the news, and Claire did not make it any easier by prattling brightly on various points of the wedding ceremony and its aftermath. They had decided, said Claire, that there was to be only one speech at the reception, because once these clergymen got on to their feet they didn't know when to sit down. And there was a lot of careful planning to be done about Going Away, even if it were only for the weekend…no nonsense about confetti, old boots, and "L" signs attached to the rear of the car. Mr. Minto, as a Scotland Yard detective, was to see about all that sort of thing. It was another quarter of an hour before Mr. Minto could get a word in edgeways, and by that time he felt even more uncomfortable about what he had to say.

"Where is the prospective bridegroom now?" he asked.

"Running about doing some business," said Claire. "The man thinks of nothing but his blooming vacuums. I hope he doesn't dream about them. It would be very awkward if he started giving me demonstrations in bed."

"Claire!" said the clerical member of the Minto family. "Really...!"

Mr. Minto lit a cigarette and blew two neat smoke-rings before broaching the subject.

"Claire darling..." he said.

"He wants money," said his sister, "I've never heard him call me 'darling' before."

"Be serious for just a minute. I want to tell you something. Something that may—upset you a bit."

"Carry on. I can take it."

"Are you very much in love with this young man of yours?"

"Robert—have you been getting at him?"

The little priest looked worried, but did not answer.

"You have. I can see it from the fishy look in your eye. I know you don't hold with me marrying Ronnie, and you've been trying to get him to agree with you. It's a little late in the day to do that, though. I'm going to—"

"You're not!" said Mr. Minto.

"What?"

"You aren't going to marry that young man."

"Well!" said the bride-to-be. "We're not going to have a Victorian scene, are we? What's it got to do with you, Mr. Detective?"

"A great deal, unfortunately. And if I can do anything to prevent you from marrying that young man, I'll do it."

"That's very nice of you. What are you getting at?"

"Claire, my dear, I'm terribly sorry...I've found out something about him that makes it impossible for you to marry him...."

"What?"

"He's a criminal. A very nasty type of criminal too."

The priest looked across at Mr. Minto in astonishment. Claire stared straight ahead.

"What have you found out?" she asked.

"He's engaged in one of the filthiest trades any man could be mixed up in...the smuggling of dope. He's no vacuum-cleaner salesman—that's only a blind. His job is to take round supplies of drugs to poor wretches all over the country. He's not the head of the concern—not even the brains. He's just a tool...he'll probably get no more than a year or two in gaol for his sins. But you can't marry him, Claire. If I thought you were madly in love with him I might have done something for the pair of you...even knowing what Briggs has done. But I don't think you are madly in love with him. You've always dashed into things without thinking much about the consequences, Claire. I believe you dashed into this. And the consequences in this case won't be pleasant ones...I'm going to have young Briggs arrested tonight."

Mr. Minto got up and stared out of the window, playing with the tassel of the blind-cord.

"I'm going back to town tomorrow," he said. "I think you ought to come with me—stay at my place for a few weeks...."

Claire went out of the room without speaking. Mr. Minto threw himself into an arm-chair.

"Oh, lord!" he said. "Robert—you're a priest. Why the devil do things happen like this? Why the blazes did you get me to come down here, eh? I wouldn't have come within a hundred miles of the place if I'd thought I was going to be mixed up in a mess like this."

"It seems that it was as well that I did ask you," said the priest.

"You...you didn't know anything about this, did you?"

"I had my suspicions. As a matter of fact, I thought young Briggs took drugs himself. I thought I was being absurd... he stayed here a few weeks ago, you know. There was a little powder left lying in his bedroom one morning which worried me a lot. I knew it wasn't health-salts or anything like that. I never imagined it was anything as serious as this, of course. But I think it was as well that you came down here."

"Maybe. I wouldn't have liked Claire to have got tied up with a little rotter like that. She'll get over it all right. Poor kid, though…!"

"You said you were going to have him arrested," said Robert. "Is he involved in the circus business?"

"Yes. Not in the death of Anton. I've got my man for that all right."

Mr. Minto stood up. His brother did not speak.

"Yes," said Mr. Minto. "I'm arresting Joseph Carey tonight."

"You're wrong—" said the priest, and stopped.

Mr. Minto smiled.

"Thank you, Robert," he said. "I didn't say I was going to arrest Carey for the murder, did I? Good heavens, no! I'm arresting practically the entire population of this town tonight for one thing or another. And now I know whom to arrest for the murder of Anton. Thank you, Robert…."

Mr. Minto went straight back to the circus ground. It was shortly before seven o'clock. He passed the constable standing at the main entrance to the field, and the sight cheered him. The stage was set for the last act. He walked round the big tent to the tigers' cage. There were very few people about. The circus staff and performers were in their tents and caravans getting ready for the evening performance; the crowds had not yet turned up. Mr. Minto reached the cage and stared at the animals, who were huddled up in one corner of the cage.

"It's all right," said Mr. Minto, half to himself and half to any tiger who might be listening. "We've got our man."

It was just after saying this that something hit Mr. Minto on the back of the skull. Interviewed some time later, Mr. Minto gave it as his opinion that the something which hit him was either (*a*) part of the Norman ruins, or (*b*) one of the cabers which are tossed at Highland Games. Actually it was a small length of lead piping. Mr. Minto gave a little groan, his legs crumpled up underneath him, he fell on the grass and lay still.

Chapter Seventeen

Loretta left the hospital to which Lorimer had been taken and walked back to the circus field alone. She had stood beside his bed and waited in vain for him to move or recognize her. He had lain with his eyes open, staring at the ceiling. There was some hope, she was told. He might never be able to work in the circus again, but with careful treatment he might be pulled through. Loretta went away stunned. She could not imagine life without the circus.…With Lorimer a cripple, and never again the thrill of swinging right across the roof of the big tent from one trapeze to another. She walked on, and found herself back in Martin's Field. One of the stable hands muttered his sympathies and asked how Lorimer was. She did not answer. She walked past the tigers' cage and on to the corner of the field where Joe Carey's green-and-white caravan was pitched. She went slowly up the steps and pushed open the door.

Carey was standing with his back to her, staring at the far wall of the caravan. It had been battered to pieces, and Mr. Carey seemed much affected by the sight. His face was pale, and as he turned round quickly to see Loretta he was trembling.

"Oh…it's you, Loretta," he said. "My dear, I'm terribly sorry….'Ow is 'e?"

"You raised that rope," said Loretta.

"What? What are you talking about?"

"You raised that rope. I saw you standing at the ringside while our act was on. That trapeze was raised while we were doing the act. You heard that Lorimer had found out something about you, Carey…you thought he was going to tell that man Minto, didn't you? And so you kept him quiet."

"My dear girl, you don't know what you're saying. I wouldn't do anything to Lorimer. You're ill…go and lie down at your hotel. And don't worry, I'll make everything all right for you both."

"You can't make Lorimer all right…ever."

"'E'll get better. 'E's broken some bones, that's all. 'E'll get over it. 'E'll be back doing the act in no time. Don't you worry."

On the small table in the middle of the caravan Mr. Carey's evening meal was laid out, untouched. Mr. Carey was not hungry—the sight of the battered wall had put him off his food. There was a half-loaf of bread on a plate and beside it a bread-knife with a saw edge. Loretta came up to the table, still staring at Carey. Her fingers reached out for the knife. She gripped it suddenly and yelled out.

"You've killed him! You swine…you've killed him!"

Mr. Carey had a momentary flash-back to a very similar scene…to the night when that jealous Dago, Varconi, had used a knife in this very caravan owing to a little misunderstanding about the relationship between Carey and Varconi's wife. He had time for no more than a momentary flash-back, for he realized that Loretta's arm was above her head, that the knife was in her hand with the saw edge pointing down towards his face, and that here was a young woman who was mad with fury and who meant business. He gripped her arm as it came down; the knife flashed past his face and tore the shoulder of his jacket. He took a tight hold of the girl and tried to pinion her arms behind her back. She was screaming hysterically now, and lashing out with the knife. Mr. Carey did not enjoy the next few moments. Of all weapons to be killed with, a bread-knife with a saw edge was one of the last he would have chosen. He was very relieved when the body of Loretta suddenly went limp in his arms, and she flopped on the floor of the caravan. She let go of the knife in falling and it dropped across her legs, opening up the skin and making a trickle of blood ooze out on to the worn carpet. She lay quite still. Mr. Carey took out a large red silk handkerchief and mopped his forehead.

He took another look at the battered wall, and the hundreds of small white packages tumbling out of it. His mind was already made up. Carey's Circus was not due to leave the town until the Sunday morning, and was also due to open at Norwich on the Monday. Its proprietor, however, had no intention of staying on until Sunday, and less intention of being in Norwich on the following day—or in any of the places advertised by the circus's publicity manager as future halts in the summer tour. He was getting out now while the going was good…at least, he hoped that the going was good. Geography had never been one of Joe Carey's strong suits, and he wished he knew which was the port nearest to this town where one could run up the gangway of a ship bound for the continent without too many questions being asked. The main thing, however, was to get out of the town and, in the first place, out of Martin's Field.

He was wearing his evening-dress in readiness for the evening performance. He took a light waterproof from a peg at the back of the caravan door and slipped it over his tails. There was a fairly big cupboard fitted along one wall of the caravan; Mr. Carey went up to it and made sure that it was locked. Then he went out of the caravan, leaving Loretta still lying on the floor inside.

The first of the crowd for the evening performance were just beginning to queue up, waiting for the ticket-office to open in half an hour. He turned up the collar of his water-proof and made his way across the field to the far exit. The thought occurred to him that it would be a nice gentlemanly thing to warn Dodo of the turn which events had taken; the thought also occurred to him that if he wasted his time being gentlemanly, he might quite easily find himself face to face with a pair of handcuffs. He broke into a trot, and realized the drawbacks of full evening-dress as a garb in which to make a getaway. Never mind, he had got out of corners before and he would get out of this one. He reached the gate and pushed it open. He felt better as soon as he was on the other side of the gate. Until, that is, he noticed the police constable ambling towards him.

The constable was of the large and heavy type, built on lines similar to the Rock of Gibraltar. The type one had a sporting chance of getting the better of in such matters as exceeding the speed limit or driving through pedestrian crossings. Mr. Carey did not welcome him, however. He was in no mood for constables, however heavy.

"'Evening, sir," said the policeman, affably enough.

"Good evening," said Mr. Carey.

"Nice evening, sir."

"Very nice."

"Going to have a full house tonight, sir?"

"I 'ope so."

"Well…good evening, sir."

"Good evening, constable."

Mr. Carey walked on. The deep depression which had set in on seeing the policeman had lifted slightly; the outlook, if still unsettled, seemed a little brighter. Minto could not have got the local police on to the job, at any rate, otherwise the constable would hardly have wasted his time chatting about the weather. Mr. Carey then realized that the constable, with what seemed a great excess of zeal, was following him. He kept always a hundred yards or so behind, but there was no doubt that he was on the trail. If Mr. Carey quickened his pace, the constable—with much puffing and panting—accelerated accordingly. If Mr. Carey paused to inspect the contents of a shop window, the bobby found something equally interesting in another shop window further along the street. Mr. Carey bobbed up a side street; the bobby bobbed also. Mr. Carey turned quickly into Bank Street. The bobby followed.

Bobby or no bobby, Joe Carey was determined to get word to a pretty young girl who worked in that pawnshop that, though God might be in His heaven, all was not right with the world. Once he had given her warning, he did not very much care what happened. He could spend the rest of the evening leading this persistent policeman a dance. Sooner or later, judging from the weight and girth of the policeman, he would be able to shake him off. The first thing to do was to pay a quick visit to the pawnshop and get the girl out of this. Mr. Carey almost ran down the full length of Bank Street. Arriving at the door of the pawnshop he found another guardian of law and order stationed outside it. Mr. Carey swore and passed on.

The policeman at the pawnshop was of a different type altogether from the policeman shadowing Mr. Carey. Leaner, younger, and definitely more athletic in appearance. It was most annoying for Mr. Carey to find that, after a brief discussion, the two policemen had changed jobs. The leaner and more athletic specimen was now engaged in following him, and the heavier, more old-fashioned sample had been relegated to the task of mounting guard over the pawnshop.

He now stood leaning against a lamp-post with his helmet in his hand, wiping sweat from his brow. The younger man seemed capable of shadowing Mr. Carey as far as John o' Groats, if necessary.

Mr. Carey wisely gave it up and made his way back to the circus field. He was dogged by policeman No. 2 all the way, and when he arrived he found a third constable walking up and down in front of the other entrance to the field. It seemed to Joe Carey to be an ideal night for bringing off a nice quiet smash-and-grab in the town—every policeman seemed to be interested in the circus and in nothing else.

He made his way to Dodo's dressing-tent, and was told that the clown was already in the big tent. The performance was not due to begin for another half-hour; there were still only a few people in the tent. The sections of the huge cage for the tigers' act were being assembled all round the ring, for the tigers were to appear first at the evening performance. Mr. Carey found Dodo talking to one of the chocolate-sellers in the middle of the ring. He dismissed the attendant and got down to business.

"We're sunk," said Mr. Carey. "They've found the stuff."

"Where? In the caravan?"

"Yes. The wall's been 'acked to pieces."

"Minto, I suppose?"

"I expect so. There's a guard of policemen all round the field. I went out just now and was followed right through the town."

"You weren't trying to get away, were you?"

Mr. Carey was shocked.

"I was trying to get word to the girl at the shop. You don't think I'd clear out and leave you, do you?"

"Yes," said Dodo. "I know you would. Where's Minto?"

"'E's all right. 'E won't trouble us tonight. It's these

damned local police I'm worrying about. What are we going to do?"

"Clear out, of course."

"That's not so easy. 'Ow are you going to do it?"

"Johnston's car. He leaves tonight for Norwich to fix up hotel bookings, doesn't he? He can take us."

"They'll stop the car when it leaves the field."

"No, they won't. We can make Johnston step on it all right. Sit in the back seat with a revolver between his shoulder-blades, and Johnston won't worry about policemen or speed limits."

"All right. We'll try it. When?"

"We'd better do it during the show. Meet me outside my tent—after the sea-lion turn. I'll fix up things with Johnston. Oh, hell!"

"What's the matter?"

"I thought you said Minto wouldn't trouble us tonight?"

Joe Carey swung round. Mr. Minto was making his way into the ring, looking very pleased with life. He had a fairly large lump on the back of his head covered with a wad of sticking-plaster, but apart from this he was looking remarkably healthy. He was having some little difficulty in getting inside the ring, for the attendants were fixing up the last section of the big cage and he had to dodge his way through a great number of ropes, steel bars, and human beings.

"Good evening," said Mr. Minto. "House is rather slow in filling up tonight, isn't it?"

"Yes…it's this Lorimer business," said Carey. "The news 'as got round the town. Puts people off."

"You've had bad luck this visit, haven't you?"

"I'll say we 'ave. I don't want to see this town again in a 'urry."

"I don't expect you will," said Mr. Minto. "Has the circus ever been to Devon?"

"Yes," said Joe Carey. "Exeter—a few months ago."

"I wasn't meaning Exeter. I was meaning Dartmoor."

Carey and Dodo exchanged glances.

"Just what are you getting at, Mr. Minto?" asked the clown. "I wish to hell you'd stop beating about the bush and come out into the open."

Mr. Minto did not answer. He had just noticed something which interested him. The last section of the big cage had been assembled and the ring was now completely surrounded by the steel bars. The attendants had cleared off. As soon as they had gone, a girl in a thick coat ran in from the wings of the tent and did something to the small door which formed part of the last section...the door through which Anton's successor entered the ring to do his act and through which, if lucky, he left the ring at the end of the act. Mr. Minto would not have sworn to it, but he had a strong feeling that the girl had locked the door. The girl was Loretta.

"Talking of coming out into the open," he said, "can we get out of here all right? We seem to have been shut in by this cage, don't we?"

"That's all right," said Carey; "there's a door over there. Come on, Minto...what the 'ell are you getting at?"

Again Mr. Minto did not answer. He heard in the distance a sound which did not appeal to him at all—an angry roaring. He also heard the clang of a steel door, and he saw—straight ahead of him—the face of the first tiger as it came lurching down the tunnel and into the ring. Carey and the clown had their backs to the tunnel. Mr. Minto walked very quickly to the door leading out of the ring.

"Where are you going?" asked Dodo.

"Home," said Mr. Minto. "Look behind you."

He reached the door, and found it locked.

The rest of the tigers came down the tunnel and into the ring. The few early arrivals scattered about the tent were not quite sure what was going on. They consulted their watches and told one another that the show had begun twenty minutes too soon. The band, getting into their places to while away the time with more or less sweet music, leaned over the rail of their platform and refused to believe their eyes. Mr. Minto looked quickly round the tent. It was one of the boasts of Carey's Circus that they had so many attendants that the big tent always looked full, even when business was bad. Not one of those attendants appeared to be in sight now. Mr. Minto was alone in the world…with the exception of Carey, Dodo, and six tigers.

The tigers were all in the ring now. They grouped themselves together around the entrance to the tunnel, weighing up the position. They had their eyes on Mr. Minto, who was the only one of the three men in the ring to have moved— not a wise move, as Mr. Minto was now thinking. It may have been merely imagination, but Mr. Minto was pretty sure that the largest of the tigers put out a healthy tongue and deliberately licked its lips in anticipation. Feeling rather pleased with himself for remaining so calm, Mr. Minto walked back to where Carey and Dodo were standing in the centre of the ring. If there was going to be any unpleasantness, he preferred it to be three against six, instead of one against six. The tigers followed him round with their eyes. And then—or so it seemed to Mr. Minto—they saw, for the first time, Dodo.

The next moments seemed very long ones to Mr. Minto. In reality the whole unpleasantness was over in less than ten seconds.

The clown was in his costume, ready for the show. A red-and-yellow costume similar to the one he had worn on the night of Anton's death. The beasts stopped weighing up the position and began to slouch across the ring to where the three men were standing. The men parted company—Mr.

Minto retreated back to the locked door of the cage, Carey along the opposite side of the ring. Only Dodo stood his ground, and Mr. Minto, after awarding him full marks for his courage, realized that it was not courage at all. The clown was petrified with fear.

The tigers came straight on towards him. They paid not an atom of attention either to Mr. Minto or Joe Carey... Dodo was their man, and they got him. The biggest of the animals paused for a second in its walk, relaxed its muscles, and sprang. The others took their cue from him. Dodo let out one horrible scream, and the rest was drowned in the roars of the six tigers.

Mr. Minto banged on the bars of the cage and yelled for help. At the other side of the ring, Carey yelled and swore. The people already in the audience, realizing at last that they were getting something extra for their money, stood up and added to the babel. After what seemed an eternity, but was actually only a few seconds, attendants rushed in from all directions. Four shots were fired. The big tiger leapt in the air with a snarl of rage, and rushed wildly round the ring. He passed a little too close to where Mr. Minto was standing for that gentleman's liking. Mr. Minto leapt higher than he had ever done in his life and clung for dear life to the bars of the cage. Visions of various jungle films he had seen, in which tigers kept climbing up trees to get hold of the heroine's legs, swam before him. The tiger in this case, however, was too hurt to waste time over a detective's legs. It dashed round the ring and then ran quickly up the tunnel and into its cage. The other animals, frightened by the shots, followed it. Mr. Minto heard a door clang outside the big tent. It seemed to him sweet music.

"Now then," he said to an attendant outside the ring, "would you mind letting me out of this?"

Having put himself on the comfortable side of the bars, he went to find Loretta. She was standing in the wings, staring through the plush curtains into the tent.

"Did you lock the door of that cage?" he asked.

"Yes."

"And did you let those beasts into the ring?"

"Yes."

"Oh! I just wanted to know. If it's of any interest to you, I am not insured against tiger-mauling."

"He tried to kill Lorimer…and you let him do it. I wish they'd torn you both to pieces."

"They seem to have done that to one of us."

"Not Dodo…Carey, I mean. He found out that Lorimer was going to tell you something—you made him think that, I suppose. He tried to kill him. He altered the ropes for the trapeze during our act this afternoon. Lorimer's in hospital now. He may not live…he'll never do circus work again. The little swine…he killed Anton…he thought that Lorimer knew he'd done it…he kept him quiet.…"

"Carey didn't kill Anton," said Mr. Minto. "Didn't you watch how those tigers behaved? They're intelligent beasts, those tigers. They've been waiting for an opportunity like this ever since Anton's death—and you gave it them. The opportunity to get even with the man who killed their trainer. If Carey had killed Anton, don't you think they would have gone for him in the ring just now? They didn't. They left him alone—and me, thank God!—and they went for Dodo. They got their revenge all right."

"You mean…Dodo murdered Anton?"

"That's right. And you'd better get out of the road. Here's the local Superintendent.…"

Superintendent Padgeham rushed up considerably worried. He had just received a rather wild report to the effect that Mr. Minto had mauled one of the tigers, and he was anxious to find out the truth.

"Glad to see you, Padgeham," said Mr. Minto. "You're just in time. You can make those arrests now. There won't be any performance tonight."

"Are you all right, sir?"

"Good heavens!" said Mr. Minto. "I believe the man's human. Just imagine that—a superintendent worrying about the life of a Scotland Yard upstart! I'm all right, thanks, Padgeham. Is the clown dead?"

"No. Badly mauled about—but still living."

"Good!" said Mr. Minto. "I don't want him to die—just yet. Padgeham, do your stuff. Arrest Joe Carey for being the head of a very efficient organization for the smuggling and selling of dangerous drugs all over the country. Arrest the Winters for allowing the pawnshop to be used as a clearing-house for the drugs, and for aiding and abetting in the distribution of the stuff. Arrest young Briggs for acting as one of Carey's agents, and that young attendant who goes round with the chocolates and cigarettes for the same thing. There'll be a lot more, but that's enough to be going on with. Oh—*and* your dirty old magistrate for receiving illicit drugs and having the nerve to sit on the bench on the same morning."

"And the clown—Dodo?"

"You can arrest what's left of him for the murder of Anton and the attempted murder of Lorimer," said Mr. Minto. "And take good care of him, Padgeham. Nurse him well. He's got an appointment with the hangman, and he'll have to be back in his usual health for that."

Chapter Eighteen

Mr. Minto came down to his breakfast at the Station Hotel feeling—apart from the lump on the back of his head—at peace with the world. He sat down at his usual window-table, removed the vase of carnations which always got in the way of his food, folded his *Times*, and beamed kindly on the aged waiter as he shuffled wearily across to take his order.

"Good morning, sir," said the waiter. "And what shall it be this morning, sir?"

"This morning it shall be porridge," said Mr. Minto.

"You said you didn't trust the chef with porridge, sir."

"This morning I would trust him with arsenic," said Mr. Minto. "Porridge it is, lumps and all. With a little boiled cod, double bacon and eggs, with fried tomatoes, black coffee, toast and marmalade to follow."

"Yes, sir," said the waiter. "Will the other gentleman be coming down, sir?"

"The other gentleman?" said Mr. Minto, and realized that the waiter was referring to Dodo. "No…he's left the hotel."

"Nothing wrong, I hope, sir?"

"He's been called away on some legal business, I understand."

The waiter shambled off to the serving-hatch and relayed Mr. Minto's order.

Mr. Minto studied his morning paper. Wars and rumours of wars; revolutions and uprisings; the breaking-up of conferences and the hatching of new ones to take their place; most important of all, Yorkshire out for less than a hundred runs on a sticky wicket. What hope of fame had a little affair like the death of Anton in the face of such competition? But Mr. Minto found it at last—Illicit Drug Organization Exposed. A neat little paragraph, ending up by congratulating Superintendent Padgeham and the local constabulary on a smart capture. Mr. Minto had, of course, bought the wrong newspaper. In all the others there would be inch-and-a-half headlines and blotchy photographs of the Superintendent. He read the paragraph through, and then passed on to the more sensational news about Yorkshire.

He was in the middle of the cricket crisis when Robert arrived.

"Sit down," said Mr. Minto. "How's Claire?"

"She's much better this morning," said the priest. "I think she realizes her—um—escape. Did everything go well last night?"

"Splendidly. I was hit on the head with a piece of lead piping—and very nearly attacked by the tigers."

"Good gracious!" said Robert. "What on earth happened?"

"Have some coffee, Robert. It's always considered correct for a detective to explain the crime and solution once the thing's over. So have a cup of coffee, and make appropriate remarks whenever I pause."

"What sort of remarks?"

"You could say 'How clever of you!' every now and then," said Mr. Minto, attacking a particularly obstinate lump in his porridge.

"I see...."

"The awkward thing about this business," said Mr. Minto, "was the fact that there were two crimes to solve. The murder of Anton and the drug-smuggling racket. They were mixed up with each other, of course; but the drug part of it didn't come to light until fairly late on in the case. We seem to have hit on one of the most complete organizations for the smuggling of drugs that's been known for a long time. When you come to think of it, a circus was an ideal place from which to distribute illicit drugs. Always on the move—*personnel* unknown to the police—every facility for getting the wretched stuff broadcast. Padgeham and I had a long chat with Joe Carey last night. He wasn't inclined to talk at first, but after a while he got quite conversational.

"He started this business in a small way; he's built it up to an enormous concern. Until a year or two ago he distributed the stuff only on his own. Whenever the circus visited a town, he sold a supply to the poor wretches who were ready to buy it. The business prospered—Carey found himself making almost as much out of the sideline as out of the circus. He took Dodo into partnership. He established a number of depots for the distribution of the stuff in towns where there was a big demand—small businesses which no one would possibly suspect of having anything to do with the smuggling of drugs…a tobacconist's shop in Liverpool, a pawnshop here, and so on. He even went the length of having personal representatives, going round with the circus to help distribute the stuff. Young Briggs was one. He seemed a perfectly ordinary vacuum-cleaner canvasser. I don't expect he knows one end of a vacuum-cleaner from the other. Wherever the circus went, young Briggs was there with his little case, calling on customers.

"Believe me, Joe Carey had it all worked out to a nicety. You could get the stuff in all sorts of different ways…collect it late at night at his own caravan, get it through the pawnshop in Bank Street, have a visit from young Briggs, or get it smuggled to you by one of the circus attendants during an actual performance. A really efficient organization. Waiter!…"

The waiter dragged his body across.

"My cod, please," said Mr. Minto. "Well, business got so bright in the drug line that Carey decided to give up the circus. He planned to sell out to Anton, who'd always been hankering after running a show of his own. The drug sideline was to continue, of course. Dodo was to run that, under Carey's supervision. The deal was just going through when Anton—I don't know how—found out what was going on. He refused to have anything to do with the deal, and threatened to spill the beans to the police. Very awkward for Messrs. Dodo and Carey.

"I believe Anton found out about the drugs on the day the circus arrived here—last Sunday. At any rate, on the Sunday night he visited Carey in his caravan and the pair of them had words. Fortunately for us, Lorimer—the trapeze chap—heard the words, or some of them. Anton, I expect, threatened to tell the police next day. Carey told Dodo what was going to happen. They watched Anton all the next day like a couple of hawks and didn't let him get a chance to pass on his information. They got to know that Anton was going to tell Lorimer what he'd found out. And Dodo took the matter into his own hands and decided that Anton must be silenced. He murdered him. Ah…thank you, waiter."

Mr. Minto took a peck at his cod and then looked across the table at his brother.

"He did murder Anton, didn't he?" he asked.

"I believe so," said the priest. "It was Dodo who confessed in the church that morning."

"That's a relief! The way you've been carrying on this week, I wouldn't have been at all surprised if you'd said, 'No—it was someone else altogether.' Dodo murdered Anton that night during the supper-party. He planned the thing very carefully. He knew that two other people at least beside himself were going to leave the supper-tent, and he arranged things so that suspicion could fall on either of them. He had me all tied in knots for quite a while, the little swine!

"Joe Carey had told Lorimer that Anton was having an affair with his wife…I don't believe there was a great deal of truth in that, but it was enough to make Lorimer mad with jealousy. As a matter of fact, he says he set out that night with the idea of killing Anton himself—which didn't make things any easier for the poor detective.

"Dodo was going to shoot Anton, and he needed a revolver. He tried to get Lorimer's, in order that suspicion might be thrown on him; he found that Lorimer had already taken out the revolver himself. The other man who was going to be suspected was Miller—the fellow who made such an outburst during the supper-party. Dodo got hold of his revolver from the ring-master's tent and used it to kill Anton. He shot him thrice and then dragged his body inside the tigers' cage. He thought, of course, that the beasts would finish off the job and cover up all trace of the crime. He threw the revolver into that little stream which runs through the field, and then he ran back to the tent and gave the alarm. If ever you commit a murder, Robert, be sure to be the first to tell the police about it. The person who finds the body is the last person they think of suspecting. Waiter…bacon and eggs, please."

Mr. Minto sat back and glanced once again at the distressing news about Yorkshire while the waiter removed an empty plate and put a full one in its place.

"Now then…Dodo suffered a little damage when he placed Anton's body inside the cage. He got a scratch across his lip, and a piece of his costume was torn off—a piece which I subsequently found. I asked him about that, and he said that he'd tried to drag Anton out of the cage as soon as he'd found what had happened, and had been set upon by the tigers. Quite a feasible explanation. But then he made the mistake of giving away his torn costume to one of the other clowns—who, in turn, popped it."

"Popped it?" said Robert.

"Deposited it in a pawnbroker's establishment. The one at 288, Bank Street, which entered into the affair later on. I don't know whether Carey knew right away that Dodo had committed the murder; at any rate, he asked me to look into the business instead of getting in the local police. Maybe he thought I was as dumb as I looked. And right away either Dodo or Carey made a mistake…Dodo told me that he went to Carey's caravan for a drink after leaving the supper-tent; Carey told me that he wasn't in his caravan at all, but was away in the town visiting friends. They were both suspects.

"But the prime suspects at the time were the other two people who had left the supper-party—Lorimer and Miller. Lorimer asked for trouble by losing his nerve and clearing out. And when Miller was mauled by those tigers, I honestly thought he'd done the deed.

"The thing that had impressed me about the tigers' behaviour was the fact that they *didn't* maul their trainer when his body was chucked in beside them. They respected him all right—maybe it's going a bit too far to say that they loved him; but, at any rate, they hardly touched him when they knew he was dead. I got it into my head that they wouldn't treat the man who had killed Anton in the same way. And neither they did. Unfortunately they ill-treated Miller first, and that put me on the wrong scent. It seems that Miller and the tigers had never been on very good terms…and I wouldn't put it past Dodo to have roused the beasts into a fury before they went on for their act that afternoon. In any case, they killed Miller; and when I found the confession in Miller's pocket, I thought the case was over and done with. Then you stepped in and said that Miller wasn't the man. Waiter...more toast, please...."

"The confession, though...I can't understand that."

"Neither could I, at the time. Chiefly because I didn't use my brain. That confession was Dodo's second mistake. He wrote it himself, in a fairly good imitation of Miller's handwriting. He planted it in Miller's clothes—but he planted it in the wrong clothes. He put it in the suit Miller had been wearing at the supper-party the night before. The wording of the confession indicated that it had been written just before Miller went on to do his act with the tigers that afternoon....If Dodo had only thought, he'd have put it in the suit Miller was wearing that day. And the other big mistake he made was to use a fountain-pen to write the confession. Have a look at that, Robert."

Mr. Minto handed a small piece of paper across to his brother, who studied it carefully.

"'Now is the time for all good men to come to the aid of the party'," said Robert. "I don't see what that has to do with the case."

"I wrote that—with Anton's fountain-pen. If you notice, the two halves of the nib aren't true. The pen's probably been dropped at some time, and one half of the nib is a little out of position. The writing on the confession was exactly the same as this. In other words, it had been written with Anton's fountain-pen. It couldn't have been written by Anton, it was written by the person who took charge of Anton's belongings—Dodo. Waiter!..."

The ancient waiter stopped picking his teeth and threaded his way across to the window-table.

"This coffee's cold," said Mr. Minto. "Bring us some more, please."

"Yes, sir."

"The first indication I had of the drug business was when I paid a visit to the house above the pawnshop in Bank Street. Joe Carey had told me that he had been there at the time of the murder. I got Padgeham to give me a report on the people staying in the house, and it was such a good report that I got fishy at once. I went to see them—carefully disguised as a housing inspector. They made a great fuss about an invalid sister who was living in the house at the time—said she was very ill and suffering from paralysis, and that I couldn't go into the room where she was. I went in. She wasn't nearly so paralysed as that waiter of ours. She was drugged.

"I got suspicious about the people in that house. They told me the stairs leading down to the pawnshop were never used, when it was quite obvious that they'd been used fairly recently. As soon as I heard that Dodo's costume had been put into pawn in the shop below, I made an excuse and had a look at it. I got severely choked off by the girl who looks after the shop. I couldn't think how she knew I was a detective, although she made some rather insulting remarks about the size of my feet. It turns out that she was Carey's illegitimate daughter by the woman Winter, and of course Carey had told her all about me and what was going on. Thank you, waiter....Some fresh coffee, Robert?"

The waiter made some meek remark about clearing away the table in preparation for lunch. Mr. Minto waved him aside.

"Then Claire's young man entered into things. On the second night of the circus's visit, when I was down keeping an eye on Joe Carey's caravan, I saw someone come up to the caravan and then go off into the town. I followed him; he went to the pawnshop. I was perfectly certain that I'd seen the man before. The next night, when I saw him again, I was even more certain. It was young Briggs. I checked up the dates of Briggs's visits to various towns—Claire told me that—and found that they coincided exactly with the tour of the circus. Like Mary and her little lamb, wherever Carey's went young Briggs was sure to go. I spent yesterday morning going round with young Briggs—or, rather, behind him—and I saw him deposit his vacuum-cleaner case in the pawnshop. I got hold of it...the bag of the vacuum contained a goodly quantity of drugs, all ready packed up for distribution.

"And I also got hold of Dodo's costume. I've had the blood on the costume analysed overnight...there were three different stains of blood on it. Two human stains, and one animal. The animal blood came from the tiger who had a sore paw which was still bleeding slightly. One of the human stains was of Dodo's own blood, from where Peter had scratched him. The other blood was Anton's...and if we hadn't anything else to go on, those three stains are quite enough to get a verdict of 'guilty' for Dodo."

Mr. Minto paused.

"How very clever of you," said his brother.

"Thank you," said Mr. Minto. "I was wondering when you'd remember to say that. Now then...I was pretty sure that either Carey or Dodo had killed Anton, but I didn't know which. I got poor Lorimer to help me find out. I arranged that Carey should get to know that Lorimer had found out about the drug business, and that he was planning to spill the beans to me. I gave Lorimer a revolver to protect himself with and cleared out. I never imagined that they'd do such a filthy trick as they did—altering the length of the trapeze drops and trying to kill him that way. They damned nearly killed the girl; it was only in trying to save Loretta that Lorimer fell and smashed himself up."

"How is he?"

"He's all right, thank God. He's broken some bones but he'll be all right. Carey evidently told Dodo that Lorimer was going to talk, and Dodo manipulated the trapeze ropes. Loretta thought that Carey had done it himself, but Dodo has confessed to doing it. The funny thing is that Lorimer found out that there was going to be an attack on me, and tried to warn me. In doing so, we found another member of the gang. Lorimer gave a note to one of the attendants— the fellow who sells chocolates and cigarettes in the cheap seats during the performances. The attendant was part of the gang, and naturally didn't deliver the note. He took it straight to Dodo, and Dodo put Lorimer out of action and prepared to do the same to me. Incidentally, I found out that the attendant sold more than chocolates and cigarettes…I bought a neat little parcel of dope from him myself at the matinée yesterday. Go on…say something…."

"Um…very clever," said Robert. "Very clever indeed."

"Thank you. As soon as Lorimer's accident happened I dashed over to Carey's caravan and found the main source of supply. The back wall of his caravan is hollow, and in the cavity there's enough dope to ruin half the country. After that I was all set for the kill—but I still didn't know whether Carey or Dodo had murdered Anton. I hadn't the results of the analysis of the clown costume then, remember. I got the local police force on the job—had them surround the circus field and follow anyone who tried to make a getaway. Carey had a shot at it, but didn't get very far. I think he meant to get to the pawnshop and warn the girl before things got too hot. In any case, I went back to the circus ground about an hour before the evening performance, and got this…."

Mr. Minto bowed his head and showed the bump.

"Dodo did it, plus a length of lead piping. Poor little Dodo…he made another big mistake then. He lugged me into Carey's caravan, and the pair of them locked me up in

a cupboard. At least, I suppose they did, for that's where I
found myself when I came to. And on the other side of the
cupboard Carey was having a very embarrassing time with
Loretta. She'd got it into her head that he had been responsible for Lorimer's crash, and she was going for him good
and strong. With a bread-knife, of all unpleasant things.
Carey got her quietened down—I think she fainted—and
cleared off to make a getaway with Dodo. I'd had enough of
the cupboard. I banged and thumped and yelled, and after
a while Loretta came to and let me out. Then I had a nasty
few minutes. Loretta said that I'd let her husband be killed,
and got hold of the bread-knife again. Never be alone in a
caravan with a woman and a bread-knife, Robert. It isn't a
nice situation at all."

Mr. Minto pushed his cup and saucer away from him,
lit a cigarette, and put his elbows on the table.

"I went straight to the big tent. The show hadn't begun—
there were only a few people in the place. Carey and Dodo
were in the middle of the ring, discussing escape. I went and
joined them. The attendants were putting up the big cage
all round the ring, and when they'd finished Loretta had a
bright idea. She locked the door leading out of the ring and
let the tigers loose inside with us. She was mad—she thought
she'd get two birds killed with six tigers…Carey for causing
her husband's accident and me for allowing it to happen.

"The tigers didn't pay any attention to Carey or me,
though. They went straight for Dodo. They'd been waiting for this sort of chance. Earlier on in the week, when
Dodo and I passed their cage on our way back to the hotel,
they'd shown pretty clearly what they thought of the little
clown. And this time they didn't waste a second. Another
minute, and Dodo wouldn't have been in a position to
stand his trial. Which he will, for the murder of Anton
and the attempted murder of Lorimer. He'd got control

of the drug business—with Carey selling out he was fairly safe from prosecution if anything went wrong—and when Anton found out and made up his mind to expose the whole thing, Dodo was desperate. It meant 'Amen' for him. He shot Anton and counted on the tigers to cover up his crime. Those tigers have brains, though. I take no great credit out of this case. I couldn't have solved it without you, Robert. And I certainly couldn't have solved it without the tigers. Waiter!…"

The waiter came out of a reverie and sauntered across to Mr. Minto's table.

"When's the next respectable train to town?" asked Mr. Minto.

"Eleven-thirty-five, sir," said the waiter. "And a very good train at two-ten."

"And what's for lunch?"

"Scotch Broth, sir. Roast Beef and Yorkshire. Stewed prunes and rice, or bread-and-butter pudding, sir."

"In that case, ask them to get my bill ready," said Mr. Minto. "I'm leaving on the eleven-thirty-five."

To see more Poisoned Pen Press titles: